SIL

ST

OVER 100
GREAT NOVELS
OF
EROTIC DOMINATION

If you like one you will probably like the rest

NEW TITLES EVERY MONTH

If you want to be on our confidential mailing list for our Readers' Club Magazine (with extracts from past and forthcoming titles) write to:

SILVER MOON READER SERVICES

The Shadowline Building
6 Wembley Street
Gainsborough
DN21 2AJ
United Kingdom
or
sales@babash.com

or telephone
01427 816710
(UK office hours only)

NEW AUTHORS WELCOME

Please send submissions to
Silver Moon Books Ltd.
PO Box 5663
Nottingham
NG3 6PJ
or
editor@babash.com

First published 2004 Silver Moon Books
ISBN 1-903687-49-7

A Slave for the Sinfinder

By

Jonathan Tate

Also By Jonathan Tate
Sinfinder General

CHAPTER 1

The lank-haired rustic dropped to the soil, his face turned upwards, his eyes begging - imploring a mercifulness that could not be found in the Sinfinder's heart.

"Please, Matthew!" he choked from between frothy lips. "Please have mercy on my lady wife. My Clara has not been herself of late - she has been tormented by the very Devil himself!"

Matthew Hopkirk, the self-styled, self-appointed Sinfinder General, glowered down at the miserable wretch crawling at his feet.

He casually lifted a boot and crunched it into the chest of the yokel, shoving him against the ground.

"Then Beelzebub must be cast out, thou snivelling cur!" he growled. "It is God's work which I am doing here, Zeb Carter - fighting to purge this wicked female of her sin, and to help her find the light that lies beyond the horned shadow of Satan."

The burning orange sun was slowly rising above the horizon as the Sinfinder General and his party trudged their way towards the summit of the steep hill known as Devil's Mount.

Staggering behind him, their arms fastened behind their backs, the chains running between their neck collars effectively tethering them to one another, came Laura, Sally and Lucinda, urged onwards by two of the Sinfinder's henchmen. Further back still, the villagers climbed upwards, clambering over rocks and through bracken and nettles. The menfolk brandished wildly flickering torches, the flames burning bright against the still-gloomy sky.

Up ahead of Matthew Hopkirk were more of his henchmen, carrying between them long, flat lengths of wood, and a variety of tools and implements. And at the very front of the throng, an attractive woman in her early thirties staggered beneath the weight of a heavy wooden crossbeam that rested along her shoulders, and to which her outstretched arms had been fastened.

Clara was a broad-boned female. Her shapely, naked frame wobbled splendidly as she trod a precarious path through the thick hillside vegetation.

At length, the party reached the summit. Without word from the Sinfinder, his men set about their work. Two of them unfastened Clara's wrists; another two erected one of the flat lengths of wood, a three feet-wide piece with a hole gouged from it. The woman was pulled towards the wooden flat and guided around so that she was facing away from it. One of the brutes who had untied her leaned her forward. Another pressed his hand against the white flesh of her belly and pushed backwards, until her big bottom had been fitted through the porthole-shaped opening in the flat.

A length of rope was drawn tightly across her stomach and fastened to hooks either side of her. The rope effectively clamped her body in place and secured her broad posterior in position, blooming out, as it was, from the hole on the reverse side of the flat.

Other flats were erected then, one to each side of her and one ahead of her - the latter of which had a metal ring set near its top, to which her wrists were bound.

The flats were shifted into position and fastened to one another by bolts. A roof was added, effectively boxing Clara in. Only her fleshy buttocks remained visible to those who gathered outside the grim wooden prison.

The building work completed, the Sinfinder's men stood back, leaving the way clear for Matthew Hopkirk to take centre-stage.

"For the sin of thy wildness, for thy ill temper and thy rage," the Sinfinder stated without emotion, "for the anger which thou hast displayed these last few weeks, and for the abhorrent behaviour that has so shamed thy husband, so appalled this fair community of goodly citizens..."

"Please, Sinfinder!" Zeb Carter begged once more, his

overwhelming sense of grief blinding him to the fact that he had dared to interrupt the dark-eyed Hopkirk, "My wife, my dear wife - she is not herself! She cannot help the way she has behaved!"

The Sinfinder paid no attention, but instead continued, grim-faced and sullen-voiced: "I hereby pass sentence upon thee..."

A deathly silence embraced the gathered throng, save for the sobs of the distraught yokel. The flickering flames of the torches reflected in the eyes of the villagers as they stared at Matthew Hopkirk, their jaws hanging, their breaths - when they came - shallow and laboured.

"Ye have been placed within the restraining box. There, ye shall remain while the seasons pass, and until summer is once again here. Thy husband, I trust, shall see to it that ye are fed and watered..." the Sinfinder met the tear-stained gaze of the yokel with a dark-souled, passionless stare. He indicated with his gloved hand towards the box. "Ye will find a small hatch built into the front panel," he muttered as an aside to the rustic. "Ye may hand-feed the wanton harpy by that means."

He returned his attention then to the matter of sentencing. "Thy body shall be emptied of its waste matter at dawn, and then again at dusk," he continued. "Let thy golden water flow into the ground beneath thy feet. Speak ye not to any soul who happens thy way, and beg ye not for mercy when ye do suffer for thy heinous crimes. Offer up thy fulsome hindquarters with a good grace to those who wish to make good use, and struggle ye not against the tides that will flow into thy body through the channel of that wanton orifice. Buck ye not against the tender kiss of rod, nor barter with those who seek to absolve thee of thy sin."

The Sinfinder pulled his cloak tightly around himself and glowered at his muscular henchmen. "Let her suffering begin," he murmured.

The crowd became suddenly agitated and shifted closer

to the firmly bolted box. A gruesome brute in woollen rags acknowledged the Sinfinder's command with a slow nod of his shaggy head, and lumbered towards the big white bottom thrusting out from the wooden panel. The brute spat a globule of thick mucus onto his fingers, clutched the expansive buttocks before him, and unceremoniously wrenched them apart, laying open the clammy depths of Clara's valley. Swiftly, he thrust his fingers into the shadowy groove. He anointed her back-passage with his phlegm and wrenched his trousers to his knees, unfettering a muscular length of madly throbbing cock.

Nails digging into her buttocks to achieve some element of leverage, he pushed himself into Clara's vulnerable bottom-hole.

The woman howled in agony from within her wooden prison.

"No, Sinfinder, no!" screamed her husband as he watched his wife being taken, beating at the soft earth beneath him with all his might, and screaming in rage at the sombre heavens. When his anger received no response from the skies - no divine bolt of lightning to strike dead the Sinfinder, nor even the rumble of thunder to mark the gods' dissatisfaction - he buried his head in his hands, and prayed for the courage he needed to endure the terrible shame.

All around, the villagers stood in complete silence, transfixed by the gruesome sight before them. They watched as the brute's thick length of cock disappeared from view between Clara's big buttocks, entering and re-entering her body roughly, hammering away inside her in a desperate attempt to spit its vile seed.

The beast fucked away at her bottom for what seemed an eternity, drawing from her gasps and sobs that struck a chord with all but the most cold-hearted among the gathered throng.

And when he'd completed his work, and filled her hole with his gushing come, another gruesome beast took his place. His twitching cock slipped easily into the slick, sperm-oiled anus, and slid in and out of the hole at a frenetic pace until it too had spat its juices.

In turn, each of the Sinfinder's henchmen fitted their stiffened muscles into the ravaged bum-trench, and fucked away until they had spent inside the traumatised hole.

Then it was the turn of the menfolk from the village. They roared one another on as they took turns to perform. "That's the way!" they called. "Fuck the shit out of her!"

"Split her in two!" the womenfolk screamed, "Open her arse right up, that'll learn her!" As the men took their turns, various among the women spurred them on, delivering slaps to their buttocks and urging them to thrust as hard and as fast as they could.

In time, each man spent within the slackened hole. Trails of thick white fluid, dribbling from the flooded anus, soaked the undersides of Clara's gently trembling buttocks.

When each had used the big bottom to satisfy his carnal desires, the brute who'd made the first deposit took a thick length of cane from one of his fellows, and began to briskly flog the white bum-flesh. In no time at all, he laid the heavy, swishing rattan across every inch of the exposed arse, criss-crossing the cheeks with cruel red weals.

When he dropped the implement, it was to once again inhabit Clara's hole with his throbbing length. Within seconds, he had emptied himself once more. He completed his work by landing a mighty slap across the big cheeks, which burned a ruddy crimson and glistened with the overflowing spend of two-dozen and more men.

The party turned on their heels then and the Sinfinder strode to the front of the group and headed off down the hillside. Laura, Sally and Lucinda struggled to retain their footing as they stumbled after him, their overseers urging them to move quickly through the tangle of vegetation. They trudged across a broad, fallow field, and Laura was reminded of her time at The Farm; the days spent toiling beneath a baking sun in just such a field, working to avoid the cut of the overseer's cane.

She stumbled through puddles of slush and mud behind Lucinda, whose expansive, aristocratic bottom still bore the marks of the fierce paddling it had received that very morning.

Through a creaking gate and back into the village, the party made its way along the cobbled road towards a small cottage, where a slight figure stood silhouetted in the window. The Sinfinder reached the front door, and rapped it with the brass tip of his walking stick.

"Open the door, harlot!" he growled. "Thy moment of reckoning is at hand!"

As the villagers gathered around, the door slowly creaked open, and a small red-haired woman peered out into the gloom. The Sinfinder forced the door wide and strode into the cottage, his henchmen following hard on his heels.

"No, please!", the woman cried at their sudden intrusion, and let out a frightened squeal as two of the Sinfinder's brutish servants hauled her onto the kitchen table. She was still dressed in her night attire - a long white gown, which rode up her legs as she was manhandled onto her back.

From her vantage point just inside the door, to where the three bound women had been ushered by their overseer, Laura watched as one of the brutes roughly tugged the garment upwards, laying the victim bare from her feet to her ribs. She was an attractive female. Her body beautifully toned and neatly proportioned, she was altogether slimmer and more petite than the broad and fleshy woman who had just been imprisoned on the hilltop.

"I have dealt with the other wanton harpy, and now I shall deal with thee," murmured Matthew Hopkirk, adjusting his black leather gloves until they fitted more snugly around his hands. "I am told that you and the wilful witch now incarcerated on Devil's Mount have a history of feuding. I have meted out punishment to that fat-buttocked wench, and now I shall give thee a dose of the same medicine. Thy only salvation is that I am aware it was she, not thee, who was the main perpetrator of thy feud. Otherwise, ye too would now be imprisoned 'pon the hillside."

The Sinfinder nodded his head gently. The subtle movement informed his henchmen it was time to proceed. They tugged the red-haired woman across the splintering table-top until her head hung over its far end. One of the brutes attending to her positioned himself behind her head and swiftly tugged his thick cock from the confines of his sackcloth trousers. The other lifted the woman's legs and guided them backwards, up over her head, delivering them into the vice-like grip of his companion. He yanked them wide apart, opening her up.

"Oh, Sinfinder - no!" she squealed. She shifted her body from side to side, a vain attempt to wriggle free of the ankle-hold that had left her so cruelly exposed.

The brute standing at her head, her ankles clasped in his hands, pressed his cock into her face. She knew better than to resist his urgent demand, and opened her mouth to allow the rigid muscle access.

The redhead began to suck desperately on the thick shaft, even as the other brute, taking up a position at the near-end of the table, ran his course fingers across the soft flesh of her cunt.

He began to lash her exposed buttocks then, with a thick length of cane. The woman gurgled in pain, and seemed to suck more fervently on the cock that was bunging her mouth. Ten cruel weals patterned her bottom before the brute dropped the length of rod. Ripping down his own britches, he sank his throbbing cock into the pink flesh-pot of her cunt.

Half-a-dozen hard thrusts and he emerged glistening, his muscle drenched in the woman's silvery juices. He pushed his lubricated muscle at her conveniently-exposed anus, slowly drilling the thick, wet length deep into the tiny hole. The redhead gurgled again at the penetration, her head continuing to bob up and down as she sucked and chewed at the throbbing flesh within her mouth.

The beast hammered in and out of her bottom-hole until the fires of a muscle-tensing orgasm embraced him. He groaned languidly and pumped his spend into her bowels.

Another took his place then, and made similar use of her ripe cunt and tight bottom until he, too, had ejaculated deep within her.

It was as a third man began to thrust inside her wet vagina that the redhead started to choke. Laura could tell from the way the brute at the woman's head had tensed that he had emptied himself into her mouth.

Once drained, he withdrew his softening cock from between her lips and shifted away into the shadows. Another replaced him, clasping her ankles and pushing his own length of thick muscle into her throat. The woman began her work anew, her lips and tongue toiling mightily to draw a fresh deposit of sticky fluid into her mouth and then down into her stomach.

Deposits continued to be made in her vagina and anus. The thick male stems that made use of her there spat their fluid more swiftly than those which bunged her frantically-working mouth.

In time, all the men had ejaculated inside her body. Some of the more confident among the women villagers had moved forward at the same time as their menfolk, and busied themselves fondling the captive woman's breasts and toying with her clitoris. Occasional slaps continued to scald her buttocks, delivered by female palms with a terrible venom, as though to punish her for the pleasure she was affording their menfolk.

The redhead's suffering came to an end as swiftly as it had begun. A barked instruction from the Sinfinder was all that it took to bring proceedings to an abrupt termination. The two men whose cocks were within her at the time, ramming at her mouth and cunt, swiftly withdrew, and released her from their vice-like hold.

The Sinfinder General glowered malevolently, and rapped the table-top with his stick. "Let that which has befallen thee serve to inform thy future conduct," he announced grandly as the redhead gasped for breath. Her mouth, vagina and anus were dribbling sticky come. "Learn thy lesson well, wench - or thou shalt find thyself tarred and feathered and sent to market, there to be skewered by thy shameless front hole upon a stake, and made to cluck like a common fowl for the better merriment of thy fellow citizens."

His warning given, and with a theatrical swirl of his black cloak, the Sinfinder strode towards the door, ordering the dawn raiders to follow him into the early morning sunshine of an ever-brightening summer's day...

In the months which followed, old Zeb visited his beautiful young wife in her wooden prison on the hillside three or four times a day. He fed her through the little hatch in the front panel of the restraining box, and sat on a fold-away stool which he always took with him, talking and reading to her. He would use soft cloth to gently wipe away the globules of thick semen that dribbled from between her buttocks, and inwardly curse the unidentified villagers who had used her there. With a thick ointment, he massaged the always-raw crimson flesh of her bottom and pressed damp towels against the cheeks to soothe the fires that burned within them.

But it was a terrible life for Zeb, as well as for his wife. Alone in bed at night, he craved the chance to satisfy his natural lustings, and remembered fondly how things had been before his wife's imprisonment. He recalled how he would roll on top of her, wrenching up her nightgown until her huge breasts were bare and her thick pubic bush mashed against his own; and how he would take her then, entering her roughly and thrusting like a madman until he had flooded her sopping love-slot.

And, as the summer sizzled and his own desires mounted, he found himself spending ever longer massaging the soothing balm into his wife's broad buttocks.

When he read to her, he began positioning his stool to the back of the wooden prison, so that he could look up from his book and see her big, succulent bum, thrusting out from the little porthole.

"It's such a lonely life without you, Clara," he said to her one day, lightly caressing her bottom with a blade of grass. "I lie in bed at night and yearn for you."

"I can't be much of a wife to you anymore, can I, Zeb?" she replied with a sigh, "not in here, where you can't even touch me."

"I can touch some of you though," he said. "I can still touch your lovely bottom."

"If only I could shift myself upwards - just a little bit - perhaps then you'd be able to get at me and have some pleasure. Lord knows you deserve it after what my foolishness has put you through. But I can hardly move at all... Please, Zeb - please stop tickling me. You've no idea how tormenting it is when you can't move. It's driving me mad."

"Do you prefer the tickle of the cane, my love?" Zeb released the blade of grass he had been stroking her with and began to gently stroke his wife's posteriors with his fingertips.

"You're strange today, darling," Clara said. "I feel as though I hardly know you."

"I'm desperate," he replied, bluntly. "I need a fuck."

A note of uncertainty entered the woman's voice. "You-you're not going to be unfaithful, are you, Zeb? You're not going to go looking for pleasure elsewhere?!"

There was a momentary silence before her husband gave

an answer; a silence which made Clara's stomach churn with anxiety.

"Maybe," her husband responded at length. "Maybe with one of the young village girls. What do you think?"

"No! You can't! I won't let you!"

Zeb removed his trailing fingers from his wife's bottom and gave her exposed flesh a gentle slap. "And how are you going to stop me?" he chuckled. He slapped her again, equally playfully - and teasingly squeezed her flesh.

"What's wrong with you, Zeb? Why are you being like this?"

He slapped her for a third time, harder than before, and felt his anger rising: "You get yourself imprisoned by the Sinfinder, leaving me without that which is rightfully mine to have, and you ask me why I'm being like this!" Another slap, even harder.

"Oww! Zeb, that hurt. Don't do that!"

"It's okay for the villagers to whip and fuck your bum, but not for your own husband, eh? That's about the truth of it, isn't it!" Zeb felt aggrieved by his wife's attitude towards him; it was as though, somehow, she could find the strength to endure her punishment, but was unable to understand the anguish, the sheer frustration, that he was suffering. "You don't mind total strangers coming in your arse, but I'm supposed to sit back and read you stories, push food into your good-for-nothing mouth and go without for a whole year - and all because you've got a nasty, vicious temper that you can't control! That's the truth of it, isn't it!"

"Zeb, you're being ridiculous! Just calm down, for pity's sake! You're sounding like a madman!"

"I ought to sound like a madman! I ought to just say 'to hell with you' and go and get me a nice piece of ripe, juicy fruit to give a damn good poking to!"

"No!" Clara struggled against her constraints. "What can I do to make it right, Zeb? What can I do, locked away in here!? I don't want to lose you, my darling! I love you and I promise, I promise with all my heart, I'll make it up to you!"

"Will you start right now, do you think?"

"How!?" she gasped. "How can I do anything when I can hardly move?! What can I do, Zeb? "

A sudden silence reigned, save for the faraway sound of a tractor as it rolled along one of the narrow lanes surrounding the village. The air was still and heavy, and Zeb could only imagine how hot and sweaty his wife must have been inside her tiny prison.

At length, he answered her. "I want to fuck you. I want to fuck you in your bottom."

Clara gasped in surprise. "Oh Zeb," she exclaimed, "oh - no! Not there. Not where all those bastards have been. Don't become one of them."

"I need a fuck. I'm desperate. Do you want me to take one of the village girls home?"

"Oh, Zeb - sweetheart - please, no."

Zeb was certain he detected a tremor in his wife's voice. For an instant, he felt a terrible pang of guilt. How could he consider using her as they had used her, he thought to himself. How could he heap further trauma and suffering upon her?

He looked at her big arse, neatly presented and ready for use...

...But then, he mused as his passions rose, hadn't she created this whole insufferable situation? Wasn't he, as her husband, entitled to make use of her - every other bastard in the village had done so, after all.

He murmured 'I'm sorry', and tugged his cock from within his trousers. Ultimately, he didn't care anymore. He wanted her bottom and there it was, brazenly taking the air while the rest of her sweltered inside the wooden box. He clasped her buttocks and edged them apart.

"You're going to have me there, then," Clara said, her

voice struggling to remain calm. "You've decided, have you? You've decided just how little I mean to you."

'Shut up, you foul-tempered bitch', Zeb thought to himself. "What I've decided," he grunted aloud, "is that if every other man in the village can stick his filthy cock in you, I sure as hell can. What I've decided is that you are my wife and I'll do with you what I bloody well want. Now push this great big arse right out - right out, I said! - and get ready for the hardest fucking you've ever taken."

A feeling of immense power surged through Zeb as Clara did his bidding. She may have been angry, she might even have hated him for what he was intending to do to her, but she'd followed his instruction nevertheless, just like an obedient, well-behaved wife should, he thought to himself.

He nudged his cock in between her buttocks until its head was pressing against her slushy, overused anus. Then he pushed firmly, and thrilled to the feeling of his shaft sliding into her, burrowing deeply into the clammy little hole that nestled between her two great arse cheeks.

"Be gentle," she gasped, unconsciously flexing her sphincter muscle around her husband's throbbing cock. Zeb gripped the wooden restraining-box to hold it steady and achieve some kind of leverage. Then, drawing a deep breath and revelling in the exquisite excitement of the situation, he began to fuck his wife's big bottom.

Clara groaned within her grim little prison. She braced her feet against the side panels of the box and leaned as far forward as her restraints would allow, doing her best to open up her rectum for her husband's vigorous assaults. Zeb shifted his groin backwards and forwards at a frenetic pace. His cock was slipping with ease into the well-oiled channel, foraging away in the depths of her very bowel.

"Yes!" he growled as he hammered at her. "Yes! Oh, yes!" He felt dizzy with excitement. Exultant, almost. As the sun beat down against him and the sweat dripped from his every pore, Zeb didn't give a damn if he could be seen from the village down below. Nor did he care how ridiculous he probably looked - thrusting his groin back and forth while clutching hold of a big wooden box, gasping hard for much-needed, increasingly elusive breath. He had never felt so alive, so... sordid, so bestial - and he loved it. He loved the sense of power he was feeling; the sense of complete, unquestionable control. And he loved the thought, too, of what he was doing - plundering his wife's bottom, making the foul-tempered bitch moan in pain and discomfort. But most of all he enjoyed the sheer, unadulterated pleasure of feeling truly liberated; feeling that somehow, finally, he had connected with a dark and thrilling side of himself he had never before known, never before had the opportunity to explore.

His wife's trembling voice cut through his thoughts: "Are you..." she gasped from between clenched teeth, "are you en..joying that? F-fucking me like...like a..." her head banged against the front panel, so powerfully was her husband thrusting into her, "...like a...dog?!"

"Oh...oh yes!" the rustic exclaimed. He had lost all sense of the world around him, had hardly even noticed that his wife was speaking to him. All that he was aware of now were the sensations within his cock as it ploughed into her sopping wet bottom.

"How...could you do this...to me?" Again her head slammed against the front panel, "T-treat me like a...piece...uhh!...a piece of meat?! Oh Christ, please - come! Y-you're going to...to split me open!"

With a terrible groan, Zeb pumped his spend into the big bottom, thrilling to the feeling of his cock pulsating violently as his testicles gradually emptied.

"Oh, dear lord," he murmured as he gradually withdrew the thick, spent muscle from Clara's back-passage. He staggered momentarily, his mind in a swoon, and sank to the soft warm grass, exhausted.

When he'd gathered his strength a little, he hauled himself

to his feet, leaned forward and began planting kisses on his wife's bottom-cheeks, tenderly ministering to them with his warm, wet lips. Already, his spend was trickling from her still-pulsating bottom-crack, a rivulet of gooey fluid that made its way to her inner thigh, and then onwards - down her leg, down into the darkest confines of the restraining box.

In the days and weeks which followed, he continued to feed her through the hatch in the front panel of her prison. But every time, without fail, he would have her in her big, bared bottom, claiming and reclaiming possession of the wrinkled opening from the village menfolk who continued to leave their deposits.

And as his passions increased, fuelled by the strangeness of his new 'relationship' with Clara, he grew more confident, more certain, of his desire to abuse her.

He regularly took off his belt and vigorously strapped her buttocks, making the flesh burn a vivid crimson.

He also found that, by reaching as far as he could into the food hatch, he was able to clasp and fondle her succulent breasts. As the days passed, and his anger at her terrible ill temper and her stupidity slowly grew, his fondling was replaced by savage, punishing slaps, his cruel fingers clutching and twisting her fat nipples until she squealed. And one day, his lustfulness rising to new heights, he reached inside the box and fitted her with metal nipple clamps, delighting in the sight of her handsome, noble face contorting in pain as his new toys bit cruelly into her.

Zeb had never been so excited by life. Curiously, he felt also that he'd never before enjoyed his relationship with his wife so much.

He took a lover then - the redhead with whom his wife had feuded for many years - and rolled on top of her every night, sucking on her pert breasts and sinking deep into her ripeness. And as she toyed with him afterwards, her fingers teasing his still-dribbling cock back to life in readiness for another hot-blooded poke, she talked to him and told him of her dreams...

"Wouldn't it be lovely," she would say, "if Clara were to have to stay in that nice wooden box for the rest of her days..."

And with that, her mouth would engulf him, and make him like her idea all the more...

Chapter 2

Heavy manacles snapped around her ankles, pinching the soft flesh of her legs, and she smelt the vile stench of the brutish overseers as they busied themselves preparing her.

Large, rough hands cupped her breasts, fingers clutched at locks of her hair, and she felt herself being manoeuvred into position, her back pressing against the cold hard surface of the splintering table.

She was hoisted then, hoisted high, by her ankles. A third overseer raised her legs into the air by means of a grinding, mechanical winch. He chuckled maniacally to himself as her body was dragged across the table and left to swing free in mid-air.

Her breasts dangled like fleshy water-sacks, big, bullet-hard nipples jutting towards the cold stone floor. Her thick hair was hanging about her, her knuckles scraping the ground. At head height, the flesh of her ripe wet cunt, shaved bald and dribbling her juices, glistened beneath the probing glare of a stark lightbulb that hung from the ceiling by a length of frazzled cord.

She gazed up at the man standing in front of her. He was clothed entirely in black; black boots, black britches, black smock, black gloves, black cape. His black hair fell about his shoulders, lank and greasy; his black beard, flecked here and there with whispish hairs of white, partially concealed the soulless black visage of his face, and from either side of the long nose, the deep black pearls of his eyes devoured the sight of the gently swaying woman before him.

Matthew Hopkirk, the Sinfinder General; wicked purveyor of pain and punishment to all women who fell beneath his malevolent control. A vile disciple of the devil himself. A carnal beast who showed no mercy, knew no tolerance. Hopkirk was truly alive only when perpetrating tortures upon the soft flesh of screaming women - and when he was using them like dogs, emptying himself into them, screaming to the heavens for the devils which drove him onwards to be vanquished.

As he stood there, he pulled his gloves more tightly around his spindly hands and reached for the wet flesh between the woman's open thighs. She moaned at his touch, and whinnied as he squeezed the pink mound, mauling her with tapering fingers that teased her opening; threatening to slide within her and explore the cavernous pit of her hungry cunt.

"The American is not broken yet," the Sinfinder muttered as he continued his almost obsessive kneading of the woman's pussy flesh. "She cannot yet be utilised in the circus. She must learn to obey without question first, and to co-operate with her fellow slaves."

"Yes, master," the woman gasped. Her upside-down body continued to sway gently, her thigh muscles clenching and unclenching as her wet pussy was roughly groped. "I shall take charge of her training myself. She shall be broken, I promise you..."

Matthew Hopkirk pushed two fingers inside the ripe cunt, and the woman groaned aloud as he took possession of her. He shifted his long, gloved digits inside her, and rubbed his thumb against the erect hood of her fat clitoris. Her body bucked and twisted as it instinctively sought the release of orgasm.

The Sinfinder continued to work the woman even as he looked across the room to one of his overseers and muttered, "spread her." The brute to whom he'd spoken moved sluggishly to the winching machine and began to labour with its wheel. As he turned it, the woman's legs were slowly stretched wide apart, opening even further the flesh-lake of her sex.

Matthew Hopkirk withdrew his fingers and examined the wetness that had gathered on his glove.

He took the cape from his shoulders, deposited it on the table, and moved across the room, out of the woman's field of vision.

When he returned, she took one look at the implement in his hand and began to moan softly.

The Sinfinder ran his fingers through the bunched birch rods clasped tightly in his right fist. "How I do delight in the pleasures of thy ripeness," the Sinfinder murmured. "The pleasures of thy soft flesh. Thou art my favourite bitch-hound, Katharine, and 'tis thy succulent body which affords me the greatest entertainment."

"Thank you, master," gasped Katharine Kimble, the Sinfinder's second-in-command. "It is my pleasure to please you." Katharine was a tall, beautifully shaped female. Despite her forty-one years, her body had retained its well-toned appearance. Fulsomely curved, its greatest glories were the large fleshy breasts - which boasted at their peaks two huge pink nipples - and the big, succulent buttocks - cleaved by a deep and tempting fissure, concealing from view the clammy delights of her two tight holes, both of which were so vigorously and frequently penetrated by the lustful Sinfinder.

"Tell me, Katharine, are the bitch-dogs ready for the circus?"

"I think so, master," Katharine replied, panting in discomfort as the manacles at her ankles began to bite more painfully. "The girls will continue to rehearse their various roles throughout the days, and then perform at night. I shall be watching them and assessing them. If they fail to meet the standard required, they shall be disciplined."

"And the visitors?" the Sinfinder asked, unleashing a practice stroke of the birch rod that cut through the air and made Kathy wince with anxiety. "Are those who were invited to tonight's opening show expected to attend?"

"Oh yes, master. Nobody contacted about your special circuses ever turns down their invitation."

"You must have much to do in way of preparation?"

"Yes, master, today will be busy."

"Then we should get on, so that you can return to your

work and prepare the girls for their performance."

Kathy felt her heart begin to pound like a hammer within her chest. The time of her suffering was fast approaching. As she gazed up into the black pearls of the Sinfinder's eyes, she found herself gripped once more by the familiar feeling of terror which always overwhelmed her on such occasions. A terror which found its origins in her first-hand knowledge of Matthew Hopkirk's cruelty; his unrelenting sadism...

...A first-hand knowledge that was about to be added to...

"Hear ye this..." the Sinfinder announced grandly. His eyes flitted between the three overseers who lurked in the shadowy corners of the grim little room, ensuring that he had their full attention. "Katharine Kimble, thou hast been found guilty of the most heinous crime in the eyes of thy lord, the Sinfinder General. In the darkness of the night, thou were found keeping company with the wanton bitch-dog Sadie. In her cell, while she was chained to the wall, ye were discovered partaking of the flesh betwixt her thighs and groping at her bosoms. Thy own crotch flesh showed the issue of thy lust, a flood of wetness that has not yet abated."

Matthew Hopkirk lowered the bundle of birch rods until they rested against Kathy's cruelly exposed sex. He used them to gently tease her flesh.

"As a result of thy sin," he continued, "ye shall now be flogged betwixt thy thighs until thy flesh is purified. Then, thou shalt be taken in thy wilful hole and therein fucked until thou art full of thy lord's absolving seed."

With his announcement at an end, the Sinfinder stepped back and adjusted his hold on the terrible rods, judging the extent and path of the arc through which he intended to swing them at Katharine's pink cunt. "Let God have mercy upon thee," he growled, and raised the instrument of torture over and behind his right shoulder.

He swung the wicked twigs through a perfect arc, bringing

them lashing down upon the wide-open sex before him, and thrilled at the feeling of their savage impact against the redhead's naked cunt.

Kathy Kimble felt a terrible, scorching pain engulf her and screamed in agony. The flesh of her cunt began to burn cruelly, and tears welled up in her eyes.

She wanted to draw her legs together, to hide her wet pussy from the birch twigs; to find some means of controlling the throbbing torment. But her legs were manacled and wide apart, and there was nothing that she could do to protect herself.

The birch twigs lashed her cunt again. Her screams filled the room. They mingled with her sobs, and with the frantic rattle of the chains at her ankles as her body twisted and turned in a wild, abandoned response to her suffering.

How her flesh burned! Such terrible torture!

The Sinfinder had whipped her in this way before, flaying her with the twigs until the mound of her sex had grown puffy and swollen; until she had whined in pain at even the softest touch.

"Please, master!" she'd squealed on the last occasion, as Hopkirk had pushed her onto the table-top after whipping her, "please, no! Don't have me there, I beg of you!" The Sinfinder had clambered on top of her, his alcohol-drenched breath hot against her neck, and had ripped his cock free of his britches. Katharine had shifted her body beneath him to avoid the torture of having her flayed cunt penetrated, but Hopkirk had weighed down upon her, ground himself against her, and shoved his thick hard cock deep into her hole. He'd fucked her then, even as she'd screamed in pain; fucked her and sucked at her tits, chewing the nipples cruelly while he satisfied himself within her flogged cunt.

The sensation of his hot spunk pumping into her had been almost soothing. As tears had poured down Katharine's face, the Sinfinder had dismounted her and staggered from the room, leaving her sprawled in semi-consciousness across the table, his come dribbling from her...

How Kathy now wished she had left the girl Sadie alone. Waking in the night, she'd seen visions of naked female flesh in her mind's eye, and had found herself recalling the whipping she'd administered to one of the slave girls the night before. The memory of her whip lashing naked buttock flesh had gathered a pool of juice between her legs in no time at all, and she'd felt a sudden, overwhelming urge to enjoy the pleasures of the flesh. She'd chosen Sadie for no reason other than that hers was the cell nearest to the chamber where Kathy was sleeping. For once, she'd left her whip behind, and tentatively made her way into the small chamber where the girl was chained in a standing position against the wall.

Without uttering a word, Kathy had set about making Sadie's delightfully curved body tremble in response to her touch. She'd played with her perfectly rounded breasts and felt her between her legs, teasing the bald cunt until a wetness had gathered there. Then, she'd lowered herself to her knees, and used her tongue on the girl, licking long and hard at the juices that drenched her sopping love-slit.

She'd revelled in the intimacy of the act, and grown ever more excited at the realisation of what she was doing - pleasuring a slave; kneeling before the chained girl as though it were she herself who were the submissive - eating her ripe cunt and affording the groaning female pleasures she had no right to enjoy.

When the overseers had barged their way into the tiny cell, Kathy knew that her adventure was at an end. She knew, as well, what the penalty would be for her transgression. Her cunt flesh would be submitted to the birch.

The Sinfinder loved flogging sexual organs. He had never whipped Kathy's cunt flesh so hard as to draw blood, but in her time as his deputy, she had certainly been witness to such vile excesses of savagery. She had even known him stretch out male overseers on the rack and have their cocks made erect, just for the sheer pleasure he took in birching the engorged organ and tight, swollen testicles. Then he would put the flogged overseer to work, making him fuck each slave-woman in turn with his brutally whipped and tenderised cock.

Most of all, though, Matthew Hopkirk loved to flog cunts. And when he had flogged them, he would fuck the punished pussy himself, while the naked woman trapped beneath his heaving body screamed for a salvation that came only when Hopkirk had had his way.

Kathy was close to passing out at various points during the flogging. The birch twigs threatened to tear her open, but so expert was the Sinfinder in wielding his rods of torment that no blood was spilt. The sex-lips instead grew puffy and swollen. And much to Kathy's shame, they grew wetter as well, as the thrill of being so cruelly mastered sent wave upon wave of unimaginable excitement splashing through her desperately writhing body.

Without warning, he peppered her pussy with a series of swiftly applied strokes. Through the high-pitched sounds of her own agony, Kathy could hear the watching overseers whooping and wailing with delight as the flurry of cuts made her twist and turn through a series of wild, futile manoeuvres.

The Sinfinder leaned over her, appearing between her legs, and peered down towards her face. Against the irksome glow of the naked lightbulb, he was little more than a silhouette to Kathy, his expression shrouded in a blanket of dark mystery. Was he smiling, she wondered to herself, pleased perhaps with the expert way in which he had whipped her vagina? Or did his face carry a heavy sentence of grim malevolence - a warning that his lustful sadism was not yet in abeyance?

She screamed even before the birch twigs ripped into her breasts; screamed with a fresh kind of pain. Her wretched cunt had been burning for much of the flogging he'd administered; each lash had brought merely a topping up of the pain the first few strokes had caused. Now, as he began to lash her wobbling bosoms, Kathy felt as though she were back to square one, enduring again the cruel devastation that an opening salvo of strokes could cause against tender, hitherto untouched flesh.

The breast whipping was brief but agonising. By the time the Sinfinder had finished laying his wicked twigs across her ample breasts, Kathy's flesh was cruelly criss-crossed with raw-looking weals, her nipples having been stimulated to hardness by the repeated touch of the birch.

She felt the overseers take hold of her, and briefly revelled in the sense of freedom which came with being unshackled and lowered to her feet. Yet even as the blood gushed from her head and she felt her heavy, fortysomething flesh once more adhere to the natural laws of gravity, the curvaceous redhead was being prepared for the next part of her punishment.

The overseers sent her staggering against the oaken table positioned in the corner of the gloomy cell. Their heavy hands upon her, stumpy fingers gripping her soft flesh, they bent her across the table-top and clutched morsels of her thighs, pulling them apart to once more expose her cunt.

She screamed as the Sinfinder entered her there, and carried on screaming as he fucked her with all the wild, drunken abandon he could muster. Kathy prayed for an early release from the torture she was having to endure, hoped to God that the brute inside her would spend his filthy seed quickly and then exit her.

But the Sinfinder was numbed with the effects of heavy drinking, and thrashed his cock in and out of her for a full half-hour. Each cruel thrust of his manhood burned her lacerated flesh, stretching her flayed cunt until she howled.

He pulled himself from her without having spent, and plucked his birch rods from the stone floor. As his overseers held Kathy in position, he flogged her bottom with the twigs, bringing them down against her until every millimetre of both buttocks was a vivid crimson. Hurling the birch across the room, he re-entered her, his lustre re-ignited by the flogging he'd given her bottom, and fucked her with all his strength until he'd emptied himself into her.

"The bitch-dogs must be readied," he gasped, staggering backwards as Kathy sank to her knees. "Wear ye but a corset to compact thy flesh, Katharine, and stockings to better accentuate the swell and curve of thy legs. Ensure that thy breasts and buttocks be displayed for all to see, that they shall know there are none who avoid the Sinfinder's justice. Let his fruitful seed dribble from thy wanton hole howe'er it shall. Let those who would doubt my wrath see how thou hast been made to take thy master's seed, and ensure thou dost show thy swollen hole to all who ask to see it."

His declaration made, Matthew Hopkirk drew his cloak about him and reclaimed his birch rods. "Get about thy duties, wanton bitch," he murmured, "and think ye not of the pleasures of the flesh. The Sinfinder has spoken."

He left the cell then, accompanied by his henchmen.

Kathy had heard him take but a few short paces down the dimly lit hallway before a sudden commotion broke out. The scuffing of boots against cold stone was followed by the scream of a young girl - one of the serving wenches, no doubt - and then a familiar sound indeed. "Does thy master not deserve thy respect and servitude?" Kathy heard the Sinfinder growl from along the hallway. "Dost thou seek to fan the flames of his rage? Mark ye, wench - by the time I have finished with thee, thou shalt ne'er again look so brazenly into thy master's face as just ye have done!"

Kathy closed her eyes and felt fresh tears tumbling down her cheeks. There were times, even when viewed from her exalted position as Matthew Hopkirk's deputy, when the horrors of existence in the Sinfinder's house of pain proved too much even for her steely resolve. This was undoubtedly one such time. Outside the cell, in the hallway, she could hear the birch rods swishing through the air, and that terrible, all-too-familiar cracking sound as they fell against bare female flesh.

Another vicious beating, more cruel torture - and for all who had fallen beneath the malevolent control of the Sinfinder General, the certain, irrefutable knowledge that the future would bring nothing but pain, suffering and misery.

"Back to the cell with her!" raged the Sinfinder as he lashed away with the rods. "Shackle her into position. Let us see how she screams when she feels the rods bite into her wanton hole!"

By the time Kathy had shuffled to the doorway, the cell was once again inhabited by the Sinfinder and his henchmen, laughing raucously as they grappled the terrified serving girl to the ground and snapped the shackles around her ankles.

Daring a glance back into the dingy cell, the redhead felt her stomach churn in horror as she saw the girl being winched into the same position in which she herself had been immobilised; hanging upside-down, her legs shackled and spread to expose the flesh of her sex.

Kathy hurried away down the hallway, thankful to no longer be a serving girl herself - grateful to the Sinfinder for the position of office he had bestowed upon her. As she turned into her own sleeping chamber, she heard the sound of the birch twigs cutting into cunt flesh, and listened to the awful screaming of the naked girl as she was punished.

In spite of her better judgement, in spite of her feelings of loathing and hatred for the Sinfinder and his grotesque world of dark suffering, Kathy felt her slushy, dripping love-hole suddenly become even wetter...

Fastening herself into her corset and pulling on her stockings, just as she'd been instructed, she picked up her whip from the bedside table and strode out into the hallway.

Beaten, humiliated, used and now deliriously, wickedly excited by the sounds of torture emanating from the grim little cell at the other end of the long hall, the flame-haired mistress took firm hold of the handle of her whip and strode confidently down the corridor.

It was time to beat some bottoms...

Chapter 3

In a dark and dingy chateau caught up in the clutches of wild woodland on a high hillside in southern France, a silver-haired aristocrat glared through the narrow slits of his eyes at the girl standing before him.

"Take your hands from the mound of your pussy, Beverley," he demanded sternly of her.

With a reluctance that was clearly evidenced by the expression on her face, the girl named Beverley did as she'd been instructed.

She was hairless there. The pink flesh of her vaginal slit was clearly visible between thighs pressed determinedly together; vainly attempting to conceal her womanly charms. Beverley was naked from head to feet. She had removed every stitch of her maid's uniform, and had even divested herself of her jewellery, one item of which was a small necklace, bestowed upon her by her dying grandmother. She'd also removed her ear studs, which had been a farewell gift from a friend - given to her on the eve of her departure for a new job and a new life working in the French chateau of Lord Cartwright and his wife, a woman curiously referred to as 'Mrs Reid'.

The aristocrat was seated in a high-backed chair, one leg crossed over the other, his hands at rest against his thigh. A Monte Cristo cigar was smoking away to itself between impeccably manicured fingers. "You know the routine, Beverley," he said. "You know how Mrs Reid likes it, don't you?"

Beverley nodded her head slowly. There was a sudden expression of helplessness reflected in the features of her pretty face. "Yes, sir," she confirmed politely.

"And you are here, of course, to do Mrs Reid's bidding, are you not?"

"I am, sir, yes."

"Are you glad for the day that Mrs Reid rescued you from

that frightfully dreary orphanage, and brought you here to live, amid such opulence and grandeur?"

"Oh, yes, sir, of course I am..." Beverley's voice trailed away. She lowered her head and gazed wistfully at the luxuriant carpet.

"Well, girl?" the aristocrat said, flicking his cigar ash into the ashtray that rested on a nearby table. "Is there some element of your time here that you perhaps do not appreciate?"

Lord Cartwright knew that there was, even without hearing Beverley's answer. Many times, he'd seen the suffering in her eyes when his wife had been busy having her way with her. Mrs Reid loved to humiliate young ladies, "to punish their errant bottoms and help them learn how to open their lungs and scream," was how she had so often put it in the past. For Lord Cartwright, ensuring that his good lady wife's needs were satisfied in this direction was of the utmost importance - for when she was at her most lustful, after administering some form of terrible physical punishment to one of the young ladies in their employ, she sucked him with a fervour and a passion which the Earl had never before known, and let him ride her all night if he wanted to.

"Well?" he demanded sternly. He was tiring of Beverley's cautious disposition. "If you have something to say, girl, come right out and say it! We will have no secrets here!"

Beverley shuffled her feet uncertainly.

Lord Cartwright leaned forward menacingly. His sudden movement was enough to decide Beverley on her course of action, and she choked from her mouth the explanation he'd been waiting for. "It's just the...the beatings, sir," she stammered. "The frightful beatings and...and...the other things..."

"What other things!" boomed the aristocrat. His complexion coloured impressively as did his best to strike fear into the cowering young woman standing before him.

"The other things that Mrs Reid does to me, sir..." Beverley murmured, fearful of upsetting her master further.

"What other things?! Tell me, dammit, or I'll thrash your hide myself even before Mrs Reid gets her hands on you!"

"She puts her hand up me, sir, you've seen her do it!" Lord Cartwright's increasingly aggressive tone had broken the back of Beverley's resolve. She garbled her words now, letting them pour from her as though she'd completely forgotten to whom she was speaking. "She puts her hand into my vagina and into my bottom and she moves it back and forth, sir, until I scream..."

"If you mean, Beverley Manders," snapped a female voice from the doorway behind the naked woman, "that I give your shameful openings a damn good fisting, then why don't you say so!" The diminutive figure of 'Mrs Reid' paced across the sitting room and took up a position in front of and facing the suddenly recalcitrant maid. Her dark brown eyes smouldered with a barely restrained anger as she peered at Beverley from beneath thick brows. Mrs Reid's face was craggy and sharp, and carried a terrible menace. She was a compact woman and had one of those incredibly curvaceous physiques that seemed likely to bloom into something truly magnificent once released from the constraints of her clothing. In her hand, she carried a bundle of birch twigs, with which she toyed menacingly as she looked the naked maid up and down.

"Wet yourself, girl," she instructed, and teased Beverley's exposed cunt with her wicked birch rods. Beverley did as she'd been told. She responded to the command almost immediately, and allowed her steaming amber water to pour from her crotch and soak into the carpet between her feet.

When the maid had finished, Mrs Reid folded her arms pointedly, and menacingly arched an eyebrow.

"Bad girls who wet themselves," she began, speaking in a low murmur, "must be birched on their bottoms until they learn the error of their ways. I have told you before, have I

34

not, about peeing yourself, you wicked girl?"

"Y-ye-yes, mistress," Beverley stammered, her face colouring up with embarrassment.

"So why have you chosen to wet yourself now, in spite of my warnings?"

"I'm a bad girl, mistress," sniffled Beverley, knowing only too well the game she was expected to play. "I just couldn't help myself. I had to pee."

"Then you must be whipped for being, as you so rightly say, 'a bad girl', must you not?" Mrs Reid's question was a rhetorical one. "And when you have been whipped, to ensure that you have properly learned your lesson, I intend, young lady, to feel you up! Let's see if you're as badly behaved after you've had Mrs Reid's hand up your pussy, shall we?!"

The maid could no longer contain the tears that had been welling up in her eyes. She began to sob quite openly at the thought of once more being flogged and penetrated by the terrible little woman, and felt her heart skip a beat as she inadvertently began to sniffle.

Mrs Reid hated that.

"If you do not desist from your childish sniffling at once, my girl, I shall have little choice but to use the birch upon you until it has actually opened the flesh of your bottom and made your blood trickle free! I assume you would not wish for that to happen, now, would you?"

"No, mistress," the maid whimpered. She wiped her nose and attempted to catch herself in mid-sob.

"'No mistress', indeed, girl!" snapped the redoubtable Mrs Reid. "Now get into position on that chair. Knees apart and leaning forward, supporting yourself against its back."

The pretty young maid did as her mistress instructed. She rested her knees against the seat of the chair to which she'd been directed, and ensured her legs were sufficiently far apart to allow her tormentor an eyeful of her bald, pink vagina. Mrs Reid had a relish for Beverley's cunt - and, indeed, for any cunt - which easily surpassed that of any man Beverley had ever known. The wicked little dominatrix loved to inspect the dark-haired girl's love-slot, and to "give it a good feel", as she liked to put it. She positively delighted in the activity of pushing her fingers in and out of the tight wet hole, stretching the opening until she could easily fit the whole of her hand inside the traumatised young girl.

The maid leaned forward and rested her forearms against the back of the chair, a position which caused her buttocks to swell invitingly, and nicely opened her ripe little cunt for Mrs Reid's greater pleasure.

"Is it a day for the blindfold, Lord Cartwright?" the diminutive woman asked her husband.

"I think not, my dear, I'm happy enough smoking my cigar and just watching today, I think."

The first few times Beverley had been whipped, she'd wondered why, on certain occasions, she'd been made to wear the thick blindfold which Mrs Reid had just mentioned. She'd also wondered why her wearing of it or not seemed to be a decision that was left to the silver-haired aristocrat. An older maid, who'd been in the couple's employ for a quarter of a century, finally explained it to her. "It's dependin' whether 'is lordship fancies a play with missus' charms," the dim-witted Cornishwoman had informed Beverley. "I dared peek, once, when one o' the maids were knelt on the chair and blindfolded. Sometimes, 'is lordship 'as a right urge on 'im, 'n' can't leave missus alone. Well, missus, she don't want no maid seein' her all exposed, like, so she blindfolds 'em. That way, there's no chance o' the girl seein' missus' bare arse when 'is lordship's stripped her down f'r a right good feel."

There had definitely been fewer occasions of late when she'd been made to wear the blindfold, Beverley thought to herself as she knelt in readiness on the padded seat of the chair. She wondered whether any of the other maids were being made to wear it more regularly than she was.

Somewhat ridiculously, she found herself actually worrying that that might have been the case! If it were, what would it mean - that the sight of the others, naked and being whipped, was more of a turn-on for Lord Cartwright than she was? Perhaps that were true; maybe there was something about her that left the aristocrat feeling less than excited. Wasn't she beautiful enough, or attractive enough, she wondered to herself. Maybe her bum didn't stripe-up as nicely as the other girls'.

Beverley's musings were cut short by the sound of the birch rods flying through the air, and the impact of the first terrible stroke across her curvaceous bottom. The maid gasped, and tossed her head back in instinctive reaction to the delivery. Mrs Reid was continuing with her game of supposedly punishing her for wetting herself: "Perhaps this will help you remember to go to the toilet when you need to pee," the small woman growled. "This is your last chance, my girl! If you don't mend your floor-wetting ways smartish, I shall be sending Lord Cartwright to fetch the cane and you'll be squealing to a different tune, I can promise you!"

Mrs Reid whipped the bare bottom in front of her with a power and energy that belied her physique. She brought the birch twigs down against Beverley's smouldering flesh time and time again, flaying the wriggling buttocks for all she was worth. "Back in position, girl!" she snapped whenever the pulverising rods had whipped against her bottom so hard that Beverley had temporarily lost her posture. "Strokes applied to your miserable behind when it is not properly displayed for me are strokes which do not count. Now get your bottom up and thrusting for the kiss of my birch rods!"

The terrible swishing sound of the implement flying through the air, the cruel cracking noise as it struck against soft bum-flesh, the gentle rustling as Mrs Reid shook the twigs free from one another in preparation for delivery of the next stroke, continued to fill the room for a full ten minutes.

By the time the wicked little woman put the birch to one side, Beverley's bottom was a network of vivid weals and red-raw cuts, and seemed to have swollen to twice its usual size.

In keeping with her earlier promise, Mrs Reid demanded of Beverley that she spread her legs as wide apart as possible, in preparation for receiving the dominatrix's hand inside her.

The following few minutes drew a fresh fall of tears from the maid, as Mrs Reid slowly and expertly worked her fingers and knuckles into the young woman's cruelly exposed love-channel. The rest of her hand followed soon after.

"I ought to make you 'moo' like a cow," Beverley's tormentor informed her, "a cow with the farmer's arm up inside it! Perhaps I should get Lord Cartwright to come over and milk your lovely udders, eh? What do you think?"

Beverley was suffering far too much to be able to think at all! Instead, she bucked so wildly in response to Mrs Reid's savage thrusts of her fist that Lord Cartwright was forced to assist in restraining her.

By the time Mrs Reid deigned to remove her hand from inside her maid's vagina, Beverley was hovering on the brink of unconsciousness. "Go and get dressed and resume your duties, girl," the diminutive mistress barked, "and let that be the last time I have to penetrate your body with my hand, as though you were little more than a farmyard animal! Inform the rest of the staff that myself and Lord Cartwright shall be dining in our bedchamber this evening and tomorrow morning, and that our meals are to be left outside the door."

Beverley nodded courteously and scurried from the room, her backside on fire, her cunt throbbing from the vigorous penetration she'd been forced to endure. It was nothing new for the master and mistress to dine in their bedroom after one or other among the maids had been given a whipping. "They go at it like rabbits!" the Cornishwoman had explained to Beverley. "The master, 'e's got a fierce appetite for you-know-what, an' missus 'as 'er work cut out keepin' 'im satisfied!"

There were none among the kitchen staff as taken aback as the Cornishwoman, therefore, when Lord Cartwright and Mrs Reid appeared in the dining room for a nine o' clock supper that very evening. "'er's sat on the chair real gingerly, like," whispered the Cornishwoman to the other staff after serving the couple's meal. "'is Lordship's obviously 'ad a right ol' go at 'er arse with that stick o' his, by looks of it! But I don't know why they're down 'ere f'r their tea; Usually 'e'd be at 'er like a rat up a drainpipe after he'd taken it out on 'er bum, an' after 'e'd watched 'er taken it out on one of us's bums!"

In the dining room, Lord Cartwright and Mrs Reid had eaten their meal in stony silence, both lost in a world of their own thoughts. It was only when their plates had finally been taken away, and another bottle of vintage red brought from the cellar at Mrs Reid's request, that the silver-haired aristocrat found it within himself to engage his wife in conversation.

He gazed quizzically down the banqueting table towards her, and couldn't help but notice the grim expression of bitter disappointment etched into her craggy face.

"Don't worry so much about it, my dear," he said, allowing a gentle and, he hoped, reassuring smile to play around the corners of his mouth. "After all, this kind of business has happened before, hasn't it, and we know exactly what to do."

"Oh, but, Bertie!" exclaimed his wife. Suddenly, her face had come to life, conveying an anxiety she had little chance of concealing. "Perhaps this time it won't work! Perhaps this time, you've tired of me and there will be no solution to it! To fuck me only twice, Bertie, and that after the flogging I gave to Beverley, and the one which you then gave to me! Once upon a time, such beatings would have inspired you to have had me all night and into the morning!"

"I know, my dear, I know, and I wish to high Heaven I could have found it within me to have had you again and again this very evening..."

"But what is it, Bertie? Don't you love me anymore?"

The aristocrat smiled again, and reached into his pocket for a Monte Cristo. "Love has nothing to do with it, my sweet," he assured her. "I have a voracious sexual appetite and I need to be constantly stimulated. The girls we have are charming enough creatures, but I have seen you burn their bottoms more times than I could hope to remember. I wish to see you work your birch upon fresh flesh, my darling - the solution is as simple as that, I'm sure. It's new blood on the staff that's required, and then everything will get back to normal in double-quick time, I guarantee."

"Are you sure, though, Bertie, are you really sure? I don't know what I would do with myself if you ever stopped wanting me!"

The aristocrat lit his cigar and did his best to calm his increasingly agitated wife. "I'm one hundred per cent certain of it, darling," he said. "A new girl to whip, that's all that's needed."

"Then we must get one, and soon, Bertie," Mrs Reid urged her husband, gingerly shifting her whipped buttocks on her chair as she did so. "I'll contact the orphanage, and see if they have any young ladies who're about to come of age."

"No, not the orphanage, Fran," the aristocrat interrupted. "We can do better than there. "Matthew Hopkirk is presenting his circus again," he said at length, "and I think we should be in attendance. He will have many girls from which to choose - pliable girls, all of whom will already have been broken-in, and will be well used to a taste of the rod. It's from there that we should select our new members of staff, don't you think?"

Mrs Reid allowed a sudden, rare smile to dart across her face, and Lord Cartwright settled back to finish smoking his cigar.

The aristocrat knew his wife well. He could see that suddenly all the tension and uncertainty had lifted from her, and in its place, reflected in her deep brown eyes, was the familiar lustre of old; a lustre which had burned there for as long as he could remember. The Sinfinder General's circus of sex slaves had provided the Cartwrights with fodder for their birch-rod before, and the dark-eyed aristocrat felt certain it could be the answer to their problems again.

Suddenly feeling so much lighter in mood, he took a final puff of his cigar before resting it in the ashtray, and stood up.

"Come on," he said to his wife as he glided towards the door.

"Where are we going?" she asked him, putting her napkin to one side and following her husband's lead. He spun on his heels and threw her a glance that was pure, devilish mischief. "There's nothing like the satisfaction of solving a problem to bring fresh lustre to an old man's loins," he informed her. "Now up those stairs with you, young lady. You were slurping your soup at supper, like an uncouth adolescent - and if there's one thing I won't tolerate, it's bad table manners. Suddenly, I'm in the mood to give you the spanking of your life..."

CHAPTER 4

After her own beating, Katharine Kimble had made her way down into the bowels of the mansion house. The passageway which ran under the hall had doors to left and right of it, leading into the cells where various among the slave girls were kept, chained by their breasts and their clitorises to the wall.

Shaggy-haired overseers chuckled to themselves as the red-haired woman approached. Katharine hated days when she'd been whipped. As mistress, she usually had control over all in the mansion house - short of the Sinfinder himself, of course. The exception to that rule was on the occasions when she herself had been beaten. Whenever she'd been flogged, as further penance the Sinfinder temporarily removed many of her privileges, including the privilege that forbade any among his staff to make use of her for their own gratification. During her penance, it was common practice for the overseers to make as freely with her as they wished, and Kathy knew better than to resist them - a course of action which would have flown in the face of the Sinfinder's edict.

Of course, the majority of overseers were careful about the extent to which they humiliated and abused her - mindful, as they were, of her usual status within Matthew Hopkirk's hierarchy. But those who were among the Sinfinder's favoured few, those about whom he would hear little criticism and entertain no complaint, knew that they had her where they wanted her, and revelled in the opportunity to exhibit their mastery of the flame-haired female.

Two such brutes awaited her in the corridor, their mouths breaking out in broad grins as she sauntered imperiously towards them, her whipped breasts bouncing with every step. "Open the cell in which Sarah the madwoman is being kept, gaoler," Katharine commanded, doing her best to retain an aura of control, "and assist me in my endeavours."

The rough brute to whom Katharine had spoken spluttered a phlegmy chuckle and reached out a hand towards the mistress.

"Maybe in a moment," he grunted. and spun her around, pushing her against the wall. "But for now," the red-head felt the shaggy brute's hands against her buttocks, wrenching them apart, "I think I'll have my way with you!"

Katharine felt his thick cock slide within her ravaged hole. Its movement inside her was aided by the presence of the still-dribbling spend which the Sinfinder himself had deposited there. She gritted her teeth, and did her best to impede the passage of a fresh stream of tears from the corners of her eyes.

The brute inside her hammered away like a wild beast at her tenderised sex, egged on by the cries of his fellow henchman, who screamed at him to "rip the bitch apart!".

The cock came out unexpectedly. Kathy felt herself being forced to her knees, and could do nothing to contain the sobs which engulfed her as she realised what was to happen next. Her lips locked around the glistening cock and began to suck, tongue licking at the thick, pulsating muscle in a desperate attempt to make the shaggy brute spend as quickly as possible.

As she sucked, she felt hands clasp her calves, drawing her legs apart, and knew that the second overseer had tired of his watching brief. She felt his cock slide inside her, and then, suddenly, she found herself being fucked more savagely than she could ever remember before.

The beast behind her worked like a snorting bullock, pistoning in and out of her stretched and battered cunt with a savagery that left Kathy feeling sure he would split her in two.

At length, she heard him groan, and felt his spend being pumped into her. Within seconds, her mouth was full as well, and she swallowed as hard as she could, gulping down the hot globules of sticky fluid until she had sucked the throbbing cock dry.

They slapped her then, indiscriminately. Their big hands landed across her face and her breasts, and lashed at her thighs and buttocks, their rough palms singing repeatedly against her pulverised flesh. By the time the brutes' cocks had regained their stiffness, Kathy's body burned a raw crimson. Each fucked her again then, as she lay on the cold stone floor, legs stretched wide, ramming home their advantage until they had tired of the sport.

For all her power, for all the responsibility which the Sinfinder had given her, Kathy knew only too well that she was still a woman in a male-dominated environment. As she lay on the ground, taking the cocks inside her, and felt the overseers' hot spend once more being pumped into her body, she fantasised about flaying the hide from each brute in turn, and wondered how supportive of such an action the Sinfinder would be. After all, he very much favoured the two henchmen who were so savagely making use of her; they were among his most loyal and long-serving. If she whipped them, would he accept her right, as his second-in-command, to mete out such torture? Or would it be she herself who would suffer most, hung upside-down and flogged between her thighs once again?

She didn't know, and her uncertainty made her weep all the more. The brutes who were fucking her, it was they who really held the 'whip-hand' - and they knew it. Whatever pleasures the Sinfinder had guaranteed for himself by making Kathy his 'assistant-in-torture' - in-so-doing ensuring the delights of watching his slaves being whipped and degraded by another female - the fact remained that, as a woman herself, the big-breasted redhead could never hope to be truly free of his reign of terror. She was whipped regularly too, after all, and then used by the overseers until she'd been as brutalised as any among the miserable slave-bitches.

As the miserable reality of her situation crowded in on her, Kathy hauled her battered body from the floor, and staggered against the wall for much-needed support. Thick globules of spend rolled down her thrashed thighs, and the whole of her body throbbed with the pain of the beatings she'd endured. Even as she stood there, gasping for breath, the second overseer amused himself by fondling her fleshy breasts, cruelly twisting her nipples between his fingers.

The sound of a key turning in a lock as the first overseer opened a nearby cell door was music to the redhead's ears. Her torment was over at last! The brutes had had their way, and now her original instruction was being followed; to let her into the cell of Sarah, 'the madwoman'.

Regaining her composure, Kathy moved cautiously across the corridor and past the overseers, stopping in the cell's doorway to assess the sight within. Unlike the rest of the Sinfinder's slave-bitches, the woman called Sarah was not fastened to the wall of her tiny prison by her breasts and clitoris. Instead, she was huddled in the corner of a waist-high metal cage, positioned dead-centre of the room. To the side of the cage stood a low cabinet, the top of which was adorned with a range of curious-looking implements and harnesses, as well as a number of whips and paddles.

"Poor Sarah," the mistress murmured, fixing the dark-haired woman with an icy stare. "How you must wish you'd been more compliant when first you were brought here by the master! If you had been, the Sinfinder wouldn't have certified you insane, and you wouldn't have been condemned to spending the rest of your days couped up like a chicken in that tiny cage!"

Kathy sidled across the cell, a wicked smile playing around the corners of her mouth. The beatings she'd taken had fuelled her desire to make those in her charge suffer at her hands, inspiring her to fresh heights of sadism.

And whenever she felt moved towards acts of uncontrolled savagery, she always came to Sarah's cell. The caged woman had never been truly broken, despite the cruelties perpetrated upon her. Brought to the mansion house after a life spent living in isolation in her small cottage deep in the woods, she had been tortured mercilessly at Matthew Hopkirk's behest. Yet in spite of everything that had been done to her, she'd continued to shriek and scratch like an untamed animal, her wild spirit remaining unbroken even as the Sinfinder condemned her body to day upon day of brutal punishment.

He had tired of her eventually, declaring that nobody but a madwoman could have endured such atrocities, and decreed that she was to be caged like a wild animal for the rest of her days.

Too uncontrollable to have any value to the Sinfinder's circus, it mattered little how Sarah looked, a fact which suited Kathy just fine. She could beat the hell out of her whenever she liked, secure in the knowledge the madwoman would never be seen by any but her gaoler...

...Indeed, Kathy had come to beat her now - and to use her; to make her scream.

Her long dark hair draped across her shoulders, Sarah rested against the cold bars of her stark little cage, her eyes following Kathy as the redhead circled her. The madwoman's face was masked, save for eye and nostril-slots, a fact that served to further deprive her of any meaningful identity; she was, after all, nothing more than a body to be beaten. She had no merit otherwise.

Kathy knew that the madwoman feared her. She knew it, and she loved it. She knew that, for Sarah, her presence in the cell was synonymous with pain and suffering. She delighted in the way the caged slave-bitch cowered in the furthest corner of her tiny prison whenever she came to visit her, her heavy whip swinging at her side.

Kathy allowed her eyes to roam along the contours of the naked woman's body. She could see the underside of Sarah's right foot, bearing the three brands which the mistress had burned into her flesh at the Sinfinder's command.

The woman's feet had been clamped in two vices, and her body stretched to breaking point along a high bench. Clamps had been snapped around her nipples, the long cords to which they were attached then fastened to ringlets in the ceiling. A smaller clamp, nipping her clitoris, had been attached to the ceiling by a similar means. The Sinfinder had been fucking her with his fist, commanding her to call him 'master', but Sarah had been too dull, perhaps too pain-racked, to comprehend. Her disobedience had stirred the Sinfinder to greater rage. "Heat the branding iron," he'd murmured to Kathy, and without even a flicker of emotion registering on his dark countenance, he instructed her to brand the madwoman.

Three times Kathy applied the red-hot iron to the sole of each foot, drawing from Sarah the most inhuman screams the redhead had ever heard. "Now her breasts," the Sinfinder then commanded, and Kathy did as her master bade, pressing the iron against the wickedly stretched flesh of first Sarah's right breast, then her left.

In the days which followed, the woman was returned to the chamber to be branded further still; at the Sinfinder's instruction. The final whipping which the Sinfinder had then applied to Sarah's body would forever live in Kathy's memory. He had flogged her as though she were nothing to him but a carcass, and he'd whipped her shoulders, back and buttocks until she was a tattered mass of criss-cross stripes. His lust re-ignited by the administering of so wicked a beating, he'd re-entered her then, and stayed within her all night, gently shifting himself in and out of her mercilessly ravaged cunt. As he fucked her, his attendants plied him with rough wine and fine ales, and Kathy did his bidding. She entertained him as he descended into drunkenness by dancing naked for him, playing with herself and with the cocks of his manservants, and emptying her bladder on his command.

The unpleasant memory of her own terrible shame that night was enough to deflect her attention back to the present. In light of all that had happened to Sarah, it was hard not to feel an element of sympathy for her sufferings, cold-hearted though the mistress was. Even as she'd been applying the branding iron to Sarah's flesh, Kathy had felt her stomach churn violently with fear; the fear that one day she herself might feel its burning touch. The knowledge that the wicked iron sat ready for use in the deepest, darkest chamber of the house, below the very cell in which she was standing, remained with her always; a constant fear that informed her every thought and action.

...Almost her every thought and action, anyway...

...How stupid she'd been the night before with Sadie, she thought as she instructed the guards to assist her. How foolish to behave in a way that gave the Sinfinder reason to punish her. And how could she have known, how could she really have known, what he would regard as being a suitable punishment for the crime she'd committed; the crime of feasting on the bald snatch of a trembling slave-bitch?

The very thought made her stomach somersault, and she found herself trying hard to concentrate on what the two overseers were doing, in a desperate attempt to control the nausea that threatened to consume her.

The two brutes knew what to do - they'd helped the mistress before. Their hairy arms invaded Sarah's cramped living quarters, clutching and clasping at her as she tried desperately to protect herself. In hardly any time at all they had fastened her wrists together with a long length of rope, trailing its free end out of the cage. Then, they fitted clamps to her ankles, clamps which were also attached to long cords. The two guards wrenched the cords in opposite directions, forcing her legs apart, and then pulled hard, dragging the groaning woman across the floor of the cage until they had pulled her legs clear of the bars.

Kathy sauntered across to the low cabinet and picked up

an enormous strap-on dildo. Moving to the cage, she crouched down and fastened the object in place around the particular iron bar that was lined up perfectly with Sarah's cruelly exposed crotch. Standing back, she issued a curt command to the two overseers to pull as hard as they could on the ankle cords. Sarah slid a few more inches across the surface of her prison and then gasped in agony as she was suddenly impaled on the huge substitute cock.

Kathy moved to the opposite side of the cage, stooped down, and picked up the trailing end of the rope with which Sarah's wrists had been tied. She wrenched hard on it, and moved further and further away from the cage, stretching Sarah's arms in the process. The slave-woman's body was soon stretched in the shape of the letter 'Y'. Sarah groaned as the mistress tugged on her length of rope, drawing her body almost clear of the dildo. The two overseers then pulled on their cords, impaling Sarah once more, before the mistress again pulled the rope she was holding, and once more hauled the woman's body almost clear of the giant cunt-ravager.

The tug-of-war then proceeded with an ever greater frenzy, causing the dildo to be slammed time and again into Sarah's squelching slit. The savagery of each violent penetration made her howl like the wild animal everybody thought that she was.

The gruesome dildo-fucking continued until Kathy's arms could no longer find the strength to pull on her length of rope. As Sarah lay groaning in discomfort, the two overseers unfastened and removed the dildo, then pulled her body a few inches further towards them so that her crotch was mashed against a bar of the cage. They pulled on their lengths of cord then, in order to raise her legs, and fastened them to two of the bars running across the top of the cage, in-so-doing forcing Sarah's body into an 'L'-shape. Then, they pulled her buttocks clear of the cage, a cheek to either side of one of the bars, which was pressed firmly into her cleft. A rope slung around her waist and then fastened to the bar ensured there was no chance of her withdrawing her buttocks from their vulnerable position.

Kathy pulled her whip clear of the hip holster in which she kept it and stood back, sizing up the madwoman's buttocks. She began to lash the exposed cheeks, allowing her whip to uncoil lazily against the naked flesh, rejoicing in the familiar cracking sound of leather against skin.

Kathy loved to use her whip; she loved its movement through the air; the terrible, echoing sound as it struck its target; the inevitable screams it drew from its victim's throat. And she loved the way it made her feel whenever she whipped someone; the hot, lustful feeling that burned between her legs; the sheer, unadulterated excitement. Christ, yes, how she loved to flog!

She whipped Sarah's bottom until all the strength in her arm had deserted her. By the time she'd finished, the exposed bum-flesh was criss-crossed with savage weals. So hot did she feel, she even wondered whether she dared visit another of the slave girls, and make use of her for her own sexual pleasure. But her fear of being caught and once more exposed to the cruelty of the Sinfinder's birch - or perhaps something worse! - proved sufficient to dissuade her.

Before she'd decided quite what to do to gratify herself, Kathy's mind was thrown into turmoil by the sudden overbearing presence of the two overseers. The brutes had been standing at a distance throughout Sarah's whipping, watching intently as the mistress went to work on the bare bottom presented before her. Suddenly, though, with the whipping at an end, the beasts had emerged from the shadows, their lust revived! They grabbed at her again, snorting like animals. The brutes hauled her to the cage and bent her over it, squashing her heavy breasts against the top bars.

A cock was within her almost before they had brought her writhing body under control. It rammed her cunt hard,

50

thrusting at her with a wild, abandoned savagery. She felt the gristle throbbing inside her, felt the thick spend being pumped into her ravaged orifice, and then briefly felt the pleasure of cold air, as one cock left her and before the second invaded. Once it had slithered into her, it fucked her hard, hammering at her squelching slit until it, too, had been emptied of its fluids. The brutes lashed her buttocks with thick leather paddles, then, swatting her jiggling cheeks until her whole bottom burned a fiery crimson.

By the time they escorted the mistress from the cell, Sarah the madwoman had awakened. Released from her shackles, she was once more huddled in the corner of her cage. Within ten minutes of Kathy's departure from the cell, the Sinfinder sent word that the flame-haired mistress's penance was at an end, and that she was once again restored to her position of power and authority.

No longer having need to be apprehensive about who might choose to do what to her, Kathy returned to her chamber and did her best to empty herself of the vile fluid which the overseers had deposited within her. Then she determined to exact her revenge; not upon the pair who'd used and beaten her - as favourites among the Sinfinder's hoards, they were frustratingly always outside her sphere of control - but on others among the overseers, others who had less or no sway with the master. There was a lank-haired boy named Adam, she remembered, a boy admitted to the Sinfinder's motley crew of ill-mannered brutes at the request of old Bill, the landlord of the local hostelry, who did much to assist Matthew Hopkirk in his quest for new girls for his circus. Adam was old Bill's nephew, and had taken well to his new role as an overseer...

Now Kathy would see how well his bottom took to the sting of her paddle...

And then she would fuck him, and fuck him hard - and, for once, she would actually delight in the feeling of hot male spend filling her hungry cunt...

Chapter 5

The neck collars were removed, the frayed cords which had been tightly drawn around their wrists, loosened and discarded.

Yet even as Laura revelled in the few brief moments of freedom she was being afforded, she knew what her fate was to be. Sally had already been fastened back into position. Next to her, a bearded overseer was busily securing Lucinda.

A hand pressed against the small of the American's back, urging her across the dimly lit stone cell to the far wall. There, just as had happened to the other two women, Laura was made to face the brickwork. Her wrists were once again secured together and then fastened to a metal ring attached to the wall just above head height. Lower down, two other fittings nestled into the cold brick. Attached to these were short metal chains, at the ends of which were fitted cruel-looking clamps with serrated edges. The overseer attending to Laura took hold of one of the clamps and pressed it open. He clasped her right breast, gently teased her nipple to hardness, and fitted the clamp over it. Laura winced and grimaced as the sharp metal dug into her aroused flesh. He repeated the procedure with the second clamp and her left nipple.

The overseer dropped to his haunches and took hold of a third tiny clamp, positioned at hip-height. Reaching between Laura's legs, his fingers massaged and groped at her soft vaginal flesh, forefinger and thumb masterfully teasing her clitoris to hardness. Pressing her gently in the small of her back once again, encouraging her to push her groin towards the wall, he carefully closed the third serrated metal clamp around her proudly erect clit.

Laura cautiously shifted forward, shuffling her feet nearer to the wall in an attempt to find the least uncomfortable position.

"Fucking Jesus," she murmured to nobody in particular. She turned her head and looked at her two companions. Both had been fastened to the wall in a similar manner, and stood with their heads bowed in a show of compliance. Their spirit was broken, there was no doubt about it. They were now the obedient property of the Sinfinder General, and would never again dare to think for themselves, let alone fight for their freedom.

Laura felt terribly alone. Her own spirit had not yet been broken, in spite of the terrible traumas of life on the Farm. Once handed over to the Sinfinder General, to be trained to perform as a sex slave in his bizarre circus, she had come to realise that - if anything - life was set to become even grimmer.

She had so far spent only one night in the Sinfinder's tumbledown mansion house; a sleepless one at that, standing face to the wall, just as she now found herself - her wrists fastened, her nipples and clitoris cruelly clamped to restrict her movement to a bare minimum. The overseers had come for her and her two companions in the darkness of the night. They had unfastened them, refastened them, and led them from their cell and out of the huge, bleak house. The brutes had made them trek across hard cobblestones and muddy fields in the wake of the Sinfinder, to see the big-breasted woman be imprisoned on the hilltop.

Now they'd been returned to the cell; returned to their bondage. Was this what Laura's life would be now? Hour upon miserable hour spent staring at the crumbling brickwork of a dank cellar, while her eyes watered from the discomfort of the metal clamps gripping her breasts and genitals?

Maybe the tedium of her situation was something to be grateful for. After all, she couldn't imagine life elsewhere in the house, away from the confines of her cell, proving too pleasant an experience either. She was fast losing all hope of ever escaping her wretched existence.

If only she and Sally hadn't decided to head out to a country pub that fateful night. Or maybe if she'd turned the car left, not right - or right, not left, she didn't know which - they wouldn't have got lost; wouldn't have stumbled upon the village, and found themselves imprisoned, first on the Farm and now in the Sinfinder's house.

Laura closed her eyes and wondered if anybody was looking for her back in the real world. She'd been good at her job - she was the marketing manager of a design agency - and had enjoyed a highly active social life, but there was nobody special. Nobody who wouldn't eventually lose interest in wondering where she'd disappeared to - who wouldn't ultimately assume she'd maybe just 'opted out'.

Opted out. Christ, what she wouldn't give to have the facility to do that right now, she thought to herself.

It was at that moment that the heavy wooden door to her cell creaked open...

One way or another, it seemed to Laura, she was just about to be opted in...

She twisted her head to try and see who'd entered the dingy room. Two of the Sinfinder's hulks shuffled across the cold stone floor, almost immediately disappearing from Laura's field of vision. She heard a noise that sounded like a bucket, or some other such object with a metal handle, being placed on the floor, and then she heard a swishing sound.

A sharp crack, followed by a high-pitched whinnying that emanated from Sally's mouth, rent the air. Laura felt her stomach perform somersaults. From the corner of her eye, she had seen Sal's body jerk in reaction to the stroke, and couldn't bear to imagine the excruciating pain the sudden movement must have caused to her clamped nipples and clitoris. Another swish, the draft from which fanned her back, and it was Lucinda's body that reacted this time, lurching backwards suddenly, stretching the flesh of her breasts and her sex.

Laura swallowed hard, gritted her teeth and tensed her muscles. Must keep still, she determined, no matter how much grief my ass gets. Her fingers folded around the metal ring to which her wrists were fastened and she braced herself. She heard a swishing, felt something hard and heavy impact on her bare bottom, and grimaced as her body twitched in response. The pain, as it seared through her buttocks, was tempered by the sharp, agonising sensation she felt in both her nipples and her genitalia. "Christ!" she moaned, her eyes filling with water as her breasts, her clitoris and her bottom burned savagely.

One of the brutes was upon her then, unfastening her wrists and unclamping her nipples and the flesh of her sex. He clutched a thick handful of her hair and tugged her away from the wall, using his raw power to twist her around and unbalance her, so that she staggered backwards, and down towards the floor.

Her fall was broken by the presence of a wooden bucket beneath her. The brute, careful to retain control of her tumbling body, expertly guided her into a seated position, her bottom wedged inside the bucket.

"Hands on your head and put it down and forward!" he commanded. Laura did as she was told, taking the opportunity to gently rub her skull where the overseer had tugged at her hair. "Now," he growled, "shit!". Simultaneously with the command, Laura felt a whip crack against her back, which had been beautifully presented for the overseer's ministrations by her hands-on-head, head-bent-forward posture.

The command had caught her by surprise, and a sudden, desperate attempt to follow the instruction proved unsuccessful.

"Come on, you little minx!" the man warned, bringing the whip hissing down across Laura's shoulders with a casual flick of his wrist, "get that arse working! Strain, you bitch! Let's have a nice full bucketload!"

"I can't," Laura muttered, continuing to flex her muscles, "I just can't!"

"Can't..?" said another voice from somewhere over by the door. "Or won't?". The voice which Laura heard took her by surprise. It was female, and familiar. She twisted on her bucket to see who'd entered the room, an act which earned her another lash of the whip.

Standing just inside the room was Kathy Kimble, the buxom, flame-haired woman who was assistant to the Sinfinder himself, and to whom Laura had been introduced on her arrival at the house the day before.

Sullen-faced and bare-breasted, the tall, imposing woman was wearing high-cut, black leather panties, dark stockings and suspenders, and high-heeled shoes. At her hip, she carried a thick leather paddle. But it was the instrument she held in her gloved hands that both intrigued and disturbed Laura the most. It was a length of plastic piping, at one end fitted with a nozzle, at the other with a heavy sack of fluid.

Rough hands hauled the American from her bucket, forcing her forward onto the floor. Almost before her knees had cracked against the slabs, her legs were being wrenched apart, her head pushed down until the side of her face was pressed against the cold stone surface. Hands continued to grip her, holding her in her unseemly position. A knee, pressed against her skull, kept her head against the slabs; one pair of hands clasped her around the waist; the other held her buttocks apart, opening her right up.

"I thought you might be difficult," Kathy Kimble muttered. "But we have ways of dealing with bitches like you. Make sure you hold her nice and still for me, gentlemen."

"No!" Laura moaned, trying hard to slither from her kneeling position and close up her ass. Momentarily, she felt the cold nozzle against her anus. Before she had even had time to draw breath, it had been pushed past her ring of resistant muscle and was being edged slowly into her. She felt the piping follow, and gasped as the nozzle was pushed firmly into her bowel.

There was a brief pause, after which she became aware of a warm fluid being slowly released into her guts. She groaned as she felt her body filling up, and was aware of her stomach slowly bloating. The sensation seemed to last an eternity. The vice-like grip of the two muscular overseers ensured she was unable to effect even the slightest movement of her bottom during the ordeal, allowing the flame-haired mistress to empty the entire sack of fluid into her rectum.

"Get your dick out!" Kathy snapped as she drained the bag and ran her hand backwards and forwards across the smooth expanse of Laura's bloated midriff. The brute to whom she had addressed the instruction released his hold on the American's waist and wrenched his trousers down to his thighs. "Let's get her up and over the bucket - then stand in front of her, you big bad brute, and give her something to chew on."

Laura breathed a sigh of relief as the piping was swiftly withdrawn from her bottom-hole. Between the three of them, the manservants hauled her from her kneeling position into a squatting posture, her backside hanging over the bucket. "Don't let her sit down," the mistress instructed the second overseer. "Take her weight and hold her in a squatting position. I want to see her arse." The overseer nodded his head obediently, braced himself, and gripped Laura under the armpits, holding her in a position that ensured her bum remained several inches above the bucket.

The mistress turned towards the first overseer, who had obediently followed her initial command to take up a standing position in front of Laura.

"Get your dick in her mouth," she commanded. Her hand clasped the American's jaw and cheeks, applying pressure to encourage her mouth open. "Right - open wide at both ends, Laura. Let's see if you can suck and shit, shall we!"

Even before the redhead had finished speaking, Laura had lost all control of her sphincter muscle and begun to deposit in the bucket. Without further ceremony, the brute in front of her pushed his cock inside her mouth, ramming it against the back of her throat, urging her to suck. She did the best she could in the circumstances, licking and chewing at the swollen gland as tears rolled down her cheeks.

Standing to her left side, the mistress was clutching Laura's buttocks, holding them wide apart. The redhead had bent right over so that her head was level with Laura's rear end, allowing her a perfect view of the spectacular evacuation. She cast a cursory glance over her shoulder towards the man who stood before Laura, his cock bunging her mouth: "Take my pants down, you big brute," Kathy said, wiggling her broad bottom to further entice the hulking man-beast.

The shaggy overseer required no second bidding, and reached to his side, taking hold of the mistress's black leather panties and peeling them clear of her large buttocks. "Now feel my juicy cunt, you randy monster!"

From the corner of her eye, Laura saw two of the brute's stumpy fingers sink from view into the mistress's pink flesh-pot. The bare-breasted redhead began to coo ecstatically, wiggling her buttocks in response to the thick digits that twisted and turned inside her. She thrust her magnificently curvaceous bottom backwards, forcing the man's fingers further into her love channel. "Diddle my arsehole with your thumb!" she commanded. "That's it! Force the tip inside my bum!"

Laura's mind was a whirl of emotions. Squatting over a bucket, her weight supported by the second overseer and her buttocks held wide apart, she was consumed by an unbearable shame.

Yet even as her ordeal proceeded - even as three pairs of eyes watched her perform the most private, most shameful of acts into a wooden bucket - she felt herself stirring sexually. The feeling of having a dick in her mouth, the close proximity of the mistress's big bare ass, the sight of the brute's fingers jamming the redhead's sex, the squelching of the mistress's cunt in response to the rough penetration, all combined to generate a bizarre, unnerving tingle deep within Laura's loins.

And there she was thinking her captors were the perverts! Christ, how much more kinky could she be!? Feeling horny while being made to evacuate her bowels in front of total strangers!...

...Eventually, thankfully, the flow from her ass came to an end. The mistress disengaged herself from the man's fingers and wrenched her leather pants back into place. "Come on, you disgusting beast," she growled at him, "I haven't got all day - empty those big hairy balls into the bitch's mouth." She clutched hold of his swollen testicles with one hand and began to squeeze and pinch them roughly. Her other hand reached behind him, her fingers pushing between his buttocks and gently tickling his anus. Within seconds, Laura felt a hot jet of semen splash against the back of her throat. She continued to suck, knowing that she would be expected to draw all of the sticky fluid from his thick cock and - of course - to swallow it down into her stomach.

The other overseer released her then, and on the redhead's instruction, Laura was forced back onto her knees while her bottom cleft was sponged and gently scrubbed clean.

"I'll take custody of her now," the mistress said at length. "The Sinfinder wishes to see her, and we mustn't keep him waiting, now, must we?"

Scraping her hair back and adjusting her leather pants, Kathy loomed menacingly over the still-kneeling Laura. "Get off your elbows and support yourself on your hands instead," she instructed. "Keep your back nicely level. I'm going to see how good you are at being a little horse."

The red-haired woman swung her stockinged leg over

Laura and lowered her splendidly broad bottom onto the woman's back. She grasped a thick handful of Laura's hair, tugging her head upright, and pulled her paddle from the waistband she wore approximately half an inch above her pants. Reaching behind her, she pressed the implement's noduled surface against Laura's bottom and gently moved it over the soft, smooth flesh in a teasing, circular motion.

"Now learn, and learn well, my little mare," she said. "Bad horses get their naughty rump-ends spanked very hard. If you don't do as your mistress tells you, then she will paddle your lovely flanks for you until you are whinnying and neighing for mercy. Do you understand?"

Laura knew the score, or thought she did, and replied meekly; 'Yes, mistress'.

The paddle slapped down firmly against her bottom. "What a clever horse you must be!" exclaimed Kathy. "A talking horse! My word, what a novelty. Correct me if I'm wrong, but I don't think horses speak, do they?..." after applying the spank, she had recommenced the paddle's gentle circular motion against Laura's bottom cheeks, "...Perhaps I'm wrong, but I was under the impression they made a neighing sound. Isn't that so?"

There was no way Laura was going to fall into the trap of answering the mistress this time! Instead, mindful of the fact that there was nothing she could do about her situation she shut her eyes, swallowed her pride and made a short, high-pitched neighing noise.

She could hear the overseers chuckling to themselves behind her, and felt her face flushing with embarrassment.

"Now that's a good horse! Horses should neigh, shouldn't they? They should give out great big neighs - great big huge loud ones - or they should, quite rightly, expect to have their bottoms paddled, shouldn't they?"

"Neiggghhh!" exclaimed Laura, in a much louder voice this time.

Blank out the sniggering, she thought to herself; forget

those two hairy fucking bastards. Do what has to be done, Laura; do what you have to do to make sure that that frigging paddle does nothing more than just caress your ass!

"Right, my feisty little mare, let's get going, shall we? Trot to the door, please."

Laura shifted herself carefully through ninety degrees, aware that she needed to at all times offer a firm support for her big-bottomed cargo. She clenched her teeth, and tentatively edged her right arm and her left leg forward. She shifted her weight, and followed up by moving her left arm and her right leg in the same manner. Slowly, she progressed on hands and knees towards the door, taking great care to make no sudden movements which might have thrown her paddle-wielding rider.

Behind her, the overseers continued to snigger, and Laura suddenly became conscious of the magnificent view they would be getting; not only the mistress's big, leather-clad buttocks, but also her own ass cheeks - naked and no doubt blotchy - mashing provocatively against one another as she shuffled like a wretched animal across the stone floor.

The mistress directed her out of the cell and along a grim-looking corridor. The house smelt musty, the walls were damp, the lighting dingy. Laura felt as though she had arrived in hell. The paddle smacked against her bottom again, the redhead unhappy with her silence. "Neigh, you little bitch!" she growled. "Neigh like the obedient horse you are."

Laura once more made the peculiar, high-pitched noise that had reduced the overseers to sniggers, and grimaced as her rider tugged hard at her hair, steering her through a wide open door...

...By the time they re-emerged in the corridor some twenty minutes later - Laura still on her hands and knees, Kathy seated on her back - the American had been depilated. Inside the room, she'd been made to get to her feet and then lie down on a table-top beneath the stark glare of a naked, low-hanging lightbulb. A short, greasy man nonchalantly soaped her pubic hair, before expertly using a razor blade to remove the thick triangular bush, making her skin properly smooth by finishing off with an electric shaver.

Laura was then told to raise her legs until her knees were above her face. The man used the shaver to deal with a few fine, wispy hairs that had sprouted along the lower portion of her bottom cleft. After that, he clasped each of her sex lips in turn, inspecting both sides of the pink flesh for any signs of stray hairs. Satisfied with his highly professional job, he pronounced Laura comprehensively shaven.

In truth, Laura had known the depilation was coming. Both Sally and Lucinda's groins were hairless; it simply wouldn't have made any sense if she'd been allowed to retain her pubic bush. As she struggled along the corridor, the mistress began to feel her between her shifting legs, fingers examining her soft, bare vagina.

She directed Laura into a dark, cavernous room. The American shuffled through the open doorway, wincing as her knees scuffed against the stone slabs. The mistress seemed to be getting ever heavier to Laura, and in a strange kind of way, she was almost glad to have reached their destination.

One look around the room, however, and she made a swift re-evaluation of her feelings!

Various contraptions, most of which were fitted with chains, clamps and other bondage devices, lurked in the shadowy corners. And at the far end of the room, slouching disinterestedly in a high-backed chair, was the unmistakable figure of Matthew Hopkirk, the Sinfinder General.

"The American bitch, master," said the redhead, dismounting her charge. "Made ready for service, just as you desired."

The black pearls of the Sinfinder's eyes reflected no emotion. They glowered from within the white mask of his long and grimly-featured face, cold and staring; boding no good for Laura.

At length, when he had regarded her kneeling frame for long enough, he stretched out an arm and beckoned her with his black-gloved finger.

"Crawl to me, cur," he muttered. "Crawl to me so that I may inspect you."

Laura made her way across the stone floor, grateful to no longer be carrying her flame-haired passenger, yet anxious about the fate which awaited her.

The Sinfinder. The man who struck terror into the hearts of all who knew him. Even back at the Farm, the stern-faced Hans, the tight-lipped Gerda, had functioned only for the Sinfinder's benefit, only to please him. What kind of devil could wield such power, Laura wondered to herself. What sort of man was able to command such respect?

Her stomach churned and her guts began to ache, in spite of the cleansing they'd been given. Her skin tingled and seemed almost to crawl, and she felt herself becoming hot and flushed as the fear grew within her.

The Sinfinder held up the palm of his hand, instructing her to advance no further. "Assume a squatting position," he commanded her. Laura hauled herself up and adopted the required posture. "Open your legs."

She edged her knees apart, exposing her hairless genitalia.

"Open your sex."

Gently, Laura used her fingers to spread her pink lips, revealing the dark hole of her vagina.

Hopkirk stared at it for several seconds. "You have a ripe cunt," he murmured. "Is it juicy when you are aroused?" He looked at the American quizzically, his face contorting into a dreadful, malevolent grimace.

"Yes, sir," Laura replied. She was aware as she croaked the words from her throat that she didn't know quite how to address the Sinfinder. She remembered then that the mistress had called him 'master', and felt gripped by a sudden, terrible fear. What if she had addressed him incorrectly - if she'd been disrespectful by addressing him merely as 'sir'?

"Does your ripe cunt drip, wench?" Judging by his continuing line of questioning, Laura thought to herself, he obviously hadn't been offended - though the questioning itself was disconcerting, to say the least. "Sometimes, master," she replied, making certain to follow the mistress's lead from thereon in.

"What makes it drip?"

"When someone goes down on me, master."

The Sinfinder sat silently for a while, his eyes remaining trained upon her, his black-cowled frame slouched against the chair. Eventually, gazing down at her still-exposed vagina, he said, "Do you drip into their mouth?"

Laura's heart was hammering in her chest. She had surprised herself sometimes with her ability to respond to the intimate questioning she'd had to endure since her kidnap. Her sheer, unadulterated fear of the satanic figure sprawled majestically before her was certainly a powerful encouragement to comply. Yet the shame was still there.

She gathered her strength, breathed deeply, and prised an answer from between her own lips:

"Yes, master," she began, "I - I drip into their mouth."

"Stand up."

She did as she was told, her thigh muscles throbbing from the strain of having had to squat.

"Cup your breasts."

Laura took hold of her breasts and gently pushed them upwards, so that her nipples - semi-hard from the cold - thrust out proudly in front of her. "Do you like to have your nipples sucked?"

"Yes, master, I like to have them sucked."

"Play with your nipples, girl."

Laura stood there, in the half-light, naked and trembling, and began to gently tease her own nipples. She squeezed them between her finger and thumb; using her nails to pinch at them and make them stand proud. She pressed her palms into her breasts, squashing the flesh, and twisted the bullet-hard nodules until they stood engorged, like huge thimbles, pointing defiantly at the cowled figure lounging before her.

"Slap them."

With her palm, Laura lightly swatted her right breast, repeating the procedure on her left mound. "Slap them!" the Sinfinder repeated in a low growl. She slapped again, harder this time. Her hand fell sharply on her delicate flesh. It made a sound reminiscent of the one she had heard so many times before; of a palm against a bare bottom.

Little shocks of pain assaulted her tits as she slapped away at them. Her skin coloured a gentle pink and each breast trembled as it was struck - but the pain was endurable.

Although she wasn't hitting herself too hard, the sound of the slaps and the gentle jiggling of her bosom seemed to satisfy the Sinfinder. His eyes were exploring her naked body; resting their gaze on first her bouncing breasts, then seeming to admire the shapely contours of her waist and hips, before drinking in the erotic sight of her bald pink slit, pouting like a succulent fruit from between her thighs, fleshy and inviting.

"Put your hands on your head."

Laura reacted swiftly to the instruction; so swiftly that her palms were pressing against her skull even before her breasts had finished trembling from the final slap she'd administered to them.

Matthew Hopkirk stared contemplatively at her, his gloved, sinewy fingers stroking his firm jawline. Laura was aware that the mistress had joined her, taking up a position to her left and a little behind her.

"You are here to learn how to obey," the Sinfinder said, "and how to perform. You will suffer here, mark my words - but whether you suffer less or more..." he paused for effect, his dark eyes briefly twinkling, "...that is for you to decide." He fixed her momentarily with an icy stare, then reached down to his side and grasped hold of something. Laura couldn't see what; the object was concealed by the hanging folds of his thick black cloak.

When it came into view, she heard herself gasp and felt her heart pound anxiously in her chest.

She feared this man, now - truly feared him.

His cold, dispassionate eyes stared blankly at her, and she realised that his cruelty really did know no bounds. She knew as well that there would be no escape for her now, no respite from merciless suffering for her naked, trembling body.

She felt the flesh of her bottom begin to crawl and tingle as she gazed upon the wicked implement of torture that Matthew Hopkirk held in his hand, and she nearly wet herself.

She was about to receive the thrashing of her life...

Chapter 6

Clasped in the Sinfinder's hand was a wicked-looking birch. It was fashioned from four long, straight twigs and bound together at its base by a length of twisted wire. The twigs must each have been thirty to thirty-five inches in length, Laura surmised, and splayed outwards like grasping fingers.

Matthew Hopkirk beckoned the American towards him.

Laura's nerves began to jangle and she bit down hard on her lip, almost immediately tasting blood. Her chest was heaving; her skin, damp with fear; her eyes cradled tears that were too afraid to tumble down her cheeks.

She approached the cloaked monster with small, shuffling steps, as if she imagined that prolonging her fate might gain her an advantage. The Sinfinder readjusted himself, settling into a more upright position, and patted his thigh instructively.

She took her hands from her head, leaned across his dark frame, and clasped the arm of the broad chair in which he was sitting. With her arms supporting her weight, she lowered herself until her body was pressing against his thighs, until she could feel the thick bulge of his cock digging into the fat hood of her clitoris. The uncomfortable position in which she was draped - her head and breasts hanging over the arm of the chair, her arms tucked in neatly at her sides, her groin and abdomen raised by the thick swelling in Matthew Hopkirk's breeches - ensured her bottom was beautifully presented.

As she lay there, she could almost imagine the view which the red-haired mistress must have been avidly drinking in from her vantage point a few short paces away.

In her mind's eye, Laura could see the darkly attired figure of the Sinfinder, grim and sombre, seated in his high-backed, ornately carved chair. She could see as well the wicked bundle of birch twigs clasped in black-gloved fingers. And she could see herself, too; naked, and draped across her tormentor's legs; her breasts pointing towards the stone slabs; her bottom positioned directly beneath the Sinfinder's face - beautifully round and dreadfully vulnerable.

Laura closed her eyes, and swallowed hard to try and dislodge the lump that had risen in her throat. The terrible canings she had received on the Farm, the childish spankings she'd been made to endure, all seemed to pale into insignificance for her now.

The tears which had been hovering at the rims of her eyes began to tumbled down her face, dripping from her and splashing against the floor.

How had she come to this? How had her life transported her from the cut-and-thrust world of a high-powered job - wheeling and dealing over more business lunches than she could eat, canoodling with prospective clients late into the night at some of the City's most fashionable wine bars - to the dark and grimy room in which she now found herself?

Momentarily, she remembered herself as she once had been; in control, dressed-to-kill, flirtatious and desirable, yet cold and untouchable. Her past was a world away; her present, a nightmare. She was stretched out now, naked and vulnerable, across the legs of a vicious sadist. His fingers were massaging the soft skin of her lower back, his cock pressing against her sex.

And as for her bottom; her poor, tortured bottom! Positioned beneath the Sinfinder's nose, bare and upturned, it would soon feel the tormenting touch of the terrible birch twigs, and would dance and jiggle and cavort in wild abandonment, its spectacular display of perpetual motion brazenly exposing her secret charms for her tormentor to admire or to flog, as he saw fit.

Laura felt Matthew Hopkirk's gloved fingers glide across each of her upraised bottom mounds in turn, and bit deeply into her lower lip once again. She was, for the first time in her increasingly bizarre life, about to have her bare bottom birched...

"Plead for thy salvation, wench," muttered Matthew Hopkirk, "Plead to be delivered from the touch of the birch rod." Laura winced as the Sinfinder swished the bundle of twigs through the air. Her buttocks flinched in response to the sound, anticipating the arrival of the first stroke...

...It didn't come, and she breathed a heavy sigh of relief.

"Please, master," she murmured. "Please spare me. I don't think I can stand to be beaten on my bottom. Not with those twigs. I'm begging you to have leniency - I promise I'll be a good girl, really I do."

The Sinfinder's gloved hand gently massaged Laura's soft bottom-cheeks, his fingers dipping between her legs, pressing against the flesh of her sex. She moaned in response to the caress, hoping that he might take pity on her and decide to feel her up instead of birch her. She could hear his fingers squelching as he stroked her oily slit, and was surprised to realise that she was wet between her legs.

She tensed her thighs and buttocks as the Sinfinder pressed first one, then two fingers into the warm depths of her moist vagina; tickling the soft, warm flesh of her creamy interior. So he was going to feel her up! Pleasure before pain - some kind of silver lining at least, she mused.

As his fingers burrowed within her wetness, the Sinfinder trailed his thumb along her hot slit. Laura responded with frantic movements of her aching nether regions. She thrust her buttocks upwards at his face, arching her back as a series of delicious spasms thrilled her tingling body.

Even as she writhed across the Sinfinder's legs, Laura was aware that, somewhere out of her field of vision, the red-haired mistress still lurked. Katharine Kimble would be watching the American's squirming contortions with interest, and no doubt enjoying the sight of her slushy vagina responding to the Sinfinder's ministrations.

Laura felt her flush deepen at the thought. She hated the notion that she was inadvertently entertaining the mistress, letting her see how she responded to such intimate caressing.

Yet there was nothing she could do. Her thighs were wet with her own dribbling juices; her shaven mound, hot and sloppy. She was consumed by the delicious heat that was emanating from her genitals, and couldn't help but grind herself against her tormentor's gloved and slimy hand.

Laura began to pant and wheeze then, searching for the stupendous orgasm that she knew lurked within her, close to bursting point. She wanted her banks to break, needed the feeling of an explosive climax and the little darting ripples of pleasure that would assault her nerve-endings for long moments afterwards. She forgot herself entirely, tossing her head back in a show of wild abandonment and thrusting her whole body backwards against Matthew Hopkirk's sinewy fingers.

The mistress's fingers suddenly clutching at her locks of hair dragged her back from the brink of ecstasy.

Katharine Kimble had moved to the side of the Sinfinder's chair, directly in front of Laura's bobbing head. Her body was heaving with a barely controlled lust.

The flame-haired woman used her free hand to ease her own black leather pants over her big bottom cheeks and down her legs, until they hung at mid-thigh, an action that left her bald pink love-slot thrillingly exposed.

She tugged at Laura's hair, and pulled the American's face close to her groin. Without further delay, she thrust her pink flesh forward. Laura choked as her mistress's fat love-mound pressed against her lips, and she inhaled the sharp, pungent scent of the redhead's dripping sex.

"Lick me!" the mistress commanded, wrenching violently at Laura's hair.

Her nether orifices still throbbing in response to the Sinfinder's relentless groping, Laura reached round and clasped Kathy Kimble's broad, fleshy buttocks, drawing the mistress towards her.

She began to tongue the redhead's groin then, lashing at the big button of her clitoris until it throbbed cheekily and swelled to a spectacular size. She sucked the fat hood between her lips and nipped it with her teeth, causing the mistress to buck like a wild, magnificent horse, tossing her head backwards and exhaling a languorous, ecstatic moan. "Oh God, that's glorious! Yes - yes! Suck my wet cunt, you little yankee bitch! Lick up all my juices with that lovely long tongue! Ooooh! Eat me, darling - eat your mistress's great big cunt. That's it! Yes! Suck me - suck me, you filthy little whore!"

Laura worked her tongue at a frenetic speed, using it to diddle the engorged clitoris, and then slid it along the sopping wet flesh of her mistress's slit, towards her hot, sticky hole.

The redhead was using her fingers to hold her own vaginal lips apart, allowing her lover access to the silvery juices that were dribbling uncontrollably from her oily orifice. Laura lapped them up, her frantic efforts to please, her peculiar feelings of lustfulness in spite of the fact she was making love to another woman, causing her to become distracted from her own attempts to achieve orgasm...

Instead, she transferred her sense of enjoyment to her new activity. She revelled in the psychological thrill of what she was doing to Kathy; in the excitement of performing what for her was such a perverted act. She found herself unexpectedly delighting in the smells, the very feel, of her mistress's wet and bulging love-mound.

Her own body tingled madly, her nerve-endings jangled. A sheet of hot sweat sheathed her skin. The experience of being felt up by the sadistic brute across whose lap her wretched body madly flailed had turned her into a wild animal! She had been close...so close, to a stupendous orgasm - and much of her excitement, she knew, had been derived not from the sensual touch of her tormentor's gloved fingers, but from the terrible, undeniable helplessness of her situation.

As digits explored her, mauled her sensitive, secret flesh,

Laura had been aware that, hovering somewhere above her madly squirming posteriors, was her real destiny; four vicious twigs, bound together to create an implement with which her naked buttocks would soon become overly acquainted. And when the mistress's bald cunt had been pushed into her face, its dizzying stench, its clammy warmth and fragile softness had ignited Laura's basest, most depraved instincts. At that moment, she wanted to indulge herself as never before, to engage her lips, her teeth, her tongue in an act of shocking carnal sin. She wanted to devour the broad-hipped woman's succulent centre until it was Laura herself who became the mistress, commanding the redhead's magnificent frame with the most nonchalant flicks of her teasing tongue.

And now the redhead growled like a dog as Laura's tongue lashed at her wet flesh. The American's fingers crawled across her big, plump buttocks and teased them apart, seeking the damp, wrinkled skin of the mistress's arse-bud. The woman whinnied as her pouting crater was gently tickled, and thrust her groin hard against Laura's avidly sucking mouth. Pressing her finger into the tight, hot bumhole, the American lashed her tongue across the redhead's engorged clitoris over and over again, the repetitive hammering motion pushing the woman ever closer to a shattering climax.

"I'm coming!" Kathy screamed at length. "I'm coming! Oh, God, how I'm coming!" Laura wiggled her finger in the mistress's clammy bottom-hole, teased her bullet-hard clitty with rapid tongue strokes, and waited for the inevitable.

The redhead tensed and then trembled, her body clutched by sudden, violent spasms. Her big breasts quivered as the thrills of a delicious spend engulfed her. Her groin bucked, mashing the soft flesh of her mons against Laura's chin. Her fast-swelling pool of silvery love-juice splashed the American's skin, the scented delights of her heated climax lingering in Laura's nostrils.

The mistress sank to her knees, her body heaving from the effects of her pulsating orgasm, and began to whimper.

"Oh, master," she sniffled, "oh, master, what have I done? Oh, sir, I am so sorry for my sinful behaviour. Please, master, please - do not punish me! Punish the shameless bitch instead for mashing me against her and using her wicked tongue to bring me to a lovely spend!"

Laura lay slumped across the Sinfinder's powerful thighs, her breasts heaving, her skin hot and tingling. She had the taste of the redhead in her mouth, and could feel the juices from the woman's ripe love-hole trickling down her chin, dripping from her onto the arm of the chair.

Matthew Hopkirk withdrew his gloved fingers from her orifice and wiped them against the small of her exposed back. They were wet - drenched, it seemed, from the amount of time it took him to divest them of the silvery love secretions. Soon, the whole breadth of Laura's lower back was soaked in her own juices.

The mistress was grovelling on the cold stone slabs, mere inches from the Sinfinder's leather boots. "It was that snivelling cur who caused the spend, my lord," she sobbed. "She sucked on my pussy like the dirty dog that she is until my poor body had no choice but to succumb to the pleasures she was causing. Beat her, master - beat her until you have flayed the skin off her yankee arse!"

"Fuck you!" Laura snapped. "You pushed my frigging face in there!"

"Don't listen to her, sir! Beat her bare arse with the birch twigs, my lord! Flog her until she bleeds!"

"Silence!" the Sinfinder snapped, his gravelly command causing the redhead to tremble with fear. "I shall mete out that which ye both deserve, and ye shall know the true meaning of suffering!"

He clutched a handful of Laura's hair, the rough action drawing a startled gasp from her mouth, and pushed her head downwards over the chair arm.

"Keep thy head and thy shoulders where they are," he demanded.

His gloved fingers swiftly traced a path along her spine, tickling the soft, wet flesh of her back, then wandered briefly up and around, to gently squeeze her right breast. Laura murmured at the intimate contact...

...And then, the birching began.

His gloved left hand pressing down firmly on the centre of her back, he swished the wicked birch twigs though the air and brought them cracking down on Laura's bare bottom-cheeks. The four rods each chose their own portion of flesh upon which to land, spreading out across the expanse of her naked bum like tapering fingers, their wicked sting biting into her succulent flesh.

"Oh Christ!" she screamed in pain-racked misery, "Oh dear God, no!"

"Thou shalt learn thy lesson through the ministrations of the rod, ye naked-arsed wench!" warned the Sinfinder, allowing the four gruesome instruments of torture to slither teasingly across her burning skin before he once more raised them into the air.

The dreadful swishing sound again, and the twigs were castigating her lovely skin a second time; another four dreadful cuts, landing all at once, and burning her the length and breadth of her hot, round bottom. Two terrible, skin-slicing strokes had been delivered - and yet, because of the cruel, multi-twigged nature of the dreadful birch, Laura had received no fewer than eight cuts across her soft bottom flesh.

A third stroke, taking the cut-count to twelve, worked its deadly magic. The birch twigs splayed once more, stinging her upper thighs as well as her trembling posteriors, and making her howl in uncontrollable anguish.

She began to kick wildly as the rods struck a fourth time, threshing her legs around like a wilful child, her wet cunt squelching as she fought for freedom. All the while, the Sinfinder held her secure. He lashed her with his cruel birch rods until her quivering bottom seemed to swell to twice its size, and burn the fiery red of the setting sun.

Thwack! came the fifth stroke. The twigs molested another four portions of her madly thrusting bottom. And as she screamed, and wriggled like a little girl, she felt the mistress's arms clutch hold of her legs, pinning them firmly together so that she could neither effect an escape nor manage to make her bottom a moving target.

Thwack! A sixth stroke, and her pinioned body bucked in pain as the frightful rods tanned her naked bum flesh. She sobbed and screamed, and beat her fists against the side of the chair - but still the gloved hand pressed against her back; still the arms that clutched her legs held her secure; still, and always - perhaps forever, it seemed - the savage birch returned to her bare bottom, exploding against her skin time and again, relentlessly flogging the whole, exposed area of her desperately writhing behind.

Laura was held across the Sinfinder's knee and flogged with the birch until she was sure there could have been no skin left on her buttocks. And when she was allowed to haul herself clear of Matthew Hopkirk's muscular thighs and his lustily bulging erection, it was only in order to follow his next terse instruction.

She dropped to the ground on her elbows and knees at his growled command, and rested her head against her forearms. The mistress, who sobbed as the Sinfinder commanded her too, sank to her knees by Laura's side and adopted exactly the same position.

Their two bare bottoms thrusting into the air, the women squealed as Matthew Hopkirk briskly birched them. Hard, savage strokes stung first Laura's crimson bum cheeks, and then the broad expanse of the redhead's majestic moons, before the wicked twigs were once again laid across Laura's buttocks.

After flogging them soundly for several minutes, the Sinfinder ordered them to part their knees, and set about their flesh anew, striking them with choice, downward strokes that sent the twigs flying into their exposed bottom-clefts. The women howled as the cruel rods cut into their pink bumholes and wet vulvas - and moaned as their torturer teasingly flicked the birch at their sopping sexes, using the twigs to stimulate their fat little clitorises.

He whipped them mercilessly until the birch twigs began to snap and break apart, and even then had not enjoyed his fill of thrashing.

The Sinfinder grabbed them both by the hair then and tugged them to their feet. He escorted them across the room and deposited each of them on a wooden trestle.

Each contraption consisted of a long, narrow, horizontal beam, attached to each end of which were a pair of vertical, splayed legs. The women were made to lie along the side-by-side beams, their wrists and ankles fastened into straps already fitted to the contraption's legs. In this way, they lay flat on their stomachs, a breast hanging either side of the horizontal beam. Their ankles were fastened wide apart to the trestle's legs. Their burning bottoms hung over the end of the beam, perfectly presented for whatever wicked torture the Sinfinder next had in mind.

Matthew Hopkirk stood behind and between them, and used his gloved hands to feel their wet vulvas. They moaned softly as he touched them there. The pleasure offered by his exploring fingers was tempered by the soreness which had built up in their private parts, the result of the wicked birch strokes he'd administered between their legs.

And then, suddenly, he withdrew his digits from their naked pussies, and plucked a thick leather paddle from a hook on the nearby wall.

As the women screamed and wept, he used the implement against each bare bottom in turn, splatting their cheeks with a power and an energy that showed the women no mercy.

The floggings completed, he slumped against the wall, his chest heaving beneath his thick black cloak.

For a few moments, he observed the naked bodies presented before him, sprawled across the trestles and trembling gently as the women sobbed. Then, gathering his strength, he hauled himself upright and shifted behind Laura, his hands tugging at the cloth of his breeches.

"I must vanquish the devil within me," he murmured. "He must be cast out and defeated." His gloved fingers clasped the soaking wet flesh of her bald love-mound, squeezing it fiercely. She groaned at his action. As another wave of pain consumed her buttocks, she wondered why, deep within the pit of her stomach, she was feeling a terrible, desperate excitement.

"Tell me," her black-cloaked tormentor demanded, "tell me how ye wish to have me inside thee."

Laura's breathing became even more laboured, and she struggled hard to choke the words from her dry throat. "I'd like your big cock up me," she stammered.

"Where, thou miserable, yankee whore? Up you - where? How would thou like my cock up thy tight little cunt?"

"I'd love it," she gurgled in response. There was a part of her that genuinely meant what she said.

"Tell me then."

"I'd love for you to put your cock up inside of my pussy."

"Thy 'cunt', thou foolish little whore," Matthew Hopkirk scolded. He moved across the room and lifted down a long slender cane from where it hung on the stone wall. Returning to Laura, he unfastened her ankles and re-tied them, higher up the trestle's legs. The new position raised her buttocks, tightening the flesh, and exposed entirely to view her glistening pink slit and wrinkled anus.

Matthew took aim at Laura's bare bottom and swung the rattan through a wide arc, delighting to the sound of bamboo against succulent female buttock flesh.

Laura squealed and wriggled her hips.

"Say it again, but ensure thou use the correct words this time."

"I'd love for you to put your cock up inside of my cunt!" Laura squealed from between gritted teeth.

She felt the master's fingers at her buttocks then, separating them even more than they already were. An intrusive finger slithered inside her vagina. She gritted her teeth at the feeling of it.

The Sinfinder slowly explored the soft, warm fleshiness of her dribbling love-slit. Laura gasped when a second finger joined the first, and gasped again at the feeling of a third and fourth digit being slowly edged inside her.

"When I give thee the order," the Sinfinder said, "ye shall pee thyself; dost thou understand?"

The instruction came as a shock, but Laura's mind was already spinning and confused. The latest demand seemed entirely in keeping with the bizarre experiences she was having.

"Yes," she groaned in response from between clenched teeth. Her whole body was tense, her eyes closed and watering from the feeling of her master's fingers up inside her; feeling, probing, examining.

"Yes what?" the Sinfinder's question was accompanied by the sudden curling together of his four fingers within her body. His thumb slithered inside to join the rest of his hand.

"Yes...ahh!...Yes, master! Please! Please, no more."

"How dost thou like this, bitch-dog? Tell me ye love it. Tell me ye love the feeling of my fist up thy wet cunt."

"I love the feeling of your fist up my wet cunt."

"Piss thyself."

The water flowed almost instantly, pouring from Laura and splattering against the floor, slapping against the Sinfinder General's thighs; hot, amber and acrid.

Matthew Hopkirk pulled his hand from inside Laura and held it in the jet of urine, cleaning it. His wet palm slapped against her hip as he shifted forward and pressed his penis in between her thighs. Laura felt the thick muscle ploughing into her, pushing against her already abused inner walls. She felt as though a huge tree trunk had suddenly been forced between her legs and up inside her pussy.

"Thou art a wet little bitch," the Sinfinder spat as he withdrew and re-plunged. "The cut of the birch-rods dost suit thee well, I surmise!"

Laura groaned and gasped as the Sinfinder fucked away inside her. He rammed her over and over again, pounding into her with such force that Laura felt sure he would split her pussy wide open.

When he finally pulled his cock from within her, he did so in order to move behind the flame-haired mistress - and prepare himself for enjoying the pleasures of her fleshy love-hole.

Laura felt a sudden, biting pang of jealousy, and wondered where the hell it had come from. How was it possible, she asked herself, that after the terrible, awful flogging she had received at the hands of this man, after the miserable existence she had endured, and continued to endure, at his instruction, she could be jealous at the way he had abandoned her?

She wriggled against her bonds, agitated by what had happened, angered by her own ridiculous response to his desertion of her.

Next to her, the mistress had received their master's cock deep within her slushy cunt, and was being gently shunted back and forth along the trestle by the Sinfinder's repetitive thrusting motion.

The gentle, rhythmical movement struck time and again like a dagger at Laura's heart. The bitch, she thought to herself. The frigging bitch!

At that moment, Laura began to truly hate the mistress. She hated her for the pleasure she was affording the Sinfinder. And she hated her for the way she had stolen him from her.

And when the redhead groaned and gasped as Matthew Hopkirk filled her love-hole with his stickiness, Laura hated her even more; hated her for the fact that she had milked him; brought him to a howling, body-racking climax...

She just didn't know what was happening to her anymore!

Why in the whole, wide, miserable world - did her randy little cunt dribble its juices whenever her bottom was thrashed?

Laura didn't know.

Couldn't even contemplate.

All she knew was that, ridiculous though it seemed, there was nothing in the world that she wanted more at that particular moment in time than to have Matthew Hopkirk plunging inside her once again, his thick, hard cock pumping its juices deep into her hungry, ravaged womb...

Chapter 7

The birching Laura had received had been so severe that the Sinfinder decreed she was not to be beaten for several days. The gruesome overseers who guarded her, frustrated by their need to exercise restraint, took their pleasure of her in different ways. She became used to kneeling before one or other of the grizzled beasts, sucking into her mouth the sticky contents of its testicles. Her pussy and backside were frequently used, too. It became normal for her - as she stood facing the wall of her cell, restrained at the wrists and clamped at the nipples and clitoris - to feel thick globules of white fluid trickling from her flooded holes and dribbling down the backs of her legs.

The first time she'd been taken after her birching, Laura had entered into the experience enthusiastically. She was still in a lustful frenzy, craving the sensations which the mistress had enjoyed when the Sinfinder had emptied his swollen testicles into her. She'd found herself imagining that the brute thrusting away behind her was Matthew Hopkirk, and had pushed her bottom back to meet his strokes, delighting in the sensation of his hot spend finally filling her love-crack.

As the days passed, however, and her ardour cooled, the regular penetrations once more became grim and uncomfortable events.

She was sent each day to a young woman named Bridget, who seemed to have some understanding of rudimentary medical matters. Like her, Bridget was a slave. Born and raised in the village, she had been sent at the age of sixteen to the Farm, where her impressive obedience and beautifully curvaceous body had caught the attention of her masters. As happened with all promising specimens at the Farm, she had been transported to the Sinfinder's ramshackle mansion, where they both now resided, to be trained as a performer in his sex circus.

Laura liked Bridget, and came to enjoy her visits to the mansion's small annexe for her daily treatment. She would lie face-down on a table while Bridget used a special balm to sooth her gradually healing bottom, and would moan gently as the girl's soft fingers slipped into her nooks and crannies, mischievously teasing the tender flesh of her pink mound, and the tight little crater of her anus.

"It probably suits the Sinfinder's purpose to have you out of action for a while," Bridget revealed, as her fingers kneaded the American's buttocks. "He'll want to know he can guarantee your obedience, but he'll also want to train you to perform."

"What does that mean, honey?" Laura asked.

"We have to rehearse the little scenes that we perform for the master's special audiences," Bridget replied. "The Sinfinder will make you watch the other girls going through their paces, so that you get some idea of what'll be expected of you."

Laura recalled the series of tableaux she had been shown on her arrival at Matthew Hopkirk's tumbledown residence. The mistress had shown her a variety of scenes being rehearsed, and had even demanded Laura's participation in one. The American had been given the character of a miscreant schoolgirl, and had been turned over the knee of a blond, big-breasted 'headmistress' for a spanking. She told Bridget about the experience, and about the other scenes she had witnessed; the selfsame blond as a Victorian-age prostitute, being beaten by a policeman; Sally and Lucinda made to dress as cowgirls and take a birching from two men dressed as cowboys.

"Just like them, you'll be expected to adopt a character during the scenes," Bridget said. "You have to actually play the role you're given; the scene-setting is regarded as vital by the master. His customers don't just want to see sex scenes, they want the beatings and fuckings put in a context."

"I couldn't act to save my life," Laura stated sourly.

"You're going to have to learn fast. The master won't tolerate unenthusiastic performances."

Laura felt a strange tingle in her loins at Bridget's words. She wondered what the penalty would be for giving a poor performance. Another birching, she speculated? Or maybe he would ravage her; use her to satisfy his carnal lustings. She moaned a little louder than usual as the girl's hand fondled her between her legs.

"You're wet," Bridget said.

"I thought I might be."

"Is it my caressing that's excited you?"

Laura didn't like to disappoint the girl. Besides, she didn't feel comfortable about telling her the real reason; that she'd been fantasising about the Sinfinder birching her bottom again, so she smiled at Bridget. "Yeah, it's your caress, honey."

"We probably have a few minutes before the overseer comes to collect you," said Bridget. "Would you like me to go down on you?"

"What if you were caught?" asked Laura. In truth, she didn't know quite how she felt about the girl's offer. Once upon a time, she remembered, she would have virtually run screaming from the room at even the suggestion of another woman pleasuring her; but there was no denying the fact that times had changed. Her body was so often racked with pain from the various beatings she received, or used in a way which afforded her no satisfaction, that her attitude had changed greatly. She was no longer sure that she cared all that much how she acquired the pleasure, just so long as she occasionally had some.

"I know I might get caught," said Bridget, "and if I were to be, they would no doubt beat me. But I am sure to be beaten as a matter of procedure anyway, as are we all. At least this way I'll be sustained during my suffering by the knowledge that I have given you pleasure."

Laura looked over her shoulder at the chestnut-haired girl standing behind her. Bridget had a soft, attractive face - with huge green eyes that seemed almost to burn into the American, imploring her to acquiesce - and small but perfectly shaped breasts. As with all the girls, she had been depilated. It was when Laura looked at the thick pink lips that pouted provocatively from between the girl's legs that her mind was made up.

"Okay, honey," she said, rolling over onto her side, "that would be real nice, yeah. I'd love for you to do that."

"Lie on your back," the young woman whispered, "and raise your legs in the air."

Laura did as instructed. Bridget took gentle hold of her ankles and eased her legs right back over her head, until her knees were pressing into her breasts.

"Careful, honey!" Laura giggled. "I'm not elasticated!"

She lowered her head towards the American's exposed genitalia then, her soft hair tumbling against the backs of Laura's thighs, tickling her skin. Bridget's tongue darted from her mouth and edged along her lover's fleshy pink slit, lapping eagerly at the pool of silvery love-juice that had collected there.

"Oooh!" Laura moaned in response. "Ooh yeah, that's real nice." The girl needed no encouragement in her work. She tickled at Laura's clitoris until the little pink hood of flesh stood proudly to attention. Then she teased Laura's soaking wet labia lips with long, lashing strokes of her tongue, occasionally dipping into the gloriously distended love-pot.

The licking continued until Laura's whole body was trembling madly, and her groin was bucking wildly in response to every butterfly touch of her lover's hot, wet tongue.

"Oh, yeah," she groaned. "Oh yeah! Tickle my ass, honey...Oooh, that's real good!"

Bridget's tongue gently poked at Laura's enticingly

exposed bottom-mouth, dipping into the tight little cavity and lovingly tickling her rectum flesh. Then she commenced a series of firm tongue strokes which ran from her lover's arsehole to her clitoris - lashing the tender flesh between the two hot, throbbing areas - and then back again, causing Laura to pant feverishly as she felt an orgasm approaching.

She squealed as wave after powerful wave flowed through her. Her fleshy sex dripped with fast-gathering love juice as she revelled in the sensations of a delicious spend. "Oh, honey..." she moaned, vaguely aware that Bridget's tongue was still caressing her, licking clean her soaking love-pot, tickling at her rubbery ass-crack. "Oh, honey, yeah..."

Laura's overseer had come for her within a couple of minutes of her orgasm. Bridget had pressed her lips against the American's and given her a succulent kiss - and Laura, much to her surprise, had enjoyed responding to the hungry mouth-embrace. Their tongues had entwined, their hands had teased each other's nipples, and they had both moaned ecstatically, desperate to continue with their sensual game.

The overseer's arrival broke their spell. His lust fuelled by the sight of Laura's bare bottom, the skin still greasy from the soothing balm Bridget had applied, he twisted her arm behind her back and bent her forward over the table. Wrenching his breeches to his thighs and swiftly massaging his semi-hard cock to a full, throbbing erection, he guided the thick, purple-headed beast in between Laura's thighs and up into her cunt.

Bridget stood to the other side of the table, directly in front of Laura. Her big green eyes welled up with tears as she watched her lover being taken so roughly. The overseer growled like an animal as he spent inside the American's squelching vagina. He snatched at Laura's hair then, wrenching her up and steering her towards the door.

"Come on, you little bitch," he spat. "Time for you to go to the theatre!"

It soon became apparent that Bridget had been correct

about the Sinfinder's intentions for Laura. The 'theatre' to which the overseer had referred was actually one of the rooms of the house, one in which Laura had watched a tableau unfold when she'd first been brought to Matthew Hopkirk's mansion.

The room was very different to how she remembered it. Two sofas, a huge wooden desk and padded chair, as well as two other wooden-back chairs now took pride of place in the centre of the room. On the far wall, hung by nails hammered into the crumbling plaster, was a framed portrait of Abraham Lincoln, and a vast and badly discoloured American flag.

"This should certainly make you feel at home," commented Kathy Kimble as she led Laura by a leather cord, fastened to her neck, into the room. "Our very own Oval Office, right here in the master's house! You'd better salute your beloved star-spangled banner, hadn't you, yankee girl?" The mistress laughed at her own witticism and gave a pull on the cord.

Lucinda and Sally had also been brought to the room, pulled along by two burly overseers. "Take a seat," said the mistress, who was once again attired in black leather pants, suspenders, stockings and stilettos. She gestured to a row of padded wooden chairs, positioned on the opposite side of the room from the Lincoln portrait and American flag, and gracefully lowered her own magnificent bottom onto one of them.

When the four women had settled - the two overseers standing menacingly behind them, their stumpy fingers toying with the handles of the whips hanging at their waists - the mistress clapped her hands together and a door to the far side of the room opened.

Through it came an extraordinarily handsome man, grey-haired, approximately forty-five years of age and smartly dressed in a dark blue suit.

He was followed by a gruesome dwarf, fat and pasty,

with a seemingly permanent leer etched into his grotesquely twisted visage. He was dressed in a top hat and tails, and wore an enormous plastic sunflower in the button-hole of his jacket.

The handsome newcomer settled into the padded chair behind the desk. The dwarf scuttled to the centre of the room, and bowed courteously to the gathered audience. "Welcome, friends, to our little show," he began, revealing two rows of crumbling yellow teeth as he grimaced a ragged smile at the women. "For your delight and delectation, we this evening offer you a tale of terrible political intrigue, direct from the corridors of power." His short arm gestured as expansively as it could towards the handsome man seated behind the desk. "This, ladies and gentlemen, is the President of the United States; Mr Bob Danton, Democrat. He is a fine statesman and leader of his nation; a man most suited to the office bestowed upon him - and one who takes with the utmost seriousness his position as the most powerful man in the western world."

The dwarf clutched his head theatrically, a look of horror spreading across his contorted features. "Ah, but wherever there is ointment, good people, there is invariably a fly! Enter, his good lady wife, the redoubtable Harriet Danton."

Through the still-open doorway paced an attractive forty something woman. She had blond, shoulder-length hair, a curvaceous, broad-hipped figure, and sported a wide-mouthed smile which served to accentuate her high cheekbones and attractively piercing eyes.

"Harriet is a strong-minded First Lady of America, with a political agenda all her own. She is a tower of strength for Bob in many ways - but in others, a real thorn in his side. A lady of the South, she has good Christian values and rules their teenage daughter with a rod of iron."

The dwarf flashed another grotesque smile and stepped to one side. "Ladies and gentlemen," he announced, "welcome to the Oval Office."

Attention turned then to the two figures at the desk; Bob, lounging in his seat, strumming his fingers together pensively; Harriet, standing to the other side of the enormous, presidential table, toying with the silk scarf draped elegantly around her neck.

"You wanted to see me, Bob," she said. "I hope it won't take long; I'm showing the British Prime Minister and his wife around the White House gardens."

The President glared at his wife, a ferocious intensity in his eyes.

"My popularity's on the wane down south, Harriet," he said in a thick Alabama drawl. "Now how can that be, what with our hailing from the southern states 'n' all?"

"It'll only be a glitch, darling," Harriet offered, "these things are bound to happen from time to time."

"It's no glitch," interrupted the President. "Chuck says we've got an image problem."

"An image problem!?" Harriet seemed genuinely surprised.

Bob Danton sauntered around his desk, fixing his wife with a cold-eyed stare as he went.

"Yeah," he murmured. "It's a big problem." He paused for effect, and looked his wife up and down thoughtfully. "And Chuck tells me you're the cause of it."

Harriet drew a long breath, her eyebrows arching in surprise. "Me!" she exclaimed. "And just how d'you make that out?"

Bob Danton leaned casually against his desk and folded his arms. "You're too pushy, Harriet," he said, "too public and in-your-face. Southerners want a strong President, not a strong First Lady. They want to know that the man's in charge and that his wife knows her place."

"Well they can surely go to hell, Mr President!" Harriet snapped, slapping the desk-top with the palm of her hand. "There's no way I'm just going to slink away into the shadows like some li'l wifey with some kinda vacant apple-pie smile on my face! No way! They can just go screw themselves!"

"No, Harriet," said the President calmly. His face remained impassive, his voice measured and controlled. "I will not lose their vote. I will not risk not being re-elected because my wife does not know her place."

"They're just rednecks and hillbillies, Bob - can't you see that? These social reforms I'm working real hard to get rubber-stamped, they're what's important. That's what this job's all about!"

The President shook his head slowly, distractedly scuffing the tip of his shoe against the carpet. "Wrong again, Harriet," he said from beneath a far-from-genuine smile, "that's what my job's all about. Yours is about being there when I need your support, and bringing up our daughter Clare to be a good, God-fearin' girl."

"Chain me to the frigging kitchen sink as well, why don't you?" Harriet yelled. "Christ, Bob, haven't you heard of equal rights for women?!"

"Yeah, I've heard of 'em, and I support 'em. But this isn't about equal rights - this is about you pretending you're the President of the United States. Well, I'm here to tell you that you're not, and furthermore..." Bob Danton paused momentarily, making sure that he had his irate wife's undivided attention; "...I intend to teach you that lesson right here and right now."

Bob Danton drew himself up to his full height and purposefully straightened his tie. His eyes fixed on the First Lady, he swiftly unbuttoned his jacket.

"Lady," he said at length, "I'm gonna spank your ass!"

Harriet took a step backwards, evidently stunned by her husband's declaration. "No! Honey-pie!" she gasped, glancing quickly towards the door, as though to measure the distance to a possible escape route.

"Now I am not going to man-handle you, Harriet," the President said placidly as he removed his jacket and tossed it across the desk onto his chair. "If you do not obey me of your own volition, I will call for security and get them to prepare you."

"Oh, Bob - honey..."

"Don't try to sway me from my chosen path, Harriet," warned the silver-haired Chief Executive, with a presidential sweep of his arm. "If the most powerful man in the western world cannot spank his own wife when it's necessary to do so, then who in blue blazes can!"

"This is ridiculous, Bob - for pity's sake!" Harriet's rage of a few moments earlier had given way to utter desperation. "What about the Blakes? They're bound to wonder where I am. What the hell are they going to think when they find out what you're intending? We're talking about the frigging British Prime Minister and his wife, Bob. It'll be an international incident."

The President was carefully rolling up his shirtsleeve, baring his powerful right forearm. "I should imagine that Tom is likely to think what a good idea it is," he said. "Maybe he'll take a leaf out of my book."

He sat down on one of the wooden-backed chairs and looked at his wife. "Get your ass over my knee right now," he demanded.

"Bob, honey - please..."

"Do I have to call security?"

Harriet shuffled uncomfortably. Her face was a picture of confusion and simmering rage.

At length, her eyes glinting with anger, she huffed haughtily, murmured, 'Well fuck you, then!' and strode across the room towards her husband.

The First Lady tugged off her jacket, allowing it to slip from her arms onto the floor, and snatched at the material of her tight skirt, slowly hoisting it up her legs.

Seated in the audience watching the bizarre tableau unfold, Laura was aware that the seat of her chair was soaking wet with the love-juice dripping liberally from her sex. The scene before her was making her hot, really hot, and as her face and neck flushed, she began to realise just how mesmeric these well-played-out performances could be.

She felt her heart skip a beat as the First Lady's magnificent, sprawling bottom was gradually exposed, and felt a hot flush envelop her as she assessed Harriet Danton's undergarments. The President's wife was wearing stockings and suspenders, ensuring that the upper portions of her beautifully rounded thighs were bare. Her panties were tiny, black and frilly, concealing little more than the cleft of her bottom, and were almost immediately edged down by her husband.

What a fantastic ass, Laura thought to herself. Broad, majestic, alabaster-white, and attractively dimpled. It wobbled splendidly as the President drew Mrs Danton to him and encouraged her across his waiting lap.

The First Lady had a wonderfully deep bottom cleft! Against her better judgement, Laura found herself yearning to see the woman's fleshy pink cunt and tight pink asshole.

Harriet's palms were pressed against the carpet to one side of her husband, her white-stockinged legs stretched out to the other. Beneath the President's nose, her big bottom bloomed splendidly, the cheeks having peeled open slightly to reveal the darkness of her seemingly fathomless bum cleft.

The President began to spank her then, his large palm slapping down against first one wobbling bottom-cheek, then the other. There was a dreadful retort every time a spank was administered, and Harriet's bottom began to flush the gentlest shade of pink.

"You're lucky I don't take the hairbrush to your big ass," admonished the President as he slapped away at the First Lady's squirming bottom, "after all, that's what you use on our daughter, isn't it!"

"She needs to learn... - ow!" choked Harriet as her

husband's hand spanked down against her large posterior, "she needs - ow! oow! - to learn - how to - behave! Ahh!"

"Well so do you!" Smack! Smack! Smack! "Maybe I should take the hairbrush to your butt after all, then!"

"No! Oww! No, honey, please - I'm - oww! - I'm learning, really I am! I'm gonna be a good wife to you from now on, Bob - owww! ahh! - I promise! I'm gonna keep - real quiet an' - oww! - an' speak when I'm spoken to!"

"You sure are!" the President rasped, fighting hard to contain the increasingly frenzied movements of his bare-bottomed wife as she struggled for freedom across his knee. "If you don't, and I have to spank you again, you can bet your purple ass it's gonna go out live by satellite to the whole goddamn nation!"

The spanking continued unabated for several minutes. Harriet kicked and thrashed her legs around, vainly punched the carpet time and again with her fist, and wiggled her expansive bottom as much as she could - yet still the leader of the free world slapped her jiggling buttocks, turning her flesh from a gentle pink to a raw and burning crimson.

The First Lady's frenzied bucking became ever more spectacular. The cheeks of her upturned bottom peeled open, fleetingly revealing the pink flesh of her sex and the ring of her bumhole.

As her charms flashed into view, two more figures made their way through the door.

"Christ, honey!" exclaimed the President, delivering an enormously powerful slap across the deep divide separating Harriet's buttocks. Unceremoniously, he pushed her to the floor, "It's Tom and Charisse Blake!" The President rose and extended his hand to the equally young, similarly attractive British Prime Minister, cheekily winking in the direction of the PM's horrified wife. "Great to see you, Tom," Bob said by way of greeting. "Did you have a good time looking around the White House grounds?"

"We - we certainly did," said the Prime Minister, unable

to take his eyes from the kneeling figure of the half-undressed First Lady.

"Oh don't worry about that none, Tom," laughed the President, acknowledging his colleague's discomfiture at having stumbled upon the intimate spanking scene. "I was just taking care of a little bit of, er, domestic policy. Harriet needed to be put in her place, and, as the President - and as her husband - it was my duty to see that it happened."

Charisse Blake suddenly flared, the look of horror which had been reflected in her dark eyes being replaced by one of wild rage. "And I suppose she needed to be put in her place because she's a woman, did she!" the PM's wife snapped.

She moved swiftly across to the sobbing Harriet. Cradling her in her arms, Charisse inspected her friend's spanked bottom, wincing at the very sight of the First Lady's inflamed and swollen buttocks.

"You cruel beast!" She positively spat the words at the President. "How could you do this to your wife's bare bottom? What kind of man are you?!"

The Prime Minister looked daggers at Mrs Blake, and wagged a finger at her sternly. "Now as a matter of foreign policy, Charisse, I must insist that you hold your tongue!"

"Insist all you like!" the dark-haired Charisse barked.

The President flashed a wicked smile at the British PM; "Looks like you got yourself a feisty one there, Tom," he laughed. "If any guy ought to understand why I felt it necessary to take a hand to my wife's ass, it's just got to be you! I reckon it wouldn't hurt Charisse to have a little dose of the same."

Tom Blake's gaze flitted between his chuckling friend and his enraged wife. For a few brief moments, he was struck dumb, unable to decide how to respond. The President urged him on: "Let's teach these minxes a lesson, Tom - it'll do 'em good! Now what d'you say to that?!"

The PM smiled broadly and nodded, ignoring the almost

instantaneous whine that escaped his horrified wife's trembling lips. "You're on!" he said, and with that, the two heads-of-state turned on their wives.

Harriet, her resolve already broken, sprawled herself obediently across her husband's knee once again; Charisse put up more of a fight: "Get your fucking hands off me, you bastard!" she screamed, aiming a slap at the Prime Minister's face. The PM swung her round so that she was facing away from him and snatched at her skirt, tugging it high to reveal her splendidly curvaceous thighs.

"D'you want me to call security, Tom?" the President laughed. He was amusing himself by gently fondling the hot cheeks of his wife's bare bottom as he waited for his friend to get his own spouse under control.

"No thanks," said the PM, ripping at Charisse's tights, tearing them down her legs, "I think I can handle the situation!"

In spite of her best efforts, there was little Charisse could do against her husband's natural strength. He tore her panties down to her knees - revealing to Laura and the others in the audience the woman's shaven pink sex lips - sat down, and turned her over his legs, so that her big bottom was thrusting provocatively into his face.

The two bums on show - one white, one already crimson - were both splendidly broad and fleshy, the cheeks chubby and appealingly dimpled. In truth, Laura thought to herself from her excellent vantage point, they were two of the most beautiful examples of middle-aged female bottoms she could ever imagine seeing.

She felt another flood of love-fluid gathering between her legs as the two men started to spank their wives. Harriet immediately began where she'd left off, rhythmically kicking her legs and twisting her big broad bottom in all directions as the President's hand cracked against her flesh time and again.

Meanwhile, Charisse was attempting to use brute force

to escape her husband. In spite of her best efforts, she was held firmly in check by his steely grip, and howled out loud every time his hand spanked her two huge and trembling moons.

The women's bare bottoms wriggled magnificently as they were slapped, wobbling like two big jellies beneath the constant onslaught of stinging spanks. The PM, knowing he had some ground to make up on the President, slapped away with unreserved enthusiasm at Charisse's broad backside, his vigorous efforts soon turning her bum into a wide band of crimson, which Laura thought looked delightful framed by the white flesh of her lower back and her curvaceous thighs.

The President cast a smiling glance towards his friend, all the while continuing to slap away at Harriet's wobbling posterior: "I was saying to this little minx that she's lucky I don't take the hairbrush to her wriggly ass," he laughed. "Then she'd know she'd had a good ol' spanking!"

The PM dropped his left leg from under his wife, causing her upper body to slide towards the floor and accentuating her large and well-spanked bottom cheeks. He launched a series of choice slaps then, his hand spanking across Charisse's enticingly open bum cleft and stinging the lower portions of her buttocks. "Well, in Britain, we do things a little differently," he informed his friend. "We don't use the hairbrush so much; the cane tends to be our preferred instrument of correction."

"Well, you know, Tom, I just happen to have a length of bamboo in my desk drawer. It belonged to a Japanese politician friend of mine who accidentally left it here the last time he visited. What say we make use of it on these naughty girls' asses?"

The performers were well-drilled, that much was obvious to Laura by the speed with which the scene before her changed. The women tumbled from their 'husbands" knees - Harriet pleading, Charisse growling - and resentfully followed the President's instruction to strip. As Bob Danton fetched the cane and Tom Blake removed his jacket, the two women divested themselves of their clothes and stood like naughty schoolgirls in the middle of the Oval Office, their hands self consciously covering their love-mounds. Both women had well-rounded, sizable breasts and beautifully curvaceous figures. The sight of so much naked flesh caused another sudden gush of love-juice between Laura's legs, and she felt herself flushing with excitement as Harriet and Charisse followed the President's instruction to kneel on two of the wooden-backed chairs.

"As my guest, Tom, you should have first go," said the most powerful man in the western world. "Stripe those naughty asses, Tom - make the ladies squeal like hogs!"

"Don't mind if I do," replied the PM, shifting into position to the right-hand side of the two upturned bums.

He swung the cane through a wide arc, creating a terrible swishing sound, and cracked it down against Harriet's naked rump.

"Jesus!" she cried, "Oh God, that hurts!"

"That's a taste of British justice for you," Tom remarked. "It's why the women of Britain know their place. A few cuts of the cane on their bare bottoms soon quietens them down!"

He swung the rattan again, this time aiming at the bare bottom next to Harriet's. Charisse howled as the rod sliced into her flesh, and wriggled her bum provocatively.

"Your British women sure know how to jiggle their ass cheeks!" whooped the President. "Just look at that critter move!"

Again the swishing sound. Again the rod cracked against the First Lady's big bum, making her squeal out loud, and buck magnificently on the chair.

The PM continued to slash the naked posteriors, cruelly delivering the springy implement of punishment to each bottom in turn, until both rumps were dancing continually

- whether it was their turn to suffer a stroke or not.

As the canings continued, the President sauntered around his desk and reached into his drawer, taking from it a long-handled, wooden-backed hairbrush. "I think it's only right I administer some real American-style justice," he declared. "It's the hairbrush for you ladies next!"

Again the scene changed. Harriet lay on her back on the rug, parted her legs and swung them up into the air and over her own head, so that her knees were squashing her breasts. Charisse lowered herself on top of the First Lady then, her own legs wide apart. In this new position, the women's faces were virtually touching, and Charisse's bottom sat atop Harriet's bottom, offering the delightful sight of four crimson buttocks seeming almost to melt into one great mass of burning flesh.

The President set about his work, spanking each buttock in turn; a powerful spank to the top left cheek - Charisse's left cheek - then to the lower left cheek - Harriet's right cheek. Charisse's right buttock and Harriet's left was the order which Bob Danton followed then, before returning the cold wooden surface to the smouldering flesh of Charisse's left bum-globe. The hairbrush spanking proceeded in this methodical manner until the PM's wife was wiggling her bottom and bucking wildly on top of the First Lady, seeming almost to be riding her like a horse. Harriet, for her part, could hardly move, weighed down as she was by the bulk of her fellow sufferer.

Another barked command from the President and the two women each bent over a chair, resting their elbows against the seat. The heads-of-state took up position behind the two big bottoms. They unzipped their cocks, clutched hold of the swollen red buttocks in front of them, and edged their throbbing muscles towards the velvety pink love pouches that glistened invitingly between smooth thighs.

Cocks touched wet vaginas; prodding the sopping holes, teasing the flesh. Two wrinkled, rubbery anuses contracted in unison, and then pouted defiantly at the men, throbbing saucily.

Slowly, the cocks penetrated the wet pussies, slithering inside the creamy, glistening slits with the greatest of ease. The women moaned as the male muscles ploughed along their juicy cunt-tunnels. The rude, penetrative movement was terminated only when the cocks had been buried to the hilt.

Without further ado, the two thick muscles began to hammer in and out of the raw pink pussies. Hands stroked hot buttocks, thumbs diddled sweaty bottom-mouths, testicles slapped against thighs, and oversized breasts wobbled and jiggled, smacking and bouncing into one another as the two naked women groaned in pleasure.

The President licked his finger and pushed it up inside his woman's pouting anus. A wet British index finger promptly slid into the other female's bottom-hole. As fingers thrust in and out of the moist back-passages, and cocks ploughed the soaking pink love-furrows, the men's free hands reached down and round, and began rubbing avidly at the women's proudly stiff clitties.

Harriet and Charisse wailed even louder at the unexpected additional stimulation, and thrust their bottoms backwards into the rampaging cocks.

Soon, both females were bucking wildly, the air filled with their gasps and groans. Flesh jiggled saucily as each woman found a rhythm and slid backwards and forwards on the thick male stems.

Gradually, their breathing became more shallow, more rasping...

The President's thigh slapped against the naked thigh in front of him, trapping a trickling globule of vaginal fluid, and he felt his cock being firmly gripped inside the soft, hot pussy. The woman he was riding groaned, then suddenly tensed. She cooed in wild abandonment as a shattering orgasm consumed her. Hot jets of fluid leapt from Bob's cock, flooding the lusty love-nest.

Then the second woman wailed and trembled, finally reacting to the rhythmical thrusts of Tom's cock, which had long since spat its love fluids deep inside her fleshy hole.

The men withdrew their thick muscles from the ravaged cunts, eased their fingers from the slimy bottom-holes, and stood, heaving for breath, while the women collapsed to their knees.

Laura wanted to touch herself between the legs. She was desperate to. The scene had made her pulse race and her vagina tingle, and she desperately needed some kind of release from the terrible lust that continued to well up within her.

The mistress stood and briefly applauded the performers.

The President reached into his desk drawer again and pulled two neck collars from within, handing one to Tom. The two men then fitted the women with the collars, took hold of the lengths of cord which hung from them and led their prisoners out of the room.

"As you have seen here," the mistress explained," the more articulate and intelligent among our overseers are only too happy to participate in our little scenes."

She looked at Laura, Sally and Lucinda in turn: "Each of you is to be assigned an overseer," she revealed. "Not necessarily an articulate or an intelligent one, but your very own overseer nonetheless! And they will take responsibility for you for the foreseeable future. I understand that your overseer has already been chosen, Lucinda. As for you two," she clasped both Laura and Sally by the hair, twisting their locks cruelly until the women were grimacing with pain, "I believe your overseers are to be assigned later today....So enjoy my company while you can, ladies..." she smiled wickedly, "...things can only get worse for you from here on in..."

CHAPTER 8

"What a pretty girl!" cooed Mrs Reid, her eyes lighting up as she watched the tableau before her taking shape. Kathy Kimble followed the diminutive woman's gaze, yet remained uncertain which among the slavegirls performing in the scene had taken her client's fancy.

"Which one exactly, Lady Cartwright?" she asked politely.

"Why, that one there." Mrs Reid extended a gloved finger in the direction of the performers. "The one standing third in line, with the cascading blond hair."

It was the first performance of the Sinfinder's circus in six months. Lord and Lady Cartwright had arrived in the huge marquee tent only moments earlier, their eyes eagerly drinking in the bizarre scenes that were unfolding all around them. The tent was sprawled across one of the enormous fallow fields belonging to the notorious Farm, where girls were taught to attain the level of obedience which Matthew Hopkirk would expect from them. It was an arena positively alive with the sights and sounds of circus life.

Naked women, chained by the ankles to one another, played musical instruments in one corner of the giant fabric dome. They made music together in the style of a brass band, and were conducted by a brutish overseer, who wielded a whippy cane in place of a conductor's baton. Their music filled the capacious tent and provided a curious accompaniment to the scenes unfolding elsewhere in the big-top.

All around, spinning and turning and moving at frenetic speed, were women on unicycles, their bare breasts jiggling as they displayed their skills. Their buttocks were coloured crimson, the result of countless cane-strokes, administered by various overseers. The cuts made them squeal, causing them to teeter on the very brink of losing their balance.

Other slavegirls were being made to balance piles of plates

100

on their heads while their bottoms were repeatedly struck with wicked lengths of bamboo. If so much as a single plate were to drop, the shame-faced culprit was made to bend over where she stood and endure a vicious caning across her swollen buttocks.

In a cage to the far side of the big-top, a man attired in top-hat and tails in the style of a ringmaster used his whip to tame three wildly screaming girls, who moved around him on all-fours in the manner of prowling lions, and reared up on their legs whenever they were offered morsels of food.

The tableau unfolding before Lord and Lady Cartwright was set in a school classroom, a fact evidenced by the chalk-covered blackboard and the rows of neatly arranged desks which had been used to help set the scene. The teacher, a young man with what Mrs Reid thought to be a delightfully strict manner, had informed the schoolgirls in his charge that they had all failed their weekly spelling test, and that he intended to punish them accordingly. The girls had then been made to stand in line, bare-bottomed, and await their turn across 'Mr Phipps's' knee.

Mrs Reid had grown wet between her legs at the sight of so many naked female bottoms being thrashed. As she stood there, between Kathy Kimble and her own husband, who was erect and bulging in his trousers, she found herself truly delighting in the experience of watching each wriggling girl receiving her comeuppance. For the life of her, though, she couldn't decide which experience she was most craving for herself - to pull each girl across her own legs and whip their buttocks purple, or to be spreadeagled across the teacher's knee herself, and feel his hard, punishing hand slapping against her own peculiarly rotund bottom.

"The blond-haired girl's named Lucinda," said Kathy Kimble. "When the tableau's at an end, I'll call her over. What will you want to do with her?"

The Cartwrights looked at one another, a lustful

excitement registering in their eyes. It was Mrs Reid who spoke: "I will need a place where I can thrash her," she informed Kathy. "I think I would like to use a paddle to spank her with. Can you oblige?"

"Of course," smiled the mistress. "We have a wide range of implements from which to choose, and which most of the girls will have experienced at one time or another. Lucinda is a new arrival. She was engaged to the local lord-of-the-manor but her behaviour grew so unruly, he decided to place her in the Sinfinder's charge."

"And if we were to decide to purchase her," said Lord Cartwright, "I'm correct in thinking that she would be available?"

"Oh yes," the mistress confirmed with a generous smile. "All those who the Sinfinder has deemed ready to perform in the circus are available for sale - at the right price, of course."

"And Lucinda's price?"

"Her excellent breeding makes her rather expensive, I'm afraid, but then you are buying, how shall I put it, an aristocratic seat, when all's said and done! The going rate for her at the moment is half a million pounds."

"I would rather she wasn't spanked by 'Mr Phipps'," interjected the diminutive Mrs Reid. "I think I would like to begin with a blank canvas, if you understand my meaning, Mistress Kimble?"

"Of course, I do, your ladyship. In which case, I'll have to get her removed from the tableau rather discreetly, so as not to affect the other visitors' enjoyment of the performance. Will you excuse me for a moment?"

The flame-haired mistress left the aristocratic couple with a broad smile, and strode off across the arena. Lord Cartwright and Mrs Reid watched her as she went, their eyes fixed on her magnificently swaying bottom - on this occasion concealed beneath a tight black leather skirt. "Now there's an arse I'd love to get my hands on," murmured

Mrs Reid to her husband. "Oh, Bertie," she exclaimed, her dark eyes suddenly conveying a terrible anxiety, "do you think we'll find what we're looking for here? It's awfully expensive!"

"It's an expense we can afford, my sweet," he reassured her. "But you're right about Mistress Kimble. My cock would be as stiff as a pole in no time if I could watch you flogging the flesh off that delightful creature's bare bottom!"

"Do you think the Sinfinder would sell her, Bertie?"

"I'm certain that every wench must have her price, Fran. Perhaps later I'll make enquiries - but for now..." The silver-haired aristocrat nodded his head gently in the direction of the stage where the schoolroom tableau was taking place. Kathy Kimble was walking towards them, a broad smile playing across her face. Alongside her, the blond-haired Lucinda struggled to keep pace with her mistress, and was busily pulling her skirt back into place after having hitched it up in readiness for the spanking Mr Phipps was going to give her. "Here she is, one of our newest arrivals," Kathy declared. "Lucinda, Lord and Lady Cartwright are interested in purchasing you. They want you to go and live with them in a great big mansion house down in Cornwall, where you would work as one of their kitchen staff. I'm sure you would like that very much, wouldn't you, Lucinda?"

As Kathy spoke, Mrs Reid felt another sudden dampening of her knickers as a fanciful image flickered across her mind; the comely redheaded mistress wearing a sweet little maid's uniform, dusting ornaments, carrying trays - and then being stretched out across Mrs Reid's favourite drawing room chair, her magnificent bum-cheeks colouring spectacularly beneath the kiss of the birch-rods!

God, how Mrs Reid wanted to own that woman! She knew that she would be able to thrash Mistress Kimble's buttocks with a greater fervour than she had ever before whipped any pair of bottom-cheeks. And she remembered as well what her beloved husband had just said; that he would surely be as stiff as a pole at the sight of his loyal wife thrashing the mistress's jiggling moons. As stiff as a pole and ready to fuck Mrs Reid raw from dusk until dawn!

The flame-haired mistress directed the Cartwrights to one of the expansive 'booths' on the far side of the big-top. "You'll find a selection of crops, paddles, whips and canes hanging on the side of each booth," she smiled. "Try Lucinda out; see if she's the girl for you. If not," she smiled serenely and cast a glance around the tent, "there are plenty of others to choose from."

As the mistress sauntered away, Mrs Reid lightly touched her husband on the arm. "Yes," she muttered to him, "and I know which one I want! We must get her, Bertie! She must be ours!"

The Cartwrights took advantage of the chains they found attached to the walls of the booth to securely manacle the magnificently proportioned Lucinda. While Mrs Reid was selecting a paddle to use on the woman's fleshy bottom, Lord Cartwright happened across a blindfold, one of a number of accessories displayed on a table in the corner of the booth. "Put the blindfold on her, Fran," he urged his delighted wife.

"Oh Bertie," the diminutive whip-mistress exclaimed, "are you in the mood to feel me up!?"

"With a nice new bottom to watch you thrash, darling, I'm as horny as hell!"

Mrs Reid could hardly contain her excitement at the prospect of her husband once again loving her as he had done so many times before. "Then perhaps we won't need to purchase Mrs Kimble," she mused, as her hand wandered across the gently trembling flesh of Lucinda's broad posterior. "Perhaps this nice big bottom will prove just the ticket instead!"

Mrs Reid set about paddling the blonde's buttocks with a vigour that she had rarely displayed of late. After several minutes of thrashing, the diminutive woman felt a charge of pure adrenalin course through her heaving, panting body, and thrilled to the sudden, long-awaited touch of her husband. The silver-haired aristocrat slid her skirt up to her waist and carefully, teasingly, edged down her drenched panties, revealing to his own delighted gaze the sight of Mrs Reid's breathtakingly curved bottom; white and fleshy, beautifully shaped, and cleaved by the deepest, darkest and altogether most thrilling bottom-cleft upon which he had ever had the good fortune to lay his eyes, not to mention his hands.

His feverish excitement at the sudden displaying of his wife's bare buttocks soon got the better of the gasping aristocrat. He slipped his cock inside her even as she continued to spank the swollen bum-mounds that jiggled spectacularly before her eyes.

Mrs Reid felt her hungry cunt swallow her husband's cock into its pool of wetness and could have screamed with the sheer delight of it. She had always so much needed him to want her - she would be nothing without her Bertram - and she'd thrashed bare bottoms day and night from the moment they were married; thrashed them because that was what had always turned him on, always made him want her; watching her do that.

And it had become like a drug to her as well, and now she, too, needed it; needed to whip, to flog naked female flesh; needed to explore the dirty little holes of the women she whipped, and make use of them as though she herself were a man; taking what she wanted, when she wanted it.

But though she grew hot-blooded through thrashing Lucinda's buttocks, it was the feeling of her husband deep inside her, nudging and thrusting at her hole in spite of her furious twisting and turning, which truly transported her into a world of carnal pleasure. Even as the blond woman's buttocks turned a purple hue, even as her screams threatened to penetrate the sound-proofed booth, the enormous tent, and explode into the sultry summer air, Mrs Reid could think of little more than the intense pleasure of feeling her husband's throbbing, arrogantly stiff cock deep inside her cunthole, searching for her womb. Searching for a warm place to spill his hot, thick spend...

She continued to slap at the trembling buttocks displayed before her even as her whole body was consumed by a breathtaking orgasm...

Lucinda was superfluous to requirements from that moment on. Lord Cartwright bundled his wife across the booth to the adjacent wall and stripped the clothing from her. Within seconds, he had fastened her to the wall, snapping manacles around her wrists, and had retrieved the paddle from the floor. He began to spank his wife then, paddling her buttocks with a lust-fuelled fury until she was screaming in agony. He used the cruel leather implement against the backs of her thighs after he had fully tortured her poor bottom-cheeks. With a lust he hadn't felt for some considerable time, he repeatedly beat the expanse of flesh from beneath her bum down to her knees - and didn't stop until the area had acquired the same crimson hue as her quivering flanks.

For all her screams, and for all the tears that rolled down her tortured face, Mrs Reid wanted nothing but to be beaten harder and harder by her husband; to be beaten until he could thrash her no more, and would instead have to push his swollen cock back into her sopping wet hole, and fuck her with a savagery that would leave her in no doubt of his abiding love for her.

When the moment came, and he re-entered her, she orgasmed almost immediately. By the time he had emptied himself into her, she had climaxed for a third time, yet even then knew no desire but to be fucked and thrashed even more by her darling Bertie, and to be used by him all night long.

"Come on, Fran," he said at length, his trembling hands struggling to snap open her cruelly chafing wrist manacles, "we will return tomorrow night for the next performance, and every night thereafter, and try a different girl each time to see how we like her. But for now, my sweet..." he drew her to him and planted a kiss against her gently quivering lips, "...let's go back to the inn and let us fuck all night and into the morning."

"Oh, Bertie!" Mrs Reid gasped. "Oh, Bertie, yes! Yes, my darling! Have me, have me, please - have me until you have made me raw and I scream for you to stop. I am yours, Bertie; use me as you think fit!"

And so he did. Even as the sun rose above the distant hilltops, and the Sinfinder's slavegirls - returned to the mansion house until their next performance, the woman known as Mrs Reid continued to groan in barely suppressed ecstasy, her husband pounding away inside her.

CHAPTER 9

The huge oak desk which was the centrepiece of the Oval Office set had been replaced by two stylishly ornate sofas. A chaise longue had been positioned to the other side of the room, while three thick, elaborately patterned rugs covered much of the middle area of the wooden floor. Laura was commanded to sit down on one of the semi-circle of chairs placed at the front of the stage area.

The dwarf - who had been decreed her new master, her personal overseer - made his way swiftly centre-stage and bowed to the audience.

"Ladies and gentlemen," he began, his gaze resting upon Laura, a barely concealed lust registering in his bulging eyes. "We have for you tonight another treat for your delight and delectation; a tale set in a foreign land; a story of colonial might, and of the penalty which must be paid for the crime of empire-building. Allow me to introduce you, ladies and gentlemen, to an Indian diplomat named Vijay Sharma." A sweep of his arm, and the dwarf had directed his audience's attention to the door on the far side of the room. A spendidly broad, handsome Indian man sauntered onto the stage. His chiselled face carried about it a look of grim malevolence.

"And let me introduce you next to two royal visitors to India; Her Majesty The Queen, and Princess Tara - here on a Royal visit to the Indian capital of Bombay."

Two women entered the room. The first, shorter than the second, was a mature female with greying hair and a somewhat sour expression on her face. The second was a woman who Laura placed in her late twenties. Attractive, demure and curvaceous, her proud posture accentuated the fullness of her breasts beneath a white silk blouse.

The Indian took the gloved hand of the first woman, obviously the Queen, and gently kissed it. "While I remain always at your service, madam," he began, bowing reverentially to the grey-haired monarch, "the issue of which

I must speak will not go away."

"Speak freely, Vijay," replied the Queen. "You know of the high regard in which I hold both you personally and the Indian nation in general."

"Indeed, madam, indeed. What a pity it is that your predecessors did not share your fair-minded approach to the colonies."

"A different age, a different outlook, Vijay," Her Majesty smiled, attempting to gloss over the Indian diplomat's barbed comment. "And you oughtn't to forget that there were certain benefits which India enjoyed as a result of colonisation."

"Indeed, ma'am, that is most true. Colonisation and empire building is very much a part of your past and, I hope you'll forgive me for saying this, quite rightly so." The Indian paused, his eyes briefly flitting in the direction of Princess Tara, who stood serenely at Her Majesty's right shoulder. "What a pity," he continued at length, a flicker of a smile dancing across his lips, "that certain other - how shall I put it - intransigencies, are not also a part of your past."

The Queen looked baffled; the Princess, vacant. "I'm sorry, Vijay...I don't quite understand what you mean," said Her Majesty.

Vijay chuckled to himself, and casually slipped his hands into his trouser pockets. "No, perhaps you don't. I would not be surprised to find that your Prime Minister has indeed kept you in the dark about his movements. Well, if you do not know, let me enlighten you. Your country has secretly been trading arms to the Middle East. If the story were to break, the British Government would be forced to stand down and Britain would inevitably be ostracised by its allies and friends."

Her Majesty looked suitably stunned by the revelation. The Princess continued to show no emotion.

"If what you're saying is true," the Queen said, "the

ramifications for one's country are serious indeed."

"Trust my word, ma'am - and trust as well that I have no wish to see Britain endure such shame and embarrassment. However, I am sure you can see that I am faced with a very grave moral dilemma. There is more to this issue than the well-being of your country's reputation."

"Of course, of course," said Her Majesty, pensively. "What would one be required to do to secure your silence on this matter, Vijay?"

The grim expression on the Indian's face darkened further. "There is very much anger within my country, and within my heart, for the imperialist regime of your nation, ma'am. Anger which needs to be vented. What I would ask of you to ensure my silence may at first seem strange and shocking..."

"Ask, Vijay."

"Then I will not beat about the bush anymore. I require both you and the Princess to offer up your bodies, right here and now, that through the use of them, I may gain vengeance on behalf of my country for the colonisation that it was forced to endure."

His eyes, cold black beads, glowered impassively at the Queen, her brow furrowing with the weight of her host's demands.

"Surely, Vijay, it must be possible to come to a different arrangement? Is there nothing else that one could secure for you as...recompense? I will not insult you by offering you financial reward - I would just ask you to consider if there is anything else...anything... that you might prefer..."

The Indian smiled. "Anything I would prefer to seeing and touching the naked flesh of Her Majesty the Queen? Come now, ma'am - there are some experiences to which a price cannot be attached."

"Then at least spare Princess Tara," the monarch replied. "It's one thing to hold me responsible for the ills done to your nation, but surely Princess Tara cannot be culpable?"

Vijay folded his hands together in front of him, an expression of sympathy crossing his grim features. "Sadly, Your Majesty, the offer is non-negotiable. Princess Tara will be required to offer herself to my ministrations - or the deal is off and Britain shamed."

Her Majesty sighed, and began taking off her gloves. "Very well, Vijay," she said, "you may have your way."

"Ma'am!" squealed the Princess in protest.

"I'm sorry, my dear, but the good of the nation is of paramount importance." She peeled her gloves off and began unbuttoning her jacket. "How would you like us, Vijay?"

"Princess Tara is to sit on the sofa and wait her turn. As for you, ma'am..." he paused for effect, looking the Queen up and down, "...I require you to strip to your undies."

Tense and anxious, Tara perched herself on the edge of the sofa as Her Majesty began to undress. She slipped off her jacket and carefully folded it, placing it on the second sofa. Then she removed her skirt and petticoat.

Watching from the sidelines, Laura couldn't help but be impressed with the slickly presented tableau. The whole scene - so beautifully stage-managed and scripted - had been, to that point at least, almost entirely believable. It was only as the Queen disrobed, and Laura assessed the nature of her undergarments, that she felt an element of artistic license had been brought to bear. It was difficult for her to imagine that a mature woman, let alone a nation's monarch, would wear the kind of undergarments in which the performer in front of her was attired!

The Queen's heavy yet shapely legs were sheathed in skin-coloured stockings which terminated at mid-thigh and to which white suspenders were attached. Her big white buttocks were only part-concealed by the panties she wore; small black frilly ones that seemed to have been sucked into her bottom cleft.

Her breasts were big and heavy, the flesh spilling from a

woefully undersized black bra.

"Get your tits out," said Vijay, chivvying the roleplay along.

Almost immediately, Her Majesty's breasts were released from their constraints, and hung, bare and fleshy, like two huge water sacks. "Panties, now," the Indian demanded next, and the monarch peeled her tiny black undies down to the tops of her stockings. Predictably, her mound was entirely bald, the pink flesh of her love slit and hanging nodule of her clitoris clearly visible from where Laura was seated.

The Indian diplomat strode across the room to the chaise longue, tugging his broad belt from his trouser loops as he moved. Holding the belt, doubled-up, in one hand, he used the fingers of his other to loosen his trousers and push them down his muscular thighs.

It was all Laura could do to contain a gasp of surprise as his cock sprang into view. Thick and throbbing, it stood out a full eight inches from his groin. The foreskin had peeled back, revealing a swollen, veiny head that was already trickling with transparent fluid.

"To your knees before me, Your Majesty," he said, "and show me that you are sorry for your nation's imperialist ways."

The Queen moved awkwardly across the room towards him, the twisted panties at her thighs causing her to take smaller-than-usual steps. She sank to her knees, her big bottom magnificently displayed for Laura to admire, and took gentle hold of the massive cock twitching before her face. She slipped the thick shaft between her lips, engulfing as much of the eight inches as she could manage. For the next few moments, Laura watched the grey-haired woman's head bobbing backwards and forwards, heard the sound of her fervent sucking, and gazed at her big white bottom-cheeks.

Then the Indian rested his hand on the monarch's forehead and gently pushed her away. His cock glistened with her saliva. Laura felt a sudden, delightful sensation between her legs. She found herself craving the chance to kneel in front of such a monstrous cock herself, and feel it throbbing inside her own hungry mouth.

"Face down on the chaise longue, Your Majesty," Vijay said. The Queen stood up, her breasts and buttocks wobbling splendidly as she hauled herself to her feet, and sprawled in the required position. Her huge bottom-cheeks jutted upwards like two magnificent hillocks. The fleshy pink lips of her vagina peeked from between her thighs, which Vijay demanded were splayed as far as the width of the chaise longue would allow.

"I am going to beat you, ma'am; I am going to thrash your majestic bottom for you. The beating will absolve you of guilt. The redness of your royal moons will be your badge of redemption."

"Will you beat one's bottom hard, Vijay?"

"Oh yes, ma'am - I will beat these magnificent buttocks until they are swollen and red-raw."

"Then whip my bottom, Vijay. Absolve one of the sins of one's country with your cruel belt."

With his bare hands, he ripped the panties twisted at her thighs, and then rested his leather belt across the broad expanse of her bottom. "Trust me, ma'am, I will whip this errant royal backside of yours until you are screaming for mercy, and until I have burned the sin from you."

He began his work then, lashing the doubled-over belt into the soft flesh of the Queen's huge bum mounds. Her Majesty sobbed into a velvet cushion as her bottom was branded with broad belt marks, shifting her quivering rump from side to side in a pointless attempt to avoid the savage kiss of the leather.

Laura was breathless as she watched the scene. Her heart skipped a beat every time the belt splatted against the pinkening arse. Her love-slot poured its juices whenever she looked at Vijay's magnificent penis, swinging wildly around as he hurled the leather time and again against the big bum in front of him.

Cruel, savage strokes continued to cascade for several minutes against the Queen's enormous bottom-mounds. Each impact filled the room with the dreadful report of leather against flesh, and the tortured howls of the madly writhing monarch. Vijay beat her until every portion of her bottom burned a fiery crimson. Only then did he drop the belt to the floor and snap an instruction for Her Majesty to roll over onto her burning moons.

He climbed on top of her, then, and slotted his enormous cock into her slippery love-hole. Her legs wrapped around his waist, her arms clasped his back, and her lips embraced his, hungrily sucking his tongue into her mouth. He thrust within her, his muscular buttocks bouncing provocatively as he hammered home his advantage.

"Oh yes! Oh yes!" exclaimed the Queen. The powerful strokes of the diplomat's thick shaft increased in speed, causing Her Majesty to whinny with delight. Laura watched the heavy sacks of her breasts wobble spectacularly with every frenzied impalement, and wished it was she who was lying beneath the well-endowed Indian, her hungry sex sucking avidly on his thick cock.

"Oh, one is coming, Vijay!"

"No, ma'am," he growled, hauling himself clear of her juicy vagina, "you shall not be allowed to! Such pleasure would be inappropriate in these circumstances. You are here to be punished for your country's political crimes, and to achieve your own personal absolution. Turn over while I smack your bottom more."

Cruelly deprived of the chance to enjoy a shattering climax, the Queen couldn't help but exhale a gentle moan of disappointment. Laura understood the frustration the woman was feeling only too well. The tableau had really turned her on - and she genuinely couldn't remember the last time she'd encountered a man who she'd desired as much as she did Vijay.

The Queen did as she'd been instructed and shuffled back onto her stomach. Almost immediately, Vijay began spanking her bare red buttocks with his hand, making them jiggle delightfully. He interspersed the stinging slaps with gentle caresses of Her Majesty's sopping love-slit, drawing from her moans of pure ecstasy.

Then, he was up and across the room, moving towards the seated Princess Tara like a prowling cat hunting its prey. Almost before the princess had had time to react, Vijay had taken hold of her and pushed her face against his throbbing cock. She grimaced as its wetness soaked her cheek, and squealed as the salty head pressed firmly against her lips.

"Suck, my little princess," he murmured, edging his cock into her mouth, "suck on your master's pleasure-giver."

Princess Tara clasped the base of the heavy shaft with her hand, and began working the eight inch-length in and out of her mouth. From time to time, her tongue would lap at the throbbing muscle, teeth nibbling at the tightly stretched foreskin, before she'd once again engulf the huge, palpitating length and guide its head deep into her throat.

Vijay ripped at her blouse as she sucked him, laying bare her soft shoulders and trim stomach, and her pert, naked breasts, each one topped with a heavy pink nipple. Her long, sharp fingernails scratched at the underside of his testicles, teasing and tickling him. His powerful buttocks tightened involuntarily in response, a movement that made the watching Laura positively ache with desire for him.

And then the diplomat pulled the Princess's head away from his groin, and swung himself around onto the seat beside her. He clasped her slender wrists and pulled her across him. "No!" she whispered, "Please don't!" Despite her words of protest, she fell across Vijay's naked thighs without a struggle, and seemed to know there would be no escape for her.

Vijay pulled her ankle-length skirt up her legs, revealing

her white tights. Beneath those, and covering the full expanse of her bottom, were a pair of white silk panties. Laura couldn't help but note the modest and becoming manner in which the Princess was attired - she was dressed like a real English rose!

The Indian hardly stopped to admire her tasteful undergarments. Instead, he pulled down both her tights and pants in one uncompromising movement, ripping them clear of her soft white feet. She lay across his knee entirely naked now, save for the long flowery skirt bundled at her waist, and Laura found herself admiring the slim, leggy splendour of her beautiful white body. She had a lovely bottom; curvaceous and gently dimpled. It quivered majestically at the slightest touch and seemed almost perfectly smooth.

A truly delightful bum for smacking, the American thought to herself.

And a smacking the Indian most certainly gave it. His big rough palm covered every soft morsel of Princess Tara's bare-skinned rear, until both her gently trembling bum mounds were flushed a sunset crimson.

"Why don't you plead for mercy, Your Highness!" Vijay suggested as he slapped away at her posteriors. "I am not an unreasonable man, perhaps your pleas will soften my heart."

"Oouch! Ooh! Yes, Mr Sharma! Ahh! I will plead!" she exclaimed, her flushed face appearing for the first time from the depths of a velvet cushion. Her hair fell across her tear-stained cheek as she eased a heartfelt plea from between trembling lips: "Please, Mr Sharma," she choked, as he spanked. "Please don't smack me any more! I'll be a good girl and do whatever you want, I promise I will!"

"Ha!" Vijay scoffed mightily, applying a series of choice little slaps across the lower portions of both buttocks, "What would you do to win my favour, my little Princess?" he asked.

"I'll - I'll let you fuck me, if you wish!" she exclaimed,

as her body squirmed across her punisher's knee. "You can fuck me all night, Mr - ow! - Mr Sharma! Or I'll give you a jolly good sucking!"

"Such language for a Princess to use!" Vijay gasped in mock horror. "I should take a nice long length of cane to this lovely bottom and punish you soundly for your wicked tongue!"

Smack, smack, smack.

"Oh, no - ahh! - Mr Sharma - not the cane! Please don't cane me! I don't think I could stand it!"

"Where could I fuck you, Princess Tara?" he asked, slapping away at her left buttock as she kicked and squealed wildly across his legs.

"Here on the sofa, or - ow! - or in the bedroom!"

A powerful, punishing slap splatted against both cheeks, the sheer force flattening the flesh of the Princess's curvaceous bottom. "Silly girl!" he chided. "I mean where in your body could I fuck you!?"

"In...in my cunt, sir..." she ventured between gasps, "or perhaps in my... in my arse, Mr Sharma."

Without warning, Vijay's legs collapsed from under the Princess, sending her tumbling to the floor. He scrambled to his feet and darted behind her. "On your knees, leaning forward onto the sofa," he snapped. His hands were at her skirt, quickly unbuttoning the waistband and sliding it from her so that she was entirely naked.

Princess Tara adopted the demanded posture, her head, breasts and stomach resting against the sofa seat, her bottom upturned and tempting. Vijay knelt behind her, using his own knees to push the Princess's apart. "Hold your arse cheeks open," he panted. His thick erection bobbed up and down near the entrance to Tara's pink love-slot, occasionally tickling the soft flesh with the lightest of touches. The Princess's ringed fingers clasped the spanked flesh of her own bottom, and gently she prised her buttocks apart.

From where she sat, Laura could see the Princess's brown

bottom-hole, throbbing saucily as it was exposed to the air. Vijay anointed a finger with saliva and slipped the digit between Tara's bum cheeks, and into her anus. The Princess squealed at the intrusion, and wriggled her crimson behind alluringly.

"Oh, Mr Sharma," she moaned. "Are you really going to fuck my arse? Couldn't you put it up my cunny instead?"

"Such language from a Princess!" the Indian exclaimed once again. "You deserve to have your royal bottom buggered just to teach you to be polite. Now pull your buttocks wide apart - wide apart, I say - so that your bottom-hole is nice and open, and ready for my cock."

The diplomat's finger re-emerged from the Princess's anus. Tara pulled more firmly at the flesh of her buttocks, until the skin around her anus was stretched as tight as a drum and the dark interior of her bum cavity exposed for all to see.

The Indian pushed his way gently inside her, ignoring the Princess's gasps and squeals, until his abdomen pressed against her burning bottom cheeks and he was buried to the hilt.

Laura watched the man's powerful buttocks shift back and forth as he thrust into Tara's bottom with long, measured strokes. The American could hardly contain herself. The growing sense of excitement within her was reaching fever pitch. She began to shuffle uncomfortably on her chair, itching to be involved in the scene unfolding before her.

How times had changed, she thought to herself! A virgin in her bottom before her arrival in the strange village, she had sobbed with a terrible, mind-numbing shame the first few times her back-passage had been violated. Yet, more recently, though she'd continued to grunt and squeal every time a throbbing male cock had been plunged into her most secret and shameful hole, she'd been aware also of a tingling excitement; a thrill at the realisation of her own terrible helplessness, her inability to retain even a scrap of dignity in the face of such lurid and lustful onslaughts.

And now, as she sat and watched the tableau before her, Laura found herself actually craving the attentions of the muscular Indian's cock within her own bum!

How depraved could she get, she wondered to herself; to actually want to be ass-fucked - and in front of an audience!?

The bottom-fucking didn't last for long. Princess Tara gasped as the Indian withdrew his magnificent muscle from her traumatised sphincter. Vijay rose to his feet and quickly stripped naked, revealing his broad and exceptionally well-toned body. He moved swiftly across to the chaise longue, where the Queen was sitting, perched expectantly on its edge. He clasped a handful of her greying hair and pushed his thick stem between her lips, forcing her to take as much of his eight inches as she could. Her Majesty began to suck mightily at the muscular cock, her fingernails tickling the base of Vijay's testicles.

The Princess had also risen to her feet and glided across the room. Lowering herself to her knees behind the brown-skinned male, her slender hands rested on his buttocks and gently eased them apart. She pressed her face against his bottom, and although Laura couldn't actually see what the naked young woman was doing, it seemed a fair bet that she was licking his asshole.

The two women continued to work diligently at their tasks, hungrily devouring the magnificent Indian, who stood gently trembling between them. After a time, the Princess removed her face from between Vijay's buttocks and pushed her finger into him. With her other hand, she joined Her Majesty in teasing the giant male's testicles. She eased her digit in and out of the Indian's rectum, and planted kiss after succulent kiss against his twitching buttocks as she worked.

Before long, Vijay groaned in ecstasy. The Queen pulled his thick cock from her mouth, and held it perfectly still in front of her. The Indian ejaculated powerfully against her lips, his hot spend trickling down her chin and tumbling in thick globules to the stone floor. She carefully massaged the throbbing stem until every drop of sticky fluid had been eased from it. Then she slipped the length of muscle back into her mouth, and licked and sucked it clean.

The rapturous applause of the mistress broke the strange spell under which Laura had been cast. "Bravo!" she exclaimed, rising to her feet. She gave Laura's neck collar a gentle tug, urging her to stand as well. "Don't you think it was a magnificent show?" she asked of the American. The performers had disengaged from one another and were busily collecting together the discarded clothing that decorated the floor. "I can very easily imagine you in just such a theatrical masterpiece, Laura," the mistress enthused. "I'm sure that when the Sinfinder has decided on the correct vehicle for you, you'll show yourself to be one of our leading lights!"

Laura couldn't see it herself. She had never acted before, let alone stripped naked in front of an audience and been made to indulge in all manner of carnal sins before their very eyes! Her vagina was soaking wet, that much she knew, and the idea of being made to pleasure Vijay's magnificent cock sent thrills of excitement darting through her; but to have to perform, and to have to behave like a whore for the gratification of dirty old men with fat wallets - that was something which induced within her a very real and very terrible sense of stage fright.

"Come!" the mistress snapped, "we have other places to visit yet." Again, she tugged on Laura's neck collar, encouraging the American to follow her from the room.

Chapter 10

After a lazy morning of gentle fucking, Lord Cartwright and Mrs Reid made their way downstairs into the bar of the inn and enjoyed a leisurely lunch. The sense of excitement they both felt at having reawakened their lust seemed barely containable. Indeed, it was all they could manage to look away from one another for long enough to enjoy a mouthful of food. At length, with a couple of pints inside him and a twinkle in his eye that boded well for Mrs Reid's chances of an afternoon's passion, Lord Cartwright called old Bill the landlord over to him. He offered him a Monte Cristo cigar, which was gratefully accepted, and asked him about the possibility of setting up a meeting with Matthew Hopkirk.

"Mr 'opkirk's not an easy one to pin down an' that's a fact," chuckled old Bill. "My wife'll tell you that, won't you, love?" He called to the heavy redhead who was busily serving behind the bar. "What's that?" she asked, glancing up from the glass she was slowly filling with a pint of home-made Dragon's Breath.

"I was jus' sayin' to these folk 'ow Mr 'opkirk's 'ard t' pin down."

"He's shadowy, alright, and no mistakin'. You folks got some special business with him?"

The Cartwrights exchanged the briefest of knowing glances. "Something like that, I suppose, yes."

The redhead wiped her hands on a grubby-looking tea towel and came out from behind the bar to join her husband and their guests. "Maggie's the name," she said, extending a chubby hand to the aristocrat and his wife in turn. "You been to his latest 'show', then?"

"Yes, yes, we went along last night, actually." Lord Cartwright shuffled uncomfortably on his chair. He felt strangely ill-at-ease discussing the topic of the Sinfinder's big-top show with people he hardly knew, and yet Maggie and Bill seemed to have no such qualms.

"See anything you liked?"

The Cartwrights looked at one another again, the gentlest of smiles simultaneously flickering across their mouths. "I suppose you could say that we did, yes, but we fear it may be somewhat unattainable."

A broad grin broke out across Maggie's face, her dark green eyes suddenly illuminated with a barely contained delight. "Well if you're thinking about trying to wrestle that vile bitch from Matthew, all I's can say to you is I wish you the very best o' luck. The place'll be a lot better for seeing the back of her!"

"I'm sorry?" Lord Cartwright stammered, hardly able to believe that Maggie had so clearly perceived their intention, "I'm afraid I don't know what you mean."

"Come off of it!" the big woman chortled, digging her husband knowingly in the ribs with her elbow. "Me an' old Bill 'ere know exactly what you're up to. It's as plain as the nose on your face - ain't it, Bill?!"

"And what might it be that we're 'up to'?" the aristocrat enquired, daring the briefest of glances in his wife's direction. Mrs Reid was also looking uncomfortable - as if she knew their plan was about to made public, and that there was nothing they could do about it.

"You're after the mistress, ain't you!" Maggie laughed. "You're after buying the bitch and taking her off with you. I'm right, ain't I? That's what you've got planned?"

Lord Cartwright smiled. "You're very astute, Maggie."

"Well all I can say is I wish you the best of luck. That stuck-up strumpet gets right up my nose, sauntering around like she's the great 'I am'. Who the fuck does her think she is anyway, the fat-arsed bitch! If there's anything I can do to help you get what you want - and her won't come cheap, mind, so don't expect that her will - then you can count on me doin' it. Me an' old Bill, 'ere, we got a lot o' sway with Mr 'opkirk, an' if you want to see 'im 'bout buying 'madam', then you rest assured, we'll get a meeting set up for you!"

The arrival of three sweat-drenched overseers from the Farm - all cheerily demanding pints of ale and threatening to take their canes to Maggie's "fat behind" if she didn't serve them "sharpish'" - brought the conversation to an unexpected end. "I'll pop up to your room later," the redhead said as she ambled back to the bar, accompanied by her husband, "once I've got a meeting sorted for you."

"Thanks very much," the aristocrat smiled, and raised his drink to the ruddy-faced landlady. He turned and smiled at his wife: "Well, things seem to be moving in the right direction, at least," he said to her. "From what Maggie just said, it sounds at least as though there's the possibility of buying Mistress Kimble, even if she's likely to cost the proverbial arm and leg."

"If that Lucinda girl from last night is priced at a half-million, I dread to think what the mistress's price is likely to be."

Lord Cartwright gulped down the dregs of his pint and stubbed out the remaining length of his Monte Cristo cigar. "Let's not worry about such matters," he said cheerily. "We'll pay whatever we have to to get her. Now, get that shameful bottom of yours back up those stairs, my sweet. The sight of those gentlemen at the bar with their nice long lengths of rattan has given me a real fancy for using my own cane to stripe those misbehaving cheeks of yours."

It was a strange excitement which Mrs Reid felt in the pit of her stomach as she climbed the stairs to their bedroom. She was aware of the usual thrill of expectation which she felt whenever she was about to be soundly beaten by her beloved husband. But on this particular occasion, there was an even greater sense of anticipation coursing through her gently trembling body. There was a real feeling that she and Bertie were on the brink of doing something which would change their lives forever. In meeting the flame-haired Mistress Kimble, they had stumbled upon the answer to all of their prayers. She was a magnificent physical example of womankind, and a female who had risen to a position of great control - yet one who had nonetheless learned impressive obedience. A feisty "bitch", as Maggie had referred to her. A woman able to make enemies, to behave in a way which could induce people to hate her, yet one who really, ironically, had no control at all. One who, at a moment's notice - at the bark of a single instruction - had learned to suppress her own dominant personality, and in its place to profer her body for the pleasures of others...

...A woman, in short, who would provide a stimulating challenge for the Cartwrights - yet one who already had so instinctive an understanding of her own place in the hierarchy of things that, in truth, she would prove to be no challenge at all...

By the time Big Maggie knocked upon the door to the Cartwrights' room three hours later, Mrs Reid had enjoyed five shattering orgasms. Four of them had come while she was impaled on her husband's savagely thrusting cock - the fifth while receiving the cruel attentions of Bertie's wicked cane across her errant buttocks. For Bertie's part, he had revelled in the sensations of three mind-numbing climaxes. Even as the redhead's knuckles rapped against the heavy oak door, he was busily wiping the remnants of his most recent spend from his wife's chin, where renegade globules had dribbled from her mouth only moments earlier.

He'd thrown on a dressing gown and opened the door even before Maggie had had time to knock again. "Afternoon, sir," the redhead said. She craned her neck as her inquisitiveness got the better of her, attempting to catch a glimpse of the diminutive Mrs Reid. "And to your good lady wife, I'm sure." Realising she was to be thwarted in her nosiness, she quickly turned her attentions to the matter in hand.

"You can see Mr 'opkirk this very afternoon, I'm pleased to inform you, sir," she smiled. "If you just make your way up to the house, you'll be taken to 'im."

The aristocrat nodded his head appreciatively. "Thank you, Maggie," he said. "If you just hold on there, I'll go and get you something for your trouble." As he made to turn away from the door, the redhead gave a gentle cough. Lord Cartwright stopped in his tracks and looked enquiringly at her. "If it's all the same with you, sir," Big Maggie said, "I won't be takin' no money f'r my troubles. I prefer t' be paid in other ways, sir, if you 'n' your good lady wife wouldn't be mindin'."

"Other ways, Maggie?"

"Well, sir, I couldn't 'elp 'earin' them sounds what was comin' from your room earlier, sir - them swishin' sounds." As the redhead spoke, Mrs Reid appeared at the door alongside her husband, busily readjusting her dressing gown and tidying her hair. She nodded her head gently in Maggie's direction by way of greeting, a gesture the landlady returned in kind. "An' I was wond'rin', sir," the big woman continued, "if it were to be acceptable to your wife, o' course, whether or not you'd do me the favour of treatin' me in much the same way, sir..."

Lord Cartwright was perplexed. "I'm... sorry," he stammered, feeling as though he'd missed something. "I'm still not entirely..."

"...she wishes you to whip her, Bertie," Mrs Reid interjected, "isn't that so, Maggie?"

A smile of pure relief danced across the big woman's face. "Yes, ma'am, that's right!" she exclaimed, delighted to have successfully communicated her desire. "If it's all the same with the both of you, o' course..."

"And would it be all the same with your husband?" Mrs Reid questioned stiffly. "Another man, beating his wife for him?"

"It's the way o' things round these parts, ma'am," Big Maggie explained. "If ever old Bill 'as a problem wi' me, 'e's quick enough to take his pound o' flesh from us arse, I can assure you!"

Mrs Reid briefly allowed a gentle smile to take control of her face. "I'm sure he is, Maggie," she mused, "I'm sure he is. Well, if Bertie has no objection, I certainly don't..."

She looked towards her husband questioningly, a rare twinkle playing in her eyes.

"Uh, no. No, none," he replied, still a little taken aback by the strange and entirely unexpected turn of events.

By the time Maggie had made her way across the room, however, and Mrs Reid had fetched the cane from the floor at the side of the bed, Lord Cartwright had gathered his senses somewhat. He seemed suddenly ready to adopt the dominant manner which always so excited his wife. Maggie stood expectantly by the bed, her thick red hair tumbling around her shoulders and heavy breasts, her face alive with anticipation.

"I have my rules, Maggie," he said at length, his words accompanied by a wicked glint in the eye. "If once you accept my right to discipline you, then you accept as well my right to discipline you exactly how I see fit. No amount of pleading shall distract me from my intended path, and your punishment shall draw to a close only when I decide that you have been chastised enough. Now, do you understand that?"

Big Maggie nodded her head in acknowledgment. "Yes, sir," she said, "I understand your rules 'n' they're fine by me."

"Then let us proceed. If you would be so good as to remove all items of clothing from your waist downwards..."

Lord Cartwright and Mrs Reid set about readying her for the flogging. She was bent over the end of the bed and long lengths of cord were wrapped tightly around her wrists. Mrs Reid then drew the loose ends along the length of the bed, fastening them to the head-rest, and in so doing stretching Maggie's arms to their limit. Behind her, the buxom landlady could hear the aristocrat slicing the air with his cane. From the speed of each air-stroke, there was little doubting the Earl's intention to lay the rattan across her buttocks with all the strength he could muster!

Maggie hadn't expected to be tied up. Suddenly, she felt more vulnerable than she ever had before. As her heart pounded frantically, she wished to God she'd just taken his lordship's offer of money.

What happened next was of even greater concern to her. Mrs Reid began to massage oil into her bare buttocks; a terrible, slimy oil; cold and wet. The diminutive woman's fingers strayed where there seemed little need, and Maggie gasped as she was touched between her thighs and her buttocks, wondering at the reason for such a strange procedure.

"When my husband and I lay the cane across a shameful bottom," Mrs Reid began to explain, as though sensing Maggie's curiosity, "we like to ensure that the strokes are appreciated. This oil will heighten the pain of each cut, and ensure you'll think twice before ever again asking anyone to beat you."

The whipping which followed did indeed teach Maggie a lesson. By the time half-a-dozen strokes had landed across her wobbling bottom, she'd realised what a dreadful fool she'd been in asking for a caning. The aristocrat was a savage brute of a man, mercilessly slicing her flesh while the grim-faced Mrs Reid egged him on, imploring her husband to "thrash the big bitch's moons, Bertie!" and to "flog her fat cheeks until she pees herself!". Big Maggie twisted and turned as much as her bonds would allow. Yet no matter how spectacular the cavorting of her big white backside, Lord Cartwright's cane continued to land with unerring accuracy across the full expanse of both buttocks. After ten strokes, the Earl paused while his wife applied more oil to Maggie's bottom. "Let's get these great big cheeks nice and wet again, shall we," Mrs Reid exclaimed, "so that Lord Cartwright's cane can really make your big bum sizzle!"

The thrashing recommenced, the cane whistling through the air and cracking against Maggie's soaked and swollen bottom-cheeks with all the energy the aristocrat could muster. Another ten vicious strokes were applied, drawing howls of pain from the violently bucking redhead.

After they'd been delivered, Mrs Reid again massaged oil into the burning flesh. And again, Lord Cartwright recommenced the beating, swinging his monstrous cane at the quivering bum until his face ran with sweat and was blushing as red as Big Maggie's brutally whipped flanks.

By the time Lord Cartwright had finished pulverising his victim's bottom flesh, he was standing naked and erect, his dressing gown in a crumpled heap at his ankles. The final thirty strokes he administered were a wicked, savage assortment of flesh-ravaging cuts, delivered the length and breadth of the screaming redhead's smouldering backside. They fell without pause, Mrs Reid having finally dispensed with her phial of oil. She'd removed her own dressing gown, too, and sunk to her knees before her husband, engulfing his erect and throbbing cock in her hot mouth and sucking on the veiny muscle for all she was worth. She sucked him hard as he flogged the expanse of flesh presented before him, and delighted in the whistling sound of her husband's cane as it swept through the air above and behind her furiously bobbing head, cruelly dispensing its merciless judgment on Maggie's swollen bumcheeks.

Lord Cartwright and his wife were consumed by a frenzy of lust. It quickly became apparent to Maggie that her caning had been brought to a close only because a fresh and different desire had flashed into the mind of the silver-haired aristocrat. Disengaging himself from his wife's furiously sucking lips, he steered Maggie around the bottom of the bed until she was standing to its side, her wrists still fastened by long cords to the headrest. He settled himself on the side of the bed, then, and pulled her broad body across his knee, readjusting her until her big bottom was thrusting upwards beneath his face, almost begging him to spank it.

He set about the task with uncontained relish, his palm slapping down again and again against the landlady's hot and wobbling flanks. Mrs Reid was chirruping with delight at the scene, thrilling to the way the redhead's flesh rippled each time it was struck. As the spanking progressed, she did her bit for the cause by restraining Maggie's wildly threshing legs. She even joined in herself, striking the big bottom with her own palm between each of her husband's spanks. With two palms slapping at her, Maggie hardly had time to catch her breath between each vicious assault on her jiggling bum-cheeks.

Eventually, she was sent tumbling from the aristocrat's knee, her heavy body landing with a resounding thud against the cold wooden floorboards. Before the big woman had even had time to regain her composure, Mrs Reid had clambered onto her husband's suddenly available lap and impaled herself on his thick, dribbling cock. "Gather together your clothes, Maggie," the woman gasped as she bounced up and down on Bertie's throbbing muscle, at the same time leaning sideways to undo Maggie from the bed's headrest, "and get out of here!"

Maggie needed no second bidding. As tears poured down her face, she picked up her clothing and hurried across the room like a frightened, scampering animal. Her swollen buttocks were throbbing and burning, and, for the first time, she realised what it was to be properly beaten. She darted into her own bedroom further down the hall, and felt her stomach churning violently. The bile rose in her throat, and she staggered into the bathroom. As she collapsed, retching, in front of the toilet, she felt a fresh well of tears gathering in her eyes, and a sudden, unexpected terror gripped her heart...

She and old Bill had to leave, she knew that now! She'd been kidding herself, fooling herself into believing that she was safe - that the Sinfinder would never suddenly decide that she too should join his circus of slaves...

But how could she really feel secure? What was there to stop the dark-cowled devil's disciple from having her taken to the Farm, or transported to a life of suffering in his ramshackle mansion house? The whipping she'd just endured had certainly provided confirmation of one thing; she would never be able to survive the kind of brutality to which the Sinfinder subjected his slaves. Never in a million years.

...By the time night fell, she and old Bill had packed their bags and left the tavern...

...By the following morning, the fat old man was back in his bed, and wondering about a future without his beloved Maggie...

As they'd attempted to leave the valley for good under cover of darkness, two of the overseers patrolling the perimeters of the Sinfinder's land had stopped them. While one had contacted the manager of the Farm, the grim-faced German named Hans, the other had snapped handcuffs around old Bill's wrists and made him sit at the bottom of a tree. Then, he'd instructed Maggie to strip, forced her onto her back on the soft damp soil, and cruelly made use of her while her husband looked on.

The bespectacled Hans had arrived in his jeep within minutes, and in no time at all had made old Bill tell him what he and his wife had been planning. The German had then returned to his jeep, picked up a thick length of leather whip, and made Maggie lie face-down and spreadeagled in the soil. He'd whipped her soundly, then, across her shoulders and her back, flaying her until her flesh seemed certain to split open. Then, discarding the whip, he'd taken the thick length of rattan he always kept holstered at his side, and used it to flog her buttocks while the overseers held her down, pressing her face into the soft earth until she nearly choked.

The German beat her with the cane for fifteen long minutes, occasionally shifting from one side of her to the other to ensure that his wicked rattan struck against every morsel of her trembling flanks. When the flogging had been completed, the overseers bundled her into Hans's jeep, along with old Bill. "Maggie will be taken to the Farm for the time being," the German announced to the fat old man as he drove them away from the perimeter fencing. "You must go back to the tavern and continue as usual."

"What will happen to her?" Bill asked, casting a glance towards his wife as she lay semi-conscious in the back of the jeep.

"The Sinfinder shall decide," Hans told him. "I do not think she will be taken to the mansion house, though; she is too large and too old. I think he will have her stay with me on the Farm."

"And you, Hans," there was a tremor in the old man's voice as he spoke. He hardly dared to form the question that he knew he had to ask. "What will you... do with her?"

"I can show you no favours," the blond-haired German announced sourly. "Your wife is a too large woman, ja? She will be made to toil in the fields; her weight will be checked each morning and evening. If she does not fast lose the fat, she will be whipped, ja!" The German slapped his palm against the steering wheel as he spoke, as though to emphasise his intention to make big Maggie suffer. Old Bill began to sob gently, and wondered how his wife would cope with her new life in cruel, merciless captivity...

...He was sobbing, too, the following morning, within seconds of waking from a fitful sleep and finding himself alone in his bed. As he stared at the ceiling, he wondered where Maggie was at that precise moment in time, little more than a half-hour after dawn.

If he had known the awful truth, the old man would surely have wailed out loud in uncontrollable anguish.

Down on the Farm, in Field Four, where the female slave

131

labourers toiled from dawn until dusk, old Bill's red-headed wife was struggling hard to perform the task demanded by the gruesome overseer who stood above her, cane clutched in his chunky hand. Maggie gasped in pain as she performed her fifty-fourth press-up, and howled as the overseer's rattan struck her buttocks for a fifty-fourth time. "Fifty-four!" he snapped as he struck. "Only forty-six more to do, you fat bitch!"

As Maggie hauled her naked body up from the fallow earth for a fifty-fifth time, the early morning sunlight fell across her buttocks and thighs, exposing the pink flesh at her crotch - glistening wet with translucent fluid that dribbled freely from her overfilled cunt. Her buttocks, too, were wet with globules of sticky male spend - the overspill from her bruised and battered rectum. Flogged hard with canes, paddles and straps throughout the night, and fucked repeatedly by more brutish overseers than she could possibly recall, Maggie could hardly comprehend the change that had taken place in her life during the previous twenty-four hours.

If she hadn't attempted to leave, the likelihood was that nothing at all would have happened to her. Probably, nothing would ever have happened - she could see that now. After all, the Sinfinder had left her alone throughout her and old Bill's twenty-two year tenancy of the village pub, so why would he suddenly decide to make her one of his slaves after all that time?

She'd panicked after the whipping, that was all, and had tried to flee - and now she was paying the price. Her days as a publican were behind her; now, she was a slave. A farm labourer, to be whipped and fucked whenever the overseers had a fancy for doing so.

Now, through her own ridiculous stupidity, she truly had become the property of the merciless Sinfinder General..

CHAPTER 11

Returned to their cell, Laura, Sally and Lucinda were refastened, facing the wall, in the customary manner.

As usual, no words passed between the three women. Laura could no longer communicate with Sally anyway; her friend had become completely submissive and servile. She'd no doubt judged compliance to be a less painful method of existence than the kind of defiant attitude which Laura had attempted to retain.

As for Lucinda, although her and Laura's sufferings had seemed inextricably linked since their time together on the Farm, not even so much as a word had ever passed between them.

The constant presence of an invariably sweaty overseer at the cell door - eyes bulging with barely containable glee at the sight of so much naked and vulnerable female flesh - had also counted against the possibility of conversation.

The three women were left hanging for what seemed to Laura to be days. In truth, a matter of only a few hours had passed by the time the mistress entered the cell and gave instructions for the American to be unfastened. Laura sighed with relief as the clamps at her nipples and clitoris were removed, and grimaced in pain as she lowered her aching arms to her sides.

The afternoon she had passed chained to the wall had certainly been long, but had not been uneventful. As she'd hung there, she'd regularly heard the sounds of the two bare bottoms to her left being beaten. She'd even been able to discern which implements were being used, so familiar had she become with the regime of terror. Her own bum had been left alone - the Sinfinder had not yet passed instructions for her punishments to recommence following the terrible birching she'd received at his hands - though the overseer on duty had nonetheless made use of her. As the hot afternoon sunlight had slanted in through the high cell window, he had clasped her with his clammy hands and grunted his way to a climax, spending deep within her fleshy vagina. Then he'd cruelly corked her with some wicked contraption or other, to ensure his seed didn't bubble back out of her.

The neck collar was refitted and the mistress wrenched wickedly at the attached cord, guiding Laura to her knees. "Head down," she said, "face against the floor." There was no doubting what the instruction meant. The last time she'd been made to adopt such a posture, it had been for the purpose of an enema, administered in preparation for a visit to the Sinfinder himself. Sure enough, Laura felt a stumpy finger grease her bottom, and winced as a tube was pushed inside her anus. The warm waters flowed, her stomach bloated, and her face began to blush at the thought of the terrible shame she was about to endure.

Seconds later, she was being held in a squatting position over a bucket, the overseers and the mistress whooping with delight as a jet of waste matter squirted from her ass.

Then it was the soap and water treatment - a thorough sponging that left no morsel of bum flesh unwashed - and the command to adopt a position on hands and knees, and to crawl - no, trot, the mistress commanded - like a horse to the Sinfinder's gloomy lair. The red-haired dominatrix rode on her back, teasing her flanks with a wicked-looking crop.

Once more in the darkly lit room, the curious contraptions in semi-shadow looming like malevolent giants, Laura felt her stomach churn. The Sinfinder was slouched in his chair, just as he had been the first time the American had been brought to that dreadful place. To his right, the malignant dwarf sat at his feet, his face a twisted mask of buck-toothed evil.

Before the two dark figures, on the floor, lay a garment of clothing, carefully laid out against the stone slabs and black as pitch.

The Sinfinder pointed a gloved finger towards the

garment, fixed Laura with an impassive stare and murmured, "Put it on."

The mistress, who had dismounted the American the moment they'd entered the chamber, tapped her riding crop against Laura's bottom, encouraging her to follow Matthew Hopkirk's instruction. Laura stood up and moved tentatively forward, reaching down to pick up the strange-looking garment, wondering all the while how she was meant to fit into something so outrageously small.

The garment was made of rubber, zipped down the back. At the front, two holes had been made in the breast area, while at the back, a larger hole had been left for her bottom. Laura had seen the garment before. When first she'd been brought to the house, the mistress had made her watch a 'performance' in which Sally had appeared dressed in just such an item of clothing. She had been whipped by the man who'd played her master in the scene, and placed in an excruciatingly small wooden box, out of which only her head, feet and buttocks had protruded.

Laura felt her heart pounding in her chest as she struggled into the garment, wondering what dreadful fate might await her once she was wearing the tiny rubber suit. She fitted her pert breasts through the holes at the front, and wriggled her bottom around until her buttocks hung clear at the back, all the time gasping for breath as the tightness of the terrible rubber suit began to take effect.

The Sinfinder rose to his feet and shook the folds from his long black cloak. "I hope you have learned well the lessons you have been taught," he muttered. "I hope that you have gained much from your watching of our little shows." Ominously, he moved towards her, the black pearls of his eyes seeming almost to burn into her very soul.

What strange power did this man have, she asked herself. He was, without question, the most terrifying of entities; a satanic, pagan creature of darkness, consumed with sadistic evil.

And yet...and yet...

Though Laura could hardly comprehend it herself, she desired his attentions - grim and agonising though they were - more than she had ever desired any other man's. She wanted to be possessed by him; to be taught by him. She felt almost as though it were his right, his unequivocal right, to do with her as he wished; to cause her pain or pleasure to whatever extent he chose, and to treat her in whatever diabolical way he desired.

Even the feeling of his gloved hand slapping her across the cheek did nothing to break the mesmeric spell in which he had her so emphatically held.

"Cur!" he cried, the back of his hand flashing across her face once more, slapping against the other cheek. "It is time for thee to show how well thou hast learned thy lessons thus far." His gloved fingers clasped Laura's exposed nipples and twisted them roughly, causing the American to squeal in pain. "Do as I bid thee or I will birch these foul titties until the nipples hang limp and withered. Would ye like that, wench?"

"No, master." Laura steeled herself against the cruel stabs of pain that lanced through her breasts.

"Tell me, then, what ye would not like, slave-dog?" he spat, wrenching the big pink nodules through an excruciating one hundred-and-eighty degree turn.

"I wouldn't like you to birch my tits, master - please don't birch my tits!"

"Should I suck upon these fleshy teats instead, perhaps?"

"Oh yes, master!" Laura exclaimed, feeling a genuine thrill of excitement at the prospect of the Sinfinder's tight, lips going to work on her sore nipples, "Suck my fleshy teats, master - suck them, please!"

"And your arse, wench - what should be done to your arse?"

Tears tumbled from Laura's eyes as the vicious maltreatment of her breasts continued. In spite of the pain in her bosom, she could feel the juices once again gathering at her sex. She recalled with a form of bizarre relish the terrible birching she had endured at Matthew Hopkirk's hands. "Birch my ass!" she found herself begging, "Yeah! Get some - uhhhn!..." - another malicious twist of her erect nipples, making her groan in agony - "get some f-fresh twigs from the garden and birch the skin off of my ass!"

What the hell was she saying? What in Jesus's name was happening to her? How could the Sinfinder exercise such mind-numbing control?

Laura could feel the tears rolling down her cheeks; the terrible - yet strangely exquisite - pain within her breasts; the wetness of her love-slot, mashed against the rubber bondage suit. And she instinctively knew that she was on the verge of losing herself entirely; of leaving behind her the person she had been, and becoming instead an altogether more servile, more docile, more pathetic creature...

...A slave for the Sinfinder!

Matthew Hopkirk's fiercesome assault on her breasts ended as swiftly as it had begun. Even as the final stabs of pain coursed through her bullet-hard nipples, his hand cracked against her cheek once more, flipping her head sideways. Almost immediately, it was flipped back by another powerful slap, this time to her opposite side of her face.

"Tell me, girl," he demanded, his gloved hand punishing her blushing face with strike after dreadful strike, "What is thy bottom for?"

Even as his hand pummelled her, his gloved palm splatting against her tear-stained face with an unremitting cruelty, Laura recalled the exact same question having been asked of Sally when she had been grimly encased in the rubber bondage suit. Luckily, Laura could also remember the answer her friend had given:

"It-it's for birching, master - my bottom is for birching,"

The Sinfinder's hand was at her right breast again,

clasping hold firmly and using it to steer her around, revealing to him her bare and superbly presented buttocks. His gloved hand slapped the cheeks - first left, then right, then across the crown of both trembling hemispheres. Laura continued to gurgle her response. "And my ass is for caning, too, and for fucking hard with a nice big dick - ow! ahh! - and my ass is for licking and fingering, sir - ahh! - and-and for shitting from!"

The spanking she received was fast and sharp, making her buttocks tingle with a gently spreading heat. She felt hot and horny, and wanted a piece of dick inside her - the Sinfinder's dick! She wondered if he'd use her when he'd had his fill of smacking her ass. The enema had left her feeling wonderfully light-stomached and thoroughly cleansed, and strange though it was, she actually wanted him inside her asshole, filling her up with his throbbing cock and having his way with her. She'd lost all control of herself, that much she knew, and in her heightened state of lust, she could think of nothing hornier than the Sinfinder, the master of all he surveyed, thrusting in and out of her tight little butt; a butt specially cleansed and purified in readiness for him!

"Fuck me in the ass, master!" she gurgled, as he slapped away at her buttocks. "Fuck the shit out of me!"

Laura found herself being suddenly swung around again, her body sent tumbling to the hard stone floor. Before she'd even had time to catch her breath, the Sinfinder had pulled a bundle of birch twigs from somewhere within his cloak and had set about flogging her bare breasts. Laura screamed as the dreaded twigs splatted against her flesh, the splayed ends of the rods slicing into her still-hard nipples, sending a biting pain searing into her very core.

'Wicked harlot!" squealed the Sinfinder in an unworldly, high-pitched voice. "It is not for thee to decide how thou art treated!" Thwack! Thwack! "It is I, the Sinfinder General, who decides upon thy fate!" Thwack!

"Please, master!" Laura screamed, desperately attempting to protect her quivering breasts from the savage onslaught of the wicked rods, "Please don't beat my tits! I was wilful and rude, master! Please, I beg you, forgive me, and-and don't whip my tits any more!"

A wrench on the neck collar forced Laura onto her stomach. She felt the Sinfinder's boot against the back of her neck, mashing her face against the cold stone floor, and heard him mutter an instruction. "She is yours, Quinn."

From the sudden scuffling movements over by Matthew Hopkirk's chair, Laura knew the Sinfinder had been addressing the gruesome dwarf.

"No!" she pleaded, her lust consumed by a sudden, terrible sickness. "Not him, please!"

"Your new lord and master, bitch," muttered the Sinfinder from between clenched teeth. "It is every slave's desire to please their master, that is the Sinfinder's law; and you must do all that you can to please yours."

Behind her, Laura could hear the unmistakable sound of clothing being removed. She twisted and turned against the slabs, hoping to dislodge the Sinfinder's boot from her neck, yet realising any such achievement would ultimately be to little avail. She could feel the ends of the birch twigs gently tickling her exposed bottom, reminding her of what she would get if she were to disobey.

In truth, she considered, as she heard the sounds of the dwarf readying himself, a birching was her preferred option at that moment! But what was the point of earning herself one? Inevitably, the malevolent Quinn would still get to have his way with her, and all that her opposition would have afforded her was another set of stripes across her ass.

She felt a sudden weight against her back, and realised the gruesome little beast had clambered on top of her!

Jagged fingernails scratched against the skin of her breasts as he reached round and sought to grope her. She could feel his hot, stale breath fanning the back of her head, his hairy body shifting against hers. The little brute seemed uncertain of how best to profit from the opportunity the Sinfinder had granted him.

"Open your bottom for him," Matthew Hopkirk instructed. "Show him your hole."

"Master, please, no. I'll do anything, master - anything at all - but please don't let him have me."

"He is your master, cur - I am your overlord. Do as I say, and show your new master your hole."

Laura clasped her buttocks and prised them apart, feeling the cold air suddenly caress her anus.

A sharp nail began scratching urgently across the peripheral flesh of her asshole, the dwarf beginning an investigation of her most secret place. It was almost as though he were marking out his territory, Laura thought to herself, using his finger to feel her gently palpitating bum-mouth in preparation for using the tight little aperture. She felt his fingertip push beyond her ring of resistant muscle and enter the sanctum of her ass, wriggling like a dreadful little worm inside her.

"How do you find her, Quinn?" the Sinfinder questioned. "Is she to your liking?"

"Oh yes, Sinfinder," the dwarf squealed. "She is tight, and hot inside, and her shithole throbs around my finger, sucking it inside her. She wants me, master, she wants me inside her giving her a good fucking with my cock!"

The grizzly little man's vile words made Laura's stomach churn. She was certain she was to be sick, so disgusted was she by the frenzied attentions of the malevolent dwarf. She whinnied in sheer panic when she felt the hairy beast press his gross little body more firmly against her, stuffing his grisly cock between her buttocks and nuzzling her bumhole.

"I'll fuck the bitch's shitcrack, yes I will!" Quinn wittered to himself. "I'll fuck you, do you hear?" He edged the head of his cock past her ring of anal muscle. Laura gasped in

140

pain and despair. "Fuck you good, will Quinn!"

The dwarf's hairy little groin slapped against her bottom-cheeks and Laura knew he was buried to the hilt. He began to thrust inside her bottom almost immediately, gasping and groaning lustfully as he hammered his fleshy shaft in and out of her, hungrily seeking the release he so desperately craved. "Feel Quinn's cock in your ass. Quinn fucks you good in your hole and makes you squeal!" He giggled with delight at his own words, and snorted mightily, his body rolling back and forth as he pressed home his advantage. "I'll split your bum wide open, bitch - fill you with Quinn's seed!"

From above her, Laura could hear the Sinfinder's mocking laughter echoing around the chamber. The mistress was close by too, she could tell - enjoying the bizarre scene in which she was being made to participate. And still Matthew Hopkirk's boot pressed against her neck, clamping her flat to the floor; and still the heavy bundle that was Quinn - her lord and master, the Sinfinder had called him - writhed around against her back, and corkscrewed his fleshy cock in and out of her.

Laura felt the birch twigs tickle her shoulders.

"Ahh! I'm there!" the dwarf growled, and raked at Laura's rubber-clad back with his jagged fingernails. "Quinn is coming! He's coming!" he moaned.

"Come then, master!" Laura was desperate to end the ordeal, to use her words to spur him towards the inevitable climax. "Come inside of my tight little bum!"

She felt a sudden spurt of fluid being pumped into her rectum, and exhaled a languid sigh of relief. Quinn, his body draped across her back, continued to empty himself into her bottom for several seconds. Laura found herself wondering how so much sperm could have been held in what must have been a tiny pair of testicles, and wished to God there was some way she could empty her ass of his filthy deposit.

"Oh, Sinfinder," the dwarf moaned from between saliva-drenched lips. "Oh, Sinfinder, I love her!" Quinn slumped from Laura's rubber-sheathed back, his wet, hairy body slapping against the stone slabs as he gasped for breath.

"Then you shall have her, my misshapen friend," muttered Matthew Hopkirk. "She shall be yours to do with as you please."

"I want her forever, master," said Quinn. "I want her to be mine, for Quinn to love. She is so tight and warm."

"Then you shall take her as your wife!" the Sinfinder announced grandly.

On hearing the cowled overlord's dreadful proclamation, Laura began to writhe beneath his foot. The gentlest of moans was her only verbal response to his bombshell declaration. "Mistress Kath," he continued, addressing the flame-haired female who lurked in the corner of the chamber. "Let it be known that there is to be a wedding - of Quinn, the circus ringmaster, and the newly arrived yankee bitch. The ceremony shall take place tomorrow morning, when the two lovers shall be joined for eternity. Contact John Templeton - tell him to make the necessary preparations."

Templeton was a name which Laura recognised well enough. He was the Lord of the Manor, the man who seemed to have control over events within the village and at the Farm on a day-to-day basis. A man, like all the others, quite obviously in the Sinfinder's employ. He had also been engaged to Laura's cellmate Lucinda, until she'd committed some crime or other - Laura was unsure exactly what - and had been sent to the Farm, and then on to the Sinfinder, as punishment.

Laura's body trembled with sobs at Matthew Hopkirk's pronouncement of her wedding, and she choked a weak-willed 'no' from the very depths of her throat.

"Oh yes, my dear," the Sinfinder murmured in response to her gasped utterance, scrunching his boot even more firmly into her neck. "This time tomorrow you shall be Mrs Quinn, and will no doubt be enjoying full well the marriage nuptials with your beloved husband, upon the marital bed - satiating together the fiery lustings that burn so passionately within the loins of all young newly weds."

The Sinfinder removed his boot from the back of Laura's head, and tickled her ass with the ends of the birch rods. "Take her now, Mistress Kath," he commanded. "Though she be married on the morrow, today she remains the sole property of this house of torment, and her lessons must continue uninterrupted." The mistress approached, and helped Laura to her hands and knees. She re-mounted her, her large buttocks mashing against the small of Laura's back. She tapped her riding crop against her charge's bottom, encouraging her towards the door.

"I think the schoolgirl attire would suit the yankee harlot best, Mistress Kath," the Sinfinder advised. "Let her join you in a delightful tableau, set within the grim confines of a headmistress's office."

"It shall be done, my lord," the big-bottomed mistress said, as her human horse carried her towards the chamber door. "Return us to your cell," Mistress Kath commanded her. "There, you shall wait while the scene is set and your costume readied. I shall send for you soon."

Back in the cell, Laura winced as her nipples were cruelly clamped, her wrists manacled to the wall above her head. Her clitoris, mashed beneath the sweaty rubber suit she still wore, was inaccessible. At least she avoided the eye-watering pain of having a cruel clamp attached to her there!

There were no sobs, no noises she could have made that would have been anguished enough to express the terror with which she viewed the prospect of her bizarre wedding. The feeling of Quinn sliding around against her back as he'd pumped her ass had been almost enough to make her vomit. The thought that the miserable, malignant little beast would soon have free access to her, to make use of her however he desired, made her heart sink and her soul cry out for release from the wretchedness of her existence.

Why had the Sinfinder given her away? If he'd kept her, she could have pleased him, pleasured him in whatever ways he'd desired. And she would have done so almost happily, because her resolve had been well and truly broken. Not by the cruel whippings she had suffered, or by the many vile deposits that had been ejaculated into her body - but by her inexplicable lust for the darkly-cowled man.

Laura couldn't explain the power he held over her. Everything which had been done to her, all that she had suffered, had been at his behest. He was The One; the all-powerful Sinfinder, from which even four-legged mongrels cowered in the cobbled streets, sensing his awful, overpowering evil.

A full hour or more must have passed before the overseer guarding the cell was sent word to unfasten Laura. Again, she felt the familiar flood of relief as her nipples and wrists were released, and winced as the brutish guard slapped her on her bottom and commanded her to leave the cell. She climbed the stairs into the main area of the huge, rambling house, and was led into a small closet, where the sweaty overseer told her to change into the clothing neatly piled in a bundle on the floor.

Laura peeled the rubber outfit from her clammy body, enjoying the sudden feeling of freedom after her time inside the terrible constraint, and began to dress in the clothes that had been left for her. It was no surprise to the American to find that she was putting on a schoolgirl's uniform; the Sinfinder had instructed the mistress to dress her so. Silly though she was certain she must have looked in the garments, it was nice at least to be wearing something feminine for the first time since her ill-fated arrival in the valley.

The overseer grunted his approval of her white blouse,

blue tie and skirt, white knee-high socks and black shoes, and ushered her through a door and into another room.

"You perform with the mistress this afternoon," he said. "Once you are on the stage, you must perform at all times; that is the rule. You must pretend that you are a pretty little schoolgirl, and you must play whatever game the mistress commands. If you do not, you will be whipped." He pointed to yet another door. "Knock loudly," he instructed. "From the moment you are granted entrance, the performance has begun. You will refer to the mistress as Mrs Kimble. I will wait outside with my whip. The mistress will call me if you perform badly and are to be flogged."

Laura's skin was tingling and she felt curiously hot. She adjusted the collar of her white school shirt and straightened her tie before moving tentatively to the door. She knocked firmly, and was immediately greeted by the sound of the mistress's voice.

"Come," Mrs Kimble said. Laura gently eased the door open. Upon entering, it became clear to her that the room had been prepared to look like a Headmistress's office. Seated on the sofa at the back of the room was the grey-haired man who Laura had seen playing the President of the United States in an earlier tableau. By contrast with the well-cut suit he had worn for that role, he was now wearing casual and rather grubby-looking clothing, and seemed altogether unkempt.

"Please come in, Laura," said Mrs Kimble quietly, "and close the door behind you."

The Headmistress was standing behind her desk, a cold, impassive expression on her dour face. She was wearing an electric-blue dress that clung tightly to her magnificently curved body. Her hands were clasped together in front of her.

"I have been talking to the school caretaker Mr James, Laura," she began, gazing down her nose at the American. "He tells me that this morning, he caught you smoking in the pavilion. Now, I do not intend to ask you whether this was the case or not, because I know it to be true. Mr James is a man of great principle and moral courage. He came to tell me what he saw because he is concerned for your welfare, as indeed am I."

Mrs Kimble moved out from behind her desk and walked across to a large book cupboard positioned in the corner of the room. Laura's heart missed a beat. "I do not intend to waste time lecturing you either. This is not the first time you have been in trouble, nor, I expect, will it be the last." She opened the cupboard and took down the long, thin cane hanging inside. "So I am not going to teach you a lesson. You are clearly incapable of learning those. Instead, I am going to punish you for your crime. There is a subtle difference between those two intentions, Laura. Frankly, I care not whether you can discern that difference or not."

Laura was aware of 'Mr James' readjusting his position on the sofa. She could feel her heart thudding ever more powerfully in her chest.

"Please, miss," she murmured, realising it was time to join in with the grotesque charade, "I promise not to smoke again. Please don't cane me."

"By all means smoke again if you so desire," the Headmistress responded. "It doesn't matter to me. All that will happen is that you will be brought before me again, and I shall take great pleasure in laying a few choice stripes across your bottom. Now lift up your skirt and bend over my desk, please, Laura."

"Don't make me do that, miss," Laura whined. "Don't cane me, don't make me lift my skirt!"

"Believe me, you will be doing considerably more than that, young lady!" snapped the Headmistress. "You are going to be punished. You should be thanking me for disciplining you in this manner, rather than putting you across my knee like I do the younger girls and giving you a shameful hand spanking. At least I'm not treating you like a child."

"Please, Miss..!"

"Do as I say now, Laura, or I will have Mr James here undress you and hold you down while I'm caning your wicked backside!"

Laura could feel the tears welling up in her eyes. She was being made to feel like a naughty child, not the mature woman she actually was.

For all the whippings she had taken, there was something peculiarly embarrassing about being dressed in such ridiculous, girlish attire. It was almost as though the clothing had deprived her of her sexuality, her 'adultness'. She really did feel like a silly little schoolgirl, in the same way as she'd felt just like a naughty child on the occasions when she'd been turned over a knee and hand-spanked.

It was these feelings which made her so certain that she would die of shame if Mr James were to strip her naked.

So she pulled up her skirt and bent over the desk as Mrs Kimble had instructed, her face blushing red as she revealed her panty-clad bottom to the seated Mr James.

"That's better," the Headmistress said. "Now, I am going to take down these panties and bare your bottom, Laura."

"'No! Oh no, Miss, please don't do that. Cane me on my knickers, please! I'm begging you!"

"Silence, you wilful child! I am going to put the cane across your bare buttocks, and that is all there is to it! It's your bottom flesh I intend to thoroughly sting, not the material of your undergarments."

Without further ado, the Headmistress swiftly peeled down Laura's panties. "I am going to stripe-up this shameful bottom of yours, my girl, just see if I don't!"

Laura began to sob as her bottom was laid bare. She felt Mrs Kimble's hand resting on her ass, and trembled slightly as the Headmistress used her fingertips to gently stroke the clammy flesh within her deep cleft.

"What a lovely, curvy bottom," Mrs Kimble said

admiringly. Her finger tickled at the soft lower portions of Laura's buttocks, and for a moment the American thought she was going to slip her hand between her thighs and feel her up.

Then Mrs Kimble removed her hand altogether. Laura knew the next sensation her buttocks would feel would be the sting of the cane...

...The swishing sound that accompanied the movement of the rattan provided her with pointless warning of the impending stroke.

Laura squealed and bucked from the cut, her buttocks quivering juicily. Mrs Kimble lashed the cane down again, and then again, each time landing the implement with a sharp crack across both of the American's trembling cheeks.

Laura's buttocks first smarted, and then throbbed. Stripe after stripe was cut into the soft surface of her fleshy posteriors.

Mrs Kimble remained silent as she thrashed the cane against Laura, going about her business with a ruthless efficiency.

Laura twisted and turned but didn't dare move from her bending position, ensuring that at all times her naked buttocks were proffered for the Headmistress's cane.

Her sobs turned into full-blooded howls as she endured the final, dreadful strokes. For these, Mrs Kimble shifted her own position. She moved to the opposite side of the desk so that she was standing over Laura's head and looking directly down onto the bare buttocks in front of her. She brought the whippy cane down vertically on the American's bottom, stinging the tender flesh that sloped down into the girl's bum cleft.

"Stand up, Laura," she panted, dropping the cane to the floor. Mrs Kimble's face was flushed red, her chest heaving. Her eyes seemed strangely glazed, almost watery.

"What a bad girl I am," she gasped unexpectedly, "caning your bottom because you were caught smoking when I

148

myself have a sixty-a-day habit!" Her hands clutched the material of her electric-blue dress: "I've been such a bad girl," she gasped "I need my own wicked plums severely dealt with!"

She tugged the tight, clinging material upwards to her waist, revealing her beautifully curvaceous thighs, sheathed in tights, and the big bulge of her crotch beneath tight and tiny white panties.

Laura could hardly believe what was happening. She'd expected the cruel caning to be only the start of her torment - and yet here she was, suddenly standing on the sidelines as the mistress, in her guise of Mrs Kimble, took centre-stage! Laura watched in growing amazement as the Headmistress assumed the position in which she herself had just been, and Mr James hauled himself up from the sofa.

The American gazed down at Mrs Kimble's big bottom, thrusting provocatively upwards. The buttocks were almost totally exposed beneath the see-through nylon tights that hugged her flesh. Her panties offered little in the way of concealing her posterior, the fabric nestling snugly into her deep bum-valley.

Mr James ripped at the tights, dragging them down the Headmistress's legs and despatching the knickers at the same time. He began to slap the magnificent posteriors then, his hand swiftly covering with smacks every portion of the splendidly shaped buttocks, inducing them to quiver and tremble delightfully before him.

"Oh I'm such a naughty girl!" the Headmistress moaned. "Spank my wicked arse until it's red-hot! Treat me like the disobeying child I am!" Mrs Kimble's flesh was soon burning red, her ripe buttocks jiggling as they were crisply spanked by the muscular 'caretaker'.

Laura's chest was rising and falling as she panted for breath, unable to accept the strange scene unfolding before her. Although her eyes were drinking in the drama, she could hardly comprehend what she was seeing. She watched as

Mr James picked up the cane from the floor and delivered six vigorous cuts to the Headmistress's crimson flanks. She found herself clutching at the desk for support then as she watched him drag Mrs Kimble across the room to the sofa, spread her semi-naked body across his knee, and resume the bum-burning hand-spanking.

"You bad and shameful hussy, Mrs Kimble," he chided, his hand slapping down across the Headmistress's deep, dark buttock-divide. "I'm going to see to it that these great big moons of yours are hot and sore for hours to come!"

"Please no, Mr James!" Mrs Kimble howled. The mistress was clearly delighting in the role-play, Laura could tell that. She was thrusting her buttocks up to meet the slaps as they rained down, twisting and turning so hard that on occasions she was almost mashing her hot, trembling ass-cheeks into Mr James's face.

Laura held her breath as, at last, Mr James pushed the Headmistress to the floor and tumbled on top of her. He pulled her legs up either side of him - once more exposing to the American's view Mrs Kimble's flame-red buttocks - and tugged his thick cock clear of his trousers. Within seconds he had sunk into the heaving woman beneath him.

"That's it!" Mrs Kimble moaned. "A hot juicy fuck is just what I need now! Slap those tight, swollen balls of yours into my bum cheeks, Mr James! Yes! Yes! That's it! Spank my bottom with your great big balls! Fuck my cunt until it's as red-raw as my arse!"

Laura watched transfixed as Mr James thrust in and out of the groaning woman, burying his throbbing muscle deep inside her. After a series of juicy thrusts, he withdrew and swung his huge erection up towards Mrs Kimble's face. She engulfed the beast with her mouth and hungrily sucked on it, occasionally stopping to lick at its pulsating, purple head before once more devouring its full length.

Dragging Mrs Kimble to her knees, Mr James re-entered her from behind, his abdomen slapping against her hot bottom as he thrust in and out of her raw pink hole. Before too long the silver-haired man was pumping the contents of his swollen testicles deep inside the Headmistress's wet and hungry quim.

The ejaculation marked the end of the curious tableau, the two rutting performers disentangling their bodies and hauling themselves back to their feet. The mistress turned towards Laura, her face flushed from her exertions.

"That should suffice for this afternoon's session," she gasped. "I hope that's provided for you a gentle enough introduction into our very special 'performance art'. You can be sure that from now on, a great deal more will be demanded of you when you are on stage; the few cane stripes you've just taken across your arse are nothing compared to the devilments you will endure in the future."

The mistress's face darkened malevolently. "You should count yourself lucky," she said. "If it had been left to me, you little minx, I would have thrashed you until sunset, and had you fucked until the seed was bubbling out of you! So you are fortunate indeed that the Sinfinder is such a fair and humane man, and wishes to have you broken in gently."

In truth, Laura didn't feel fortunate at all. As she was escorted back to her cell and divested of her clothing, she thought about what the mistress had said. If she could have replaced the terrible ordeal of the following day - her bizarre marriage to a man she found repugnant - with the experience of being whipped until sunset and fucked until she could hold no more, she would gladly have done so, and regarded herself as lucky.

Chapter 12

Mrs Reid was becoming more aroused by the second. To her side, her darling Bertie shuffled uncomfortably as the material of his trousers became stretched by a thick erection. There were few times indeed when Lord and Lady Cartwright were left open-mouthed but the previous few minutes had proved to be one such occasion.

After being informed by Big Maggie that their audience with the elusive Sinfinder General had been granted, the couple had made their way to his rambling mansion house. On being admitted, they'd been guided by a shaggy hulk of a man down into the very catacombs of the property, to the damp and dismal dungeon in which they now stood. There, their gaze had met Matthew Hopkirk's for the briefest of instants, before the Sinfinder had returned his full attention to the task in hand.

He stood, birch rods in hand, behind a bulky, waist-high iron frame, stretched over which was a gently moaning female. From where they stood, Bertie and Mrs Reid were unable to see the woman's face; she was bent double over the frame, so that her buttocks were the highest point of her body. The two visitors could see from the terrible state of her flesh, cruelly criss-crossed with more weals than either of them could ever remember seeing before, that she had been thoroughly beaten by the dark-cowled figure standing behind her.

What intrigued them most, however, was the activity of one of the Sinfinder's henchmen, who stood by a crackling fire, holding a branding iron in the flames until it burned white-hot.

What happened next drew gasps from the two bemused onlookers. Even as the overseer handed the branding iron to the Sinfinder, Mrs Reid could feel the material at her crotch become suddenly, incredibly, wet. The whipped woman was going to be branded! The iron was going to be placed against her soft flesh and held there, until the Sinfinder's mark had been indelibly printed on her body! The beaten female screamed like an animal as male hands clutched her flayed buttocks and pulled them unceremoniously apart. The two onlookers feasted on the sight of her pink cunt flesh, and the tight wrinkled bumhole above it, and clutched one another's hands.

The black-garbed Sinfinder commanded his overseers to "hold the wild wench still!"

"Please, master!" she screamed, "Please, no!"

"Thy sins shall find thee out!" the Sinfinder mewed. "Thou hast attempted to take flight from the care of thy master, and now ye must pay the penalty!"

Mrs Reid instinctively pressed herself against her husband's heaving body, desperately seeking safe haven from the horror unfolding before their eyes. The Sinfinder went about his work, the black pearls of his eyes alighting on the flesh he meant to burn - the soft inner slopes of each of the woman's buttocks. He moved the iron towards the quivering flesh, his body tensing in expectation of his victim's inevitable writhings. When the white-hot implement pressed the flesh, the woman gave out a howl which penetrated the breathtaken onlookers to their very souls.

The sense of excitement in the room was almost palpable. As the flayed body bucked and cavorted, and terrible shrieks of unfathomable pain rent the dank air, those gathered in the cell felt their hearts beat faster. They felt the perspiration gathering on their skin, too. And the sheer, ecstatic delight that came with witnessing the Sinfinder's wicked demonstration of a sadism that knew no bounds.

The iron was reheated, then, and the flesh of the girl's other buttock similarly branded. As the implement pressed against the tortured woman for a second time, and the air filled with her anguished screams and the sickening smell of burning flesh, Mrs Reid clung firmly to her husband and

153

thought she would soon wet herself with excitement. "Oh, Bertie!" she wanted to gasp, though her dry throat wouldn't let her, "Oh, Bertie, we must get just such a branding iron ourselves, and brand each and every one of our wilful servants!"

Her mind was dancing with images; of Bertie wielding the horrid iron while she held down a madly wriggling maid; of the terrible hiss and the ear-piercing scream as her beloved pressed his white-hot tool against the succulent flesh of a maid's bare bottom; even of herself, tied in place on a wooden-backed dining chair, her naked bottom proffered for her husband to brand.

And then she thought of the mistress, of Kathy Kimble, bare-bummed and branded, and she groaned as a delicious orgasm swept through her. Bertie had to hold her upright as the ravages of the spend made her swoon.

What was it about the mistress, she thought to herself. What was it that had made her fall so madly in love with the idea of owning Kathy Kimble?

The newly branded woman had fainted. With his sport at an end, the Sinfinder General refastened his birch rods to the belt of his britches and turned towards Lord and Lady Cartwright. The sudden sight of the black pearls of his eyes, set deep in his craggy, malevolent face, was enough to haul the still-dizzy Mrs Reid back to reality. He approached the couple slowly, drawing his black cloak closely around him as though to further heighten his inherent sense of mystery. It was a matter of seconds before he spoke. When, finally, he deigned to make utterance, it was to Lord Cartwright that he addressed himself. "I believe that you have a special desire," he murmured, "that you have come here with the intention of making me an offer..."

The Cartwrights exchanged the briefest of glances, as though to confirm that they were both still of the same mind. "That's right, Mr Hopkirk," croaked the silver-haired aristocrat. "And in case you think otherwise, I can assure you I am no fool. I know that buying that which we want will not come cheaply, and am prepared to pay you a handsome price to acquire the, er, merchandise..."

The Sinfinder's eyes widened momentarily, and a wicked smile toyed with the corners of his mouth. "I wonder..." he mused. "I wonder whether you are really willing to pay the price that I shall ask."

"Name it, sir," Lord Cartwright demanded, suddenly emboldened. "I have every confidence that I shall meet the cost, whatever it may be!"

"Very well," Matthew Hopkirk replied, pulling his glove more tightly around his hand. "Two million pounds is my asking price for the woman you desire. Two million pounds..." he paused, his gaze shifting towards Mrs Reid, black eyes burning into her heart. "...and this woman, to do with as I please, this very night."

An expression of profound incredulity took root the length and breadth of Lord Cartwright's face. By his side, Mrs Reid put her gloved hand to her mouth and tried her best to suppress a horrified gasp. The Sinfinder showed no flicker of emotion. Instead, his gaze wandered lazily from husband to wife and back again, awaiting an answer to his terms.

"You are the very devil himself, sir!" exclaimed Lord Cartwright. "Have you no morality, man? No sense of common decency?"

"I have a great many matters which need my attention," Matthew Hopkirk muttered. "That is my offer. Take it or leave it - but if you're going to take it, then you must do so now. From the moment I leave this chamber, it is withdrawn and I will not make it again." He nodded his head gently to them both. "Now, you must excuse me. There is much to prepare before the night's revelry begins..." With that, the Sinfinder General turned on his heels and moved briskly across the dungeon, barking commands to the sluggish brutes who did his bidding.

"Wait!" cried Mrs Reid desperately. With every step the

Sinfinder was taking towards the enormous oak door, the diminutive woman could see her dream of owning the magnificent mistress quite literally receding into the distance. Hopkirk had demanded an immediate answer, an immediate acceptance of his terms, wicked and outrageous though they were. Well, if that was what he required, reasoned Mrs Reid, if that was what it took to win the flame-haired Katharine, then he would get his answer, and an unequivocal one, at that!

At the sound of her voice, the dark-cowled Sinfinder stopped in his tracks. He turned slowly, revealing a countenance considerably lightened by the wicked smile that caressed the corners of his mouth.

He knew he had the Cartwrights where he wanted them - that much was obvious to Fran - and she couldn't help but feel a rising of anger that she had so predictably bowed to his demands. But then, the Sinfinder held the trump card, of course, - and in the world of supply and demand, it was very much a seller's market.

"You can have what you wish," she exclaimed, clasping her husband's hand to signify their need for courage. "Two million pounds, Sinfinder, and..." she could hardly bring herself to confirm the deal, "..and use of me, this very evening." As she choked the words from her throat, Bertie squeezed her hand tightly, as though to confirm his support for her decision. Almost instantly, waves of relief swept through Mrs Reid. Whatever horrors awaited her, however cruel her evening at the hands of the Sinfinder proved to be, at least her beloved Bertie would not forsake her. With that one meaningful squeeze of her hand, he had let her know that he loved her still, in spite of her decision to give herself over to another man.

"And you?" the Sinfinder questioned, looking deep into Lord Cartwright's soul, "are you in agreement with your wife? Shall I... have sport with her this night?"

Even as the clutching fingers of anguish crawled across

his face, Lord Cartwright slowly nodded his approval. "Yes," he murmured. "You shall have her, Sinfinder..."

"Then leave us!" Hopkirk snapped, his eyes narrowing malevolently. "Ye are surplus to my requirement! 'tis the lady that I desire!"

Lord Cartwright looked down at the wife he adored, and through the mist of his own tears saw the tears that ran from her eyes. Then, as swiftly as he could, his heart breaking, his mind in a feverish turmoil, the silver-haired aristocrat left his wife's side and exited the miserable chamber. The sound of his sobs mingled with those of his footsteps as he hurried towards the light, scampering away from a scene he couldn't bring himself to think about but which he knew would haunt him until the breaking of a new day...

...If only Bertie had been willing to hear about the events of that night, his darling wife Francesca would happily have poured out the gruesome tale of her suffering. Perhaps in that way, she might have rid herself of the demons that danced through her mind for days and weeks afterwards.

As it was, Bertie would hear none of it, unable to endure the pain of knowing how she had been made use of. Nor would he touch her, nor look at her naked body, for fear of gazing upon the terrible evidence of Matthew Hopkirk's cruel and savage tortures. "I'll have none of it, Fran!" he growled repeatedly. "It must be as though that night did not happen, as far as I am concerned - that is the only way I have any hope of dealing with it."

So Fran suffered alone, lying awake at night, wrapped in the attire her husband made her wear to conceal her cruelly used flesh, sobbing fitfully as her mind filled with images from that dark and terrible evening. Bertie lay away from her always, his mind racked with guilt at his selfish rejection of the woman he adored. His body was hot and lustful, desiring her, needing the shattering release within his woman that he'd felt obliged to deny himself. Each night, he massaged himself until he came, and lay in his own spunk until the morning, thankful for whatever peace of mind he could achieve from his own dancing demons of conscience.

Fran checked herself in the mirror each morning and evening, hoping that her skin would heal swiftly so that she could once again display her naked charms to her husband. Bertie would want her then, she was sure; he would want her more, perhaps, than he had ever wanted her before. After all, hadn't she made the ultimate sacrifice for the sake of their marriage? Hadn't she given herself to another man, suffered cruel humiliations at his gnarled and twisted hands, to secure the purchase of the woman they both wanted; the woman who would revitalise their lust, re-ignite their voracious appetite for one another's bodies?

Bertie had crawled from their bed before dawn one morning, stealthily making his way across the gently creaking floorboards and slipping from their room. Fran thought about calling to him, letting him know that she was awake, but the growing emotional distance between them had stopped her. If only he would let her tell him, she thought to herself. If only he would let her recount what had happened to her that night, and then take her into his arms and let her sob the horrific memories out of her. "Oh Bertie!" she imagined herself saying to him, "oh, Bertie, my darling, I thought I was going to die! When you had left the chamber, the Sinfinder instructed his brutes to strip me naked. They dragged my clothes from me where I stood; they were like a pack of hungry wolves scavenging after a carcass, wrenching at my blouse, pulling at my skirt, tearing my stockings and my underwear from me. Their rough fingers groped and raked at the flesh between my thighs, squeezed my buttocks, twisted my breasts!

"They manoeuvred me, then, Bertie, laughing and growling as they clutched at my flesh, dragging me to the wall and fastening me there; my wrists to manacles high above my head, my ankles to metal ringlets in the stone floor. When they had finished their dastardly work, I was bound in the shape of an 'x', my face and breasts mashed against the crumbling brickwork.

"The Sinfinder told me then of the exquisite pain he intended to cause me. 'I shall use thee,' he said, 'until every morsel of thy flesh be screaming for salvation!'. His hands roamed all over my back and across the expanse of my buttocks, his fingers delving into the flesh-pot between my legs...

"Oh, Bertie, I have never been so cruelly felt there! He pushed his digits inside me and worked me open, widening me so that he could force another finger, then another, up into my cunt. I gasped as he pushed his knuckles into me, twisting his hand inside my pussy until I howled. 'Thy sinning hole shall be opened up for my dogs, ye wanton harlot!' he growled as his fingers crawled towards my womb. 'I shall widen thee until each rabid mongrel may force his whole snout up inside thee, and feast on thee until thy shameful cunt no longer can please men!'

As he felt me there, with his other hand he diddled my clitty, his finger and thumb squeezing and twisting the hard hood cruelly. I writhed, my Bertie, as I have never writhed before, but not through pleasure. Tears streamed from my eyes as he groped my insides, and all the while I thought only of you, and of the mistress, the coveted prize for which I was having to endure such torture.

"When he had opened my hole so wide that I could feel the air circulating within me, he withdrew his clutching fingers and once more reached beneath his cloak. 'Ye must be absolved of thy sin,' he informed me. 'My birch rods shall open thy miserable flesh and let the evil drain from thee; ye shall truly be purged and purified, and ye shall call on God for salvation from the touch of the devil-twigs. But it is God's work which I perform, ye wicked wench, and I shall flog thee until Satan has been vanquished.'

"He began to birch me then, landing the savage rods across my shoulders with such force that the twigs themselves began to snap and break! He beat me mercilessly, and shook the birch rods free of one another between every stroke. He swung the terrible implement through the air as though he were an unstoppable flogging machine, hell-bent on tearing my naked flesh until my blood ran free.

"When he had tired of flogging my shoulders, he swung his brutish weapon lower, whipping the skin of my back. As he flayed me, his lumbering servants urged him on, laughing and growling with pleasure at the sight of my suffering. 'Flog her, Sinfinder, shred her flesh!', they shouted. 'Whip her between her thighs, my Lord, then fuck her pussy 'til she screams!' 'Cover her arse in welts, master, then tear the skin from the backs of her thighs!' 'Her tits, my Lord, whip her tits until she howls!'

"The Sinfinder needed no urging from his cohorts to beat me senseless, though. He flogged and flogged until I could no longer feel my back, and then he paused momentarily to squeeze and grope my buttocks, after which he began on those. He lashed me even more soundly across my cheeks than he had my back and shoulders. He became fuelled by a terrible sexual frenzy at the sight of my buttocks dancing beneath his birch rods, and began to snort and whinny like a horse as he laid the twigs across me. My bottom-cheeks bounced and wobbled uncontrollably as he whipped them - you know how much they jiggle when beaten, Bertie! - and their wild movement as a further spur for him.

"He began to flog me anew, then, finding from some hitherto undiscovered country within himself a fresh impetus for the task, and bringing the rods down with such cruelty and venom that I soon felt as if my whole bottom were twice its normal size and about to explode!

"When he had tired of thrashing the same flesh over and over again, he began work on my thighs, lashing me time and again from below my buttocks down to my knees. He even delivered a flurry of strokes to my calves, then amused himself by teasing the flesh of my pussy with the gnarled twigs, all the while chiding me for being in league with the devil.

"Oh, Bertie, my sweet Bertie, I cannot hope to tell you how wickedly he flogged me. Not even in the dark days before you rescued me, before you took me away from the cruel ministrations of my first husband - and you know only too well how hard he was with me - had I ever been so maltreated. But the lick of his belt, the stamping sting of his brush, was like nothing compared to the Sinfinder's birch rods.

"When he had flogged raw every morsel of my flesh from my shoulders down to my ankles, he had his henchmen turn me around and refasten me, exposing for a taste of his twigs a new expanse of body to burn. With nothing more than a gentle nod of his head, he sent his lumbering brutes to work. They brought long lengths of wire and wrapped them around my breasts, pulling them tight until my skin seemed ready to split open. Then they fingered my nipples roughly, until they had grown hard - like when you lick and play with them, my darling Bertie - and attached terrible iron weights to each, so that they were stretched and painful.

"A harness was fitted over my head, a ball gag stuffed into my mouth, threatening to choke me. And then - oh, Bertie, and then - they depilated me! They shaved off my pubic hair - mindful always of the Sinfinder's instruction to avoid even so much as nicking my skin - and stopped only when I was as bald and smooth as a baby's bottom! Oh, Bertie, if only you still wanted me, I feel sure that the sight of my naked cunny would make you stiffer than you have ever been!

"When they had stripped my mons of its hair, my darling, they shuffled away to the far corner of the dungeon, leaving me at the mercy of Matthew Hopkirk. He unfastened his britches, then, and pulled his thick erection from within, its

161

head already moist with translucent fluid and red-raw from the fucking it had given the serving girl. Within seconds, the Sinfinder had pressed himself against me, his whiskey-breath heavy in my nostrils as he sucked and chewed at my neck. All the while, his spindly hands were manoeuvring my legs, pulling them apart to allow room for his throbbing cock to force its way up inside me.

He had pushed the gruesome appendage into the fleshy hole of my sex almost before I'd had time to realise what was happening. His hands at my brutally beaten buttocks, clutching the seared flesh to gain greater purchase with his madly twitching cock, he began to fuck me with savage thrusts. He pushed his muscle right up inside me, making my tortured, crudely bound breasts jiggle, causing me to bite hard into my rubber ball-gag. He fucked me where I stood, ramming me like a pounding piston, never seeming either to tire or reach a point of no return.

"As he fucked me, I closed my eyes and tried my best to imagine it was you inside me, Bertie; my darling husband making love to me, pushing home that delightful cock of yours, looking to fill me with your delicious come until I was dripping wet and full to the brim...

"But my imagination failed me, my sweet. I required too much of it. The Sinfinder was savage and cruel, and fucked me so hard that I was sure he would split my pussy wide open! All the while, he toyed with the heavy weights at my nipples and tightened the wire around my breasts, cutting off the blood supply. Behind me, he pushed a finger inside my anus and felt me there, and told me how he would 'fuck the shit' out of me once he had got me 'with child' in my 'filthy front portal of sin'!

"Oh, Bertie, never had I been so mercilessly fucked before. Even when you've been heavy with wine and have pounded away at me like a demon possessed, I have never felt so grossly violated - so... helpless - and...inhuman! I was little more than an animal to him, Bertie; little more than a dog - perhaps not even that; perhaps nothing more than a vessel in which to empty himself...

"And I hated myself for what happened next, my darling; truly hated myself with all of my heart and my mind - but there was nothing I could do to stop it. As he rammed me with all the brute force he could muster, his cock searching out my womb, hungry to fill it; as he fingered my bumhole and teased my traumatised tits; as he told me of his intention to bung my body until my holes were too battered ever to take another male cock; as he did all of these things, and his henchmen urged him on, growling, screaming, baying for my blood...I admit that I lost all control of myself! I lost control of myself and was consumed by the most overwhelming orgasm I have ever had; a thrill that engulfed my whole body and infiltrated me to my very core!

"Oh, God, Bertie, how I love you, but I just couldn't help myself! I didn't wish for it, I didn't want it or crave it; it simply happened - and happened over and over again as the Sinfinder used me that night, I could not help but cream myself, almost as though he had unlocked something carnal and grotesque that had been lurking within me, unrealised, for years.

"When he had spilt himself into my womb so many times that he could manufacture no more seed, he took a long, thick stick to my buttocks and thrashed the very hell out of me. He held me in place on my hands and knees, cowering beside him like a frightened mongrel, and beat the flesh of my poor backside until the length of wood he was wielding gave up the unequal struggle and snapped in two.

"Then, as I knelt there like a snivelling cur, he sent two of his henchmen to collect the mistress! They brought her to him naked, Bertie, her big breasts jiggling deliciously, her broad, fleshy buttocks trembling with her every enforced movement. The Sinfinder bent her over right in front of me and had the two brutes hold her in position. Then he forced his cock into her anus - without the aid of any lubricant!

The mistress screamed and writhed as she was penetrated, and gasped in anguish as he rammed her. When he had fucked at her bottom-hole for what must have been a full half-hour, he withdrew his thick muscle, its flesh glistening with slime, and forced it inside my mouth, commanding that I suck clean the whole length of the wildly throbbing cock. Behind me, an overseer thrashed my exposed buttocks with a whip, urging me to 'suck the master's cock good and clean' if I knew what was good for me.

"I gagged at the bitter taste within my mouth, and almost wretched at the thought of what I was doing! But the stick driving against my bottom reminded me that I was the Sinfinder's to command, and that very thought pulled me away from the abyss and made me perform my task with a bizarre and inexplicable fervour. Twice as I sucked at him the Sinfinder pulled his cock from my mouth, and pushed it back inside the mistress's still-waiting bottom-hole. He slammed her with a savagery that should have made my heart bleed for the poor woman; instead, it drove me to ever greater heights of excitement!

"I don't know what took hold of me that night, but as I watched that woman being flogged towards unconsciousness, I found myself suddenly, overwhelmingly, desperate to have her! After a lifetime spent lusting after the pleasures afforded by the cock, I suddenly wanted nothing more than to find myself between her red-raw thighs, my tongue dipping into her pleasure-pot, tasting her delights.

"When finally I had managed to draw one or two more globules of seed from the Sinfinder's swollen cock, I was pulled away from his groin and sent spinning across the dungeon floor. The overseers were at me then, beating my flesh with their heavy sticks, not caring where the terrible strokes fell. When they had thrashed me until my whole body burned anew, they forced me up on to my haunches and held me there, my knees pulled wide apart so that the flesh of my naked cunt, pink and wet from my delicious orgasm, was clearly visible to their grim-faced Lord. The Sinfinder slapped the cheeks of my face over and over again, until my dulled brain was reeling from the assault. Then, when he had fondled my breasts and stooped low to enjoy a feel of my bulging pussy, he gave me an instruction which made my heart pound wildly and made my open sex dribble with a fresh flooding of juices. 'Piss thyself!' he commanded, pointing a sinewy finger between my thighs. 'Empty thy bladder of its stenching waters!'

"How did I do it, Bertie? How did I ever manage to relieve myself there and then, in full view of Matthew Hopkirk and his brood of whooping, wailing thugs? As I relaxed control of my bladder, and my piss cascaded against the stone floor, a fine film of backspray soaking my thighs, I found myself hoping against hope that the mistress, sprawled on the ground behind my squatting frame, had not drifted into complete unconsciousness; that somehow, through the pain that was racking her brutalised body, she would find the strength to look up, to watch me performing like a mongrel pissing in the street. My battered face flushed even more profoundly at the very thought of her seeing me do such a filthy deed. In the brief time since that fateful night, I have wondered often why I felt such excitement at the prospect of her watching me empty myself.

"Thinking about her in the time since that night, my sweet darling, and remembering the uncontainable thrill I felt at the thought of her watching my humiliation, I have grown most wet between my thighs. And particularly so whenever my agitated mind has alighted on one particular fantasy...

"I have seen Katharine in my mind not naked, used and whipped as she was that evening, but instead as she appears when playing the part of the mistress; her bosom and buttocks accentuated by a tight corset wrapped around her midriff, her shapely, succulent thighs given greater allure by the knee-high boots she wears.

"And I have seen myself at her mercy, Bertie - a naughty little girl who has wet herself and must be punished! I have imagined her making me strip naked, and putting me across her beautiful thighs, then using a whip or a paddle to thrash my buttocks until the flesh was a gruesome mass of welts and weals.

"And I have thought of how she would make me satisfy her afterwards; how she would put me on my knees between her thighs and make me eat the dripping flesh of her pussy, lapping her until I had cleaned away all trace of her silvery emissions. Until I had swallowed her nectar down into my throat! I can't help thinking of her, Bertie - and when I do, I have felt my excitement soar to dizzying heights. I have played with myself, as I am doing now - teasing my clitty as delicious images wash across my mind.

"What happened to me that night, after I had been made to empty myself, remains even now little more than a blur. I remember being held in my squatting while a thick whip was put across my back and buttocks. I remember, as well, the Sinfinder, cruelly using a stick to apply a series of upward cuts to the flesh of my pussy. And then I recall nothing more until I awoke in a bed chamber, the Sinfinder's cock slamming away inside my cunt as I dangled over the edge of the creaking bed. Even then, even as he rammed me with all the strength he could muster, I lapsed once more into unconsciousness, my beaten body and broken mind unable to endure any more.

"Then there were the times when I awoke to find my head hanging over the edge of the bed, my face hovering inches above the floorboards. On such occasions as these, a thick cock would be plundering my back-passage, and sliding in and out of me with such ease it were as though my once-tight hole were a wet and squelching cunt, so comprehensively was I being, and had I been, made use of there!

"Oh, Bertie, I am not the woman I was, my sweet! Even

as I lie here, fingering my wet flesh, wondering where you've gone so early in the morning, I know that things between us can never be the same again! I cannot thrash bottoms for you as once I did, my darling, not when I am consumed by the fever which has taken control of me! It is my own bare bottom which must be thrashed, my precious, and it is the soft, sweet flesh of a beautiful woman which is the thing I most desire!

"I love you, Bertie, but it is the mistress who I must have, who I crave and yearn above all others; I would forsake you for her, Bertie, though it plagues my heart to say so; I couldn't help myself, really I couldn't.

"Oh, God, my darling, I can feel myself coming now, even as I think of her dripping pussy flesh! I can feel myself coming as only the Sinfinder has ever made me come! I am overwhelmed, my sweet, and can think of nothing but the scent and touch and sight of feminine flesh. And the feel of the whip against my skin, tearing me open. And of my holes, offering up their bounty as I empty myself in front of my gorgeous mistress. Yes, my darling, yes! The moment is close...very close!

"I can't deny the truth any more. I don't care that you no longer want me, Bertie - I don't care if you never touch my pussy with your cock again. It is not your cock I need anymore, my darling - it's not your cock, or any man's cock, I have ever needed. I need to eat the fleshy cunt of my mistress, that's what I need, that is what I desire! I need to grovel before her naked beauty! I need to be whipped and thrashed by her, I need her now, Bertie - now, as wave upon wave of delicious orgasm consumes my trembling body! Oh, buy her for me, my darling - buy her for me and make your beloved Fran the happiest woman alive!"

Chapter 13

Left to hang there, Laura couldn't help but think of her wedding the following day, and of the dreadful life of misery she was destined to endure with the grotesque Quinn as her husband. Tears poured down her face as she thought about her terrible future as the dwarf's wife, and she began to sob uncontrollably.

The overseers approached her, feigning concern at her tears, and promised to 'stroke it better for her'. Their hands were all over her then, fondling her breasts and fingering her sex, feeling her up inside her bottom, and then unclamping her so that they could suck her big nipples and take turns to push their faces between her legs and lick at her clitoris. Each bunged her cunt again, and left fresh deposits of hot spend inside her, once more delighting at the sight of their sticky fluid trickling from between her buttocks and rolling down her legs.

It was nighttime before Laura next heard the familiar creak of the thick stone door being opened. She heard the mistress's voice commanding the two brutes, and within seconds, she had been unfastened and steered to her hands and knees on the cold floor, the tube once again inserted into her bottom.

Another trip to the Sinfinder, she mused to herself while being held over the bucket. Her bottom was sponged and dried, and a collar fitted to her neck.

She prepared herself for the instruction to return to her hands and knees so that the mistress could straddle her back and ride her like a horse to the Sinfinder's lair. But no such instruction was given.

Instead, the flame-haired woman led her by the collar up onto the ground floor of the huge mansion house and out onto the gravel drive.

They were met there by a familiar face. Laura recognised the shaggy rustic who stood in front of her, a bundle of clothes and a pair of sandals clutched in his arms, and identified him as the husband of the woman who'd been imprisoned on Devil's Hill.

"Say nothing, just listen," the mistress said. "This is Zeb. You saw his wife interred on the hillside when you first came here. I should not be doing this, the Sinfinder doesn't know of it, but I'm going to give you to Zeb for the night. I can do nothing to stop your marriage to Quinn, and am genuinely sorry for the sufferings you are destined to endure at his disgusting hands for the rest of your life. All that I can do is to offer you this one, final night of being treated like a woman instead of a dog.

"Zeb wants to make love to you. Slip into the clothes he's holding and go with him. He will return you in a few hours, while it's still dark, and I will then return you to your cell. The overseers will simply assume that I've been torturing you all night, as is my right as mistress, and will think no more about it. Go now, and enjoy whatever pleasures you can."

Laura got dressed quickly, pulling on white panties and a long, flowing dress, and slipping on the sandals that Zeb handed to her.

Zeb was white-haired and in his fifties. A wart-ridden, unattractive man, Laura couldn't imagine gaining any pleasure from a lustful night in his bed. Yet at least in going with him, she rationalised, she'd be able to avoid the terrible beatings to which the nighttime guardsmen often subjected her, Sally and Lucinda during the hours of darkness. And besides, it was nice to be able to wear clothes again - for however brief a period before her lust-filled, white-haired lover divested her of them.

Zeb took her gently by the neck collar and led her over the gravel path and across the sprawling gardens, slipping quietly through the huge iron gates at the end of the mansion's grounds and into the small car he had parked to the other side of the country lane.

They drove for ten, maybe fifteen minutes back to the village where Laura's strange ordeal had first begun, and from there made their way up the hillside to where the rustic's wife remained imprisoned in the restraining box.

"Say nothing when we arrive at the top," he urged her. "My wife must not know that I am here. When we reach her, I want you to put this on." Zeb reached inside his corduroy jacket, pulled a long, thick object from within, and handed it to Laura. For a few moments, in the darkness, the American struggled to identify what she was looking at, and finally resorted to running her fingers across the object's smooth yet intriguingly curved surface.

She gasped out loud when she realised she'd been handed a dildo.

"What the hell do you want me to do with this?" she whispered in alarm, aware, as they approached the hilltop, of the need for quiet.

"I want you to put it on, my sweet," Zeb answered quietly, "and then I want you to fuck my wife's bottom with it."

Laura wrapped the belt to which the dildo was attached around her waist. "Pull up your dress first," Zeb said in hushed tones, "then fasten the dildo to your waist in such a way that it keeps your dress gathered up at your hips." The American did as she was told, fitting the strap-on device over the bundled material of her dress, pinning the garment in place so that her bare legs and pantie-clad bottom were on view.

How strange, Laura thought to herself, to look down and see a big cock thrusting out from her abdomen! The huge object swung rhythmically up and down as she climbed the hill. The movements somehow seemed to enhance its majesty, transforming it from a lifeless strap-on device into an object reminiscent of a throbbing, twitching length of real flesh-and-blood cock.

"Use this," he said, handing her a small tub, "to lube her hole and the strap-on dick. Say nothing. Simply fuck. Then we will go to my home and enjoy ourselves."

"Why do you want me to do this?" Laura asked.

Zeb shrugged. "The thrill of seeing her taken like that; and of seeing you take her. Because of her vile mouth, she has been imprisoned, and I've been denied the pleasures of the flesh - her flesh, at least. Now I find that I want to punish her as well, to make her pay for the effect her stupidity has had on my life."

They reached the top of the hill. By the starlight, it was possible to make out the seven foot-high restraining box, and the big bump of flesh jutting from the back of the cubicle-like construction. Laura dabbed her fingers into the pot of oil she'd been given by Zeb, and liberally doused the head and shaft of the dildo. She moved stealthily towards the imprisoned woman, then - urged on by the look of excitement she could see reflected in Zeb's eyes.

"Who's there?" asked the woman from within her wooden prison. "Who is it? Zeb, is that you?"

Laura dabbed her finger into the pot once more and, standing behind the cubicle, took hold of the two great buttocks that protruded from the porthole-shaped opening in the box's back-panel.

"Oh no!" the prisoner gasped. "Not again, please no!" Laura plied the cheeks apart and slipped her finger into the woman's bottom cleft, anointing the craggy, swollen mound of her anus.

Strange thrills of excitement stabbed their way through her stomach as she nudged her rubber cock between the captive's great white bum cheeks. Her fingernails - once long and beautifully manicured, now broken - dug into the cold flesh of the perfectly presented buttocks, searching for the leverage which would allow her to gain access to the woman's throbbing asshole.

Laura's heart skipped a beat as she heard the prisoner wail at the sudden touch of the dildo against her back-passage. Fuelled by her own rising sense of excitement, the

American gradually pushed home her advantage.

Laura felt physically sick with a strange blend of excitement and disgust; excitement at the surge of power she felt from finding herself, for once, in control; disgust at the thought of what she was about to do - to thrust her body forward again and again, to feel her own thighs slapping against another woman's naked flesh, as she sodomised her with a length of rubber dildo.

As she was about to thrust for the first time, she felt hands at the waistband of her panties. The sudden touch of fresh air against her bum followed, as the garment was peeled down to her upper thighs. Zeb's hot lips pressed repeatedly against her ass cheeks then, planting kiss after succulent kiss. When there seemed to be no let up in her lover's tender ministrations, Laura realised that she was meant to begin her pistoning movements while still receiving his luscious mouth caresses.

So she began to thrust, sending the rubber dildo deep into the big bottom before her and then withdrawing it until only the well-oiled tip remained. Then she would thrust again, and then withdraw - and every time she pulled back, she felt the cheeks of her own ass peel slightly apart, offering new flesh for her lover to pepper with impassioned kisses.

She sodomised the prisoner for several minutes, during which time Zeb's lips and tongue lashed every millimetre of Laura's bottom, teasing her throbbing holes as they rhythmically opened and closed with her every frenzied thrust.

Laura felt hot, and deliriously excited. She found herself wishing she had a real cock, and that she could enjoy the experience of a delicious spend inside the big bottom she was so wantonly impaling. Zeb pulled her away eventually, tugging her panties back into place at the same time. She waited while the rustic lashed his wife's bare bottom with his thick, doubled-over length of belt, and found herself flinching in reaction to every savage stroke the howling woman received.

Then they were off down the hillside again. The rubber dildo was still strapped to Laura's groin, her dress still pinned at her waist. As they walked, Zeb's hand gently stroked her pantie-clad buttocks...

In the rustic's house, she was immediately encouraged into the bedroom, a dim little cell with creaking floorboards and an enormous, four-poster bed that dominated much of the floor space. Without pause, Zeb tugged at his clothing, dispatching it to the four corners of the room, and stood naked before Laura - his white, fleshy body heavy with age, his thick cock twitching expectantly. Laura stripped too, knowing what was expected of her, and wondered what her next instruction would be.

When it came, it surprised even her. The fleshy rustic moved forward and dropped to his knees before her. Looking up at Laura with pleading eyes from beneath his tangled hair, he croaked a plea that caught the American entirely off-guard.

"Punish me, mistress," he said. "I have been a very bad boy..."

Laura felt her throat become dry, her heart begin to race and her sex start to ooze. Her final night of freedom from the vile Quinn was turning into an unusual and entirely unexpected experience. Back at the Sinfinder's House of Terror, she was used to being beaten - to being used by the gruesome beasts who guarded her, and by her masters, who enjoyed torturing her. How different now to find herself standing over a cowering, subservient male - a man who seemed willing to let her do anything she wanted to him.

"What should I do to you, you bad boy?" she asked, uncertain as to the rules by which this peculiar new game was meant to be played.

"You are my mistress, I am a very bad boy," said Zeb. "You must decide what punishment I deserve."

Laura hesitated for a moment, her mind in a whirl. She

was free to do as she pleased, to really enjoy herself! For the time being at least, the dreadful reality of her impending marriage to Quinn seemed delightfully irrelevant.

She decided to make the most of her opportunity.

"Bad boys like you get their bad bottoms spanked," she said. Laura thrilled to the words she was using and the dizzying sense of power they gave her.

She walked around the huddled, kneeling frame of the rustic and sat on the edge of the bed. "Get over my knee, you naughty boy. I'm gonna give that ass of yours a real good tanning!"

Zeb staggered to his feet and sprawled his fleshy frame across the American's bronzed legs. His head and torso rested against the bed; his legs were stretched out, his toes and the balls of his feet pressing against the floorboards.

Laura's gaze wandered along the man's hairy back and down to his white buttocks. She ran the palm of her hand across his cheeks, and used her finger to tickle along the line of his bottom cleft. She could feel the juices gathering at her sex, and felt giddy with power. How strange it seemed to be looking down at a bare bottom, empowered to spank it hard, to do to it as she wished; normally, it was she who was sprawled across another's knee - and her ass cheeks that were exposed to whatever cruel torments her punisher deemed appropriate.

"I'm gonna spank this ass real good, honey," she said, experimenting with a gentle slap to the crown of Zeb's left cheek. The buttock wobbled delightfully in response to her opening spank, inspiring her to deliver a second, harder smack to the opposite cheek. "You've been a bad, bad boy, and mama's gonna have to teach you a lesson!" Laura began to slap the wobbling bottom with strong, firm strokes of her hand, delivering the sharp spanks to each buttock in turn.

As she slapped away, Zeb started to writhe across her knee, his erect cock stabbing into her thigh, secreting its translucent juices against her soft skin. With her free hand, Laura reached round and under her squirming victim, her fingers wrapping around the thick length of his cock.

Slapping Zeb's bottom firmly with one hand, she began to masturbate him with her other, massaging his hard shaft with firm, forceful strokes that pulled his foreskin right back, exposing his swollen glans. The forceful caressing of his cock had the effect of increasing his writhing, until his buttocks were rising high into Laura's face, only to be smacked back into position by her rigid palm.

Zeb exhaled and bucked more wildly still, daring her to spank his bottom even harder and faster. She rose to the challenge, her face flushing red, her breasts jiggling wildly as she spanked away at the reddening buttocks cavorting in front of her.

"Get yourself off my knee and get on that bed!" she demanded.

"Fuck me, honey," she panted, as she climbed onto the bed beside him.

Zeb was upon her then, pressing his heavy body against her sweaty flesh and sliding inside her. He thrust at her savagely, burying his cock deep within the sodden trench of her love-hole, and continued to apply vigorous strokes until he was gasping for release. Within seconds, she felt his hot jets of come flooding her hole, and found herself suddenly dragged back into a terrible reality - a reality in which she was mere hours away from her wedding, and a bizarre and binding marriage to the repugnant Quinn.

Even as Zeb pressed his face between her thighs - hungrily lapping at her dripping sex, teasing her towards an overwhelming orgasm - tears rolled down her face and she began to sob. He cradled her in his arms, then, and comforted her until she had once again gathered strength. Then he returned to his task, and within minutes, Laura was howling as a shattering climax consumed her...

Returned to the mansion, she was taken by the mistress to a small annexe, and there told to bend over a rough wooden table and clasp its far edge firmly with both hands.

"You must be beaten before you are returned to your cell," the flame-haired woman said. "There must be fresh marks upon you if the overseers are to think I have spent the night torturing you. Grip hold of the table firmly and take the punishment. And never breathe a word of the great service I have done you tonight. The Sinfinder would flay the skin from me if he were to find out - and I would then do the same to you."

The mistress took up a fresh bundle of birch rods and began to flog Laura. She brought the twigs down repeatedly across her shoulders and her back, flaying the screaming woman until cruel weals criss-crossed her skin from the nape of her neck to the tail of her spine.

The first part of the flogging complete, she commanded Laura to retain her position across the table while she busied herself fastening a second bundle of twigs...

The torture began afresh within minutes, the new gathering of twigs being used across Laura's bottom, causing the American to scream for a mercy that she knew would never be granted.

A third bundle bit time and again into her thighs and calves, and a fourth - once Laura had followed the mistress's instruction to turn around and bend backwards over the table - was used across her breasts and stomach.

Made to sit on the edge of the table then, her buttocks burning against the cold wooden surface, the American followed her mistress's instruction to open her legs wide. The redhead strapped on a dildo, shifted between her captive's thighs, and pushed the length of rubber cock deep inside her sopping sex.

She forced her tongue inside Laura's mouth as she vigorously thrust into her slit, and squashed her own breasts against her lover's, gasping for barely achievable breath as a fiery passion consumed her. Her fingers at her own clitoris, she brought herself to orgasm, howling like a dog as wave upon wave of delicious climax claimed her trembling body.

Immediately afterwards, Laura was returned to her cell and re-bound to the wall, her flesh burning from the savage attentions of the birch.

She hoped that sleep would transport her weary mind and body to a sweeter place; a place where she was no longer racked with pain; no longer naked and vulnerable.

A place where the next naked body she would caress would not be that of the malignant and odious Quinn...

Chapter 14

By the early light of dawn, Lord Cartwright had journeyed to the Sinfinder's ramshackle mansion. He had hammered mightily upon the huge oaken door and eventually been admitted by a lumbering hulk of a brute, his body swathed in thick fur, his face swathed in oily whiskers. "I have come to see the Sinfinder," the silver-haired aristocrat announced to him boldly, entirely unconcerned by the earliness of the hour. The hairy brute bade Bertram follow him, and shuffled along the hallway. He opened a door and led his visitor down into the dimly lit cellars of the house, through which Bertie and Fran had passed on their way to the dungeon only days earlier.

The heavy oak doors to either side of the narrow passageways were all shut and, Bertie presumed, locked as well. As they proceeded, he couldn't help but think of the naked females who were tethered in the cells behind the doors - some perhaps sleeping fitfully; others, maybe, even as he and his gargantuan guide passed, being taken or beaten by the filthy brutes who did the Sinfinder's bidding. Bertie felt his cock stir in his britches at the thought of such scenes, and imagined himself going to work on some poor unfortunate's flesh, whipping her crimson and then entering her body, making her his to command.

In spite of such lustful thoughts he had never been unfaithful to Fran - not in the real sense of the word, anyway. There had been times, of course, when he had penetrated one or other of their maids after his wife had administered a whipping to her bare bottom, but such an action could hardly constitute unfaithfulness; not with Fran herself standing by to watch proceedings and urge him on!

With that in mind, it seemed somewhat curious to be pacing the poorly lit corridors of the Sinfinder General's home with one purpose and one purpose alone on his mind - to actually and meaningfully be unfaithful to Fran! It seemed strange to him as well to find himself propelled towards his adultery by the events of that single, isolated evening in the dungeon. After all, hadn't Fran sacrificed herself that night for the sake of their marriage? Hadn't she exposed herself to the cruel and brutal ministrations of Matthew Hopkirk simply in order to win them the prize that they both coveted above all others?

If so, Bertie pondered as he walked, why was it that he felt so mis-used, so damn jealous? No matter how many times he went through the events of that fateful night, he was incapable of ridding himself of the feeling that Fran must actually have wanted to give herself to the Sinfinder.

Was that the real issue, as far as Bertie was concerned? Did he feel as he did because Fran had transgressed the sanctity of their marriage? In truth, if he were to be brutally honest with himself, didn't he feel that, no matter how much he had wanted the mistress, no matter how much his wife had wanted the mistress, Fran should simply have refused to meet the Sinfinder's terms? Was that the plain-and-simple reason he was so damned agitated? Staying faithful to her husband should surely have been the most important thing for Fran, not securing the services of the big-breasted, broad-arsed Katharine Kimble - however delicious an idea owning such a magnificent creature may have seemed to them both.

And what did it say about his wife's love for him that she could so assuredly, so unreservedly, agree to another man having his way with her?

Yes, that was why Bertie felt angry; that was why there'd been such a savage jealousy eating away at his very innards from the moment he'd left the grim house of torture four nights previously. And that was why he was making his way through the catacombs of the Sinfinder's mansion, determined to get his revenge on Francesca for her flagrant display of inconstancy.

Near the end of one particularly long and winding corridor, Bertie could see dim light from an open cell falling

179

against the stone floor. As he approached, he became more able to distinguish the various sounds that were coming from within; a low whimpering noise punctuated by an occasional tortured groan; the sound of a male voice, slurred and muttering; and the unmistakable swish of the Sinfinder's birch rods, closely followed by the sharper sound made by the bundle of twigs cracking against naked flesh.

Arriving at the wide-open door, Bertie peered cautiously into the cell. The slave girl, cruelly fastened to the wall by her wrists, ankles and breasts, had been flogged from her shoulders down to her ankles, brutally beaten until only the flesh of her arms and the skin on her feet retained their normal colouration. There was not a single, solitary morsel of flesh, not even so much as a millimetre's-worth, that didn't burn a raw, fiery crimson, while the area of the woman's buttocks had been turned a colour more akin to purple than to red.

Bertie had never before seen the slave girl who was being so soundly whipped, and couldn't help noticing the disproportionately large size of her bottom. It was almost as though the whipping had been administered so vigorously to that particular portion of her body that it had actually caused the buttocks to become puffy and swollen! Yet what perhaps struck the silver-haired aristocrat more profoundly than anything else was the fact that, for once, the Sinfinder had dispensed with his black cowl. He stood behind the mass of smouldering crimson flesh in only his boots, britches and a baggy white shirt, much of which was covered with still-wet stains of wine.

Briefly, the Sinfinder looked up from his labours, fixing the new arrival with a glassy, bloodshot stare.

The bastard was drunk, Bertie realised.

It was only as the realisation dawned upon him that he noticed the empty wine bottles lying on the floor. There were three of them in all, resting side-by-side. Together, they bore a sickening testimony to the length of time

Matthew Hopkirk had been flogging the helpless woman. The brute had been lashing her for so long he'd had time to consume three full bottles of wine!

The very thought of the suffering the woman must have endured was enough to make Bertie's stomach turn - yet he couldn't deny, either, the raw stab of excitement that cut through him like a sharp knife. After all, he too knew what it was to whip naked female flesh. And although Matthew Hopkirk's littany of terror propelled him well beyond Bertie's own self-imposed boundaries, the aristocrat couldn't help but have a grudging admiration for the Sinfinder's uncompromising brutality.

Having ascertained who it was that had so rudely interrupted him in his work, the Sinfinder returned his attention to the task before him. "What brings thee to my chambers at so early an hour of the day?" he questioned as he continued to flog the dangling body. His speech was slurred and clumsy, confirming the extent to which the wine had claimed his senses.

Bertie swiftly became transfixed by the suddenly re-animated scene before him, his eyes drinking in every perceptible movement which the woman's body was making in response to the Sinfinder's rods.

It was all he could do to find a voice with which to answer his brutal host's enquiry. He choked the words "I've come for the mistress," from somewhere deep within his strangely parched throat.

All at once he felt concerned that he'd maybe sounded more demanding than he'd intended. "By now the money should have been transferred as you wished, and the other part of our bargain has also been fulfilled..."

The abused and hanging body twisted unexpectedly as the Sinfinder's twigs lashed across the backs of both legs. The sudden movement revealed to Bertie the inside of the woman's left thigh. It was glistening with fluid, a globule of thick white spend making its way across the scarlet skin

181

towards the stone floor.

So, the Sinfinder had done more than just whip the slave girl!

Bertie found himself wondering how many times the self-styled lord of darkness had been inside the poor woman since the flogging had commenced. Briefly, he suffered a pang of self-loathing as his own cock sprang to attention at the thought of fucking the naked wench.

"She remains with me until after the final circus show," mumbled the Sinfinder, "that was our arrangement."

"Yes, I know," Bertie responded, "but I am here to ask for access to her. Surely you must be willing to agree that she should be part-mine by now at least. The deal's struck, the money's paid, your...other requirement... provided..."

The aristocrat waited for what seemed to be an eternity for Matthew Hopkirk to reply.

By the time he deigned to speak, Bertie was as anxious as he'd ever been. He felt for all the world as though he were about to be sentenced by the hanging judge himself!

"Use her then," Matthew Hopkirk slurred. "She knows of her fate already, and will show you the respect which her new master deserves..." he looked up briefly, catching the eye of the hairy brute who'd been Bertie's escort. "Accompany Lord Cartwright to the mistress's cell," he growled, "and assist him in anything that he asks."

The hirsuit manservant made no reply but turned and led Bertie back the way they'd come. The silver-haired aristocrat breathed a sigh of relief as they made their way through the labyrinthine passages.

Once beyond the labyrinth and back at ground level, their journey was a short one. Bertie's shuffling guide led him down a short corridor, paused about two-thirds of the way along, and opened a wooden door. Inside, wrapped up in rough blankets on a crudely fashioned bed, lay Katharine Kimble. Her eyes struggled to open as the servant pulled on a frayed length of cord, his action stirring a naked, hanging lightbulb grudgingly into life.

"'tis your new master, mistress Kath," he mumbled in a broad Norfolk accent, "come to 'ave 'is way with yer."

Given his desire to appear strong and impassive in the company of his new 'purchase', Bertie edged into the room a little too tentatively for his own liking. In truth, he was uncertain how best to proceed with the mistress yet knew at the same time that he couldn't allow her to perceive his indecision. It was important that he seemed strong, that he lay down the ground rules as swiftly and effectively as possible, so that the flame-haired female understood exactly what would be expected of her by her new owners.

With that in mind, he gritted his teeth and determined to take control of the situation. "Get up at once," he demanded firmly, allowing a scowl to burn itself into the features of his face. "Get your hands on your head and your legs apart so that I may inspect you."

The mistress responded immediately, following his instruction efficiently. How anomalous, Bertie thought, that a woman who seemed so self-assured by comparison with the other girls he'd encountered in the Sinfinder's lair, should actually be so perfectly obedient! The mistress had certainly been trained well - but then, of course, without the acquisition of such a devout obedience, the Sinfinder would never have invested her with the high office she currently held.

Bertie felt a sudden groundswell of confidence in his own ability to deal with the magnificently proportioned woman. His initial anxieties had been laid to rest, at least to an extent, by her willingness to follow his commands. In their place, he found himself suddenly appreciative of the delights which awaited him - and which started with the opportunity to feel her ripe pussy.

The mistress, it turned out, had a big cunt, fleshier and squelchier than any Lord Cartwright had ever before fondled. It was even more magnificent than his wife's, and

Fran had the most beautifully bulbous mound imaginable - or so he'd thought until now!

Bertie allowed his fingers to roam the fleshy sex, and mashed his palm against it until he felt his skin become wet with the mistress's oils. Slipping a finger, then a second, inside her, he found himself breathing all the more heavily when he realised just how cavernous her fat cunthole actually was! He stared her straight in the eyes as he felt her up and told her, "You have, without question, the roundest, pinkest, deepest pussy I have ever had the pleasure of encountering, girl," he liked the little thrill which calling her 'girl' sent through him. "And I shall very much enjoy filling this filthy fat love-pot of yours on a regular basis - though I suspect that I shall have to come inside you at least half-a-dozen times in succession to fill up this delightful tank!" Bertie slipped his fingers from the mistress and used them briefly to rub the large pink hood of her clitoris. She gasped as he felt her there, her body beginning to tremble uncontrollably with a mixture of discomfort and delight. If that was her reaction to so lacklustre a fondle, he thought to himself, what would it be like when he went to work on her pussy with his tongue?!

He wiped his fingers clean on her breasts, taking the opportunity to cruelly grope the fleshy mounds. The mistress groaned softly as he twisted her huge nipples. Bertie decided then to test her endurance, turning each nipple back and forth as far as he could, wondering how long it would be before his action elicited a plea for mercy from her. As it was, he twisted her flesh so viciously that she could hardly find sufficient air to breathe, let alone speak.

By the time he tired of his wicked game, there were tears coursing down the woman's flushed face, and it was all she could do to keep her hands clamped to her head, in the way her new master had told her to.

Eager to play a new game, Bertie demanded she clasp her ankles. Bertie sauntered around the bent-over woman, his eyes drinking in the sheer magnificence of her body; her big breasts, hanging free; her soft, smooth shoulders and back, sloping upwards towards the highest point of her bending body, her gloriously rotund buttocks - broad, deep-clefted, alabaster white... and waiting for her master to perpetrate upon them whatever devilish torment he desired. Her legs, too, were beautifully curvaceous, boasting delightfully large thighs and attractively slim ankles.

"What a succulent bum you have, mistress Kath," he commented, and firmly squeezed each buttock, shaking the morsels of flesh so that the whole of her bottom wobbled deliciously. "I can hardly contain my excitement at the thought of putting my leather-bound arse-paddler across this great big arse of yours! Tell me, do you think you'd enjoy a taste of my paddler?"

"I doubt I would enjoy it, sir," the doubled-over woman gasped, "but I would endure whatever punishment you deemed it necessary to administer to my bottom."

"And when I wished to poke the little opening between your big arse cheeks..." Bertie pulled the mistress's buttocks apart to inspect her bottom-hole, "..oh my, not such a little opening, after all!" he laughed as he gazed at the protrusion of pink flesh that pouted at him like a tiny volcano. "When I wished to poke this big, bold arsecrack of yours, mistress Kath, would you squeal like a pig as I entered you, and beg me not to fuck the shit out of you?!"

"If that was what you wished, sir, then yes, I would..."

Bertie teased her bum-opening with his thumb, pushing its very tip into the exposed arsecrack. "Then why don't you tell me, girl..." he suggested menacingly.

Kath did as he bade. "If you wished to poke my arse, sir, then I would squeal like a pig as you entered me, and beg you not to fuck the shit out of me..."

Bertie caught the attention of the shaggy brute who still stood at the doorway. "I require an implement; a birch, perhaps, with which to castigate the mistress's naked arse..."

"The cupboard over there, sir," it was Kathy Kimble herself who spoke, "you'll find whatever you're looking for in there..."

Bertie snapped his fingers and addressed the shaggy brute with another instruction. "Attach her wrists to the iron ringlet in the wall. Let's see exactly what she's made of..."

The Sinfinder's shuffling henchman enjoyed performing the task he'd been given. He clasped the mistress by her right breast and left buttock, squeezing the flesh hard as he encouraged her across the room to the far wall. There, he fastened her as he'd been told, so that her arms were raised above her head, tied at the wrists, and her back and buttocks were exposed to the aristocrat's cruel ministrations. He stood back then, making way for Lord Cartwright, and felt a gentle tremor of excitement register in his dull brain as the visitor made ready to punish the mistress.

The aristocrat flogged the mistress hard. He used the birch twigs exclusively on her buttocks, leaving the bare white flesh of her broad back and shapely legs completely untouched.

Bertie thrashed the big, writhing cheeks for all he was worth. When he had flogged the flame-haired female so hard and for so long that the birch twigs had splintered and broken, he pulled his belt from his trousers, wrapped his left arm around Kathy Kimble's waist to steady the swollen target area, and began to thrash her afresh, bringing down the doubled-over strip of leather with sickening savagery.

He administered in excess of one hundred strokes before finally stopping. Then, in one slick, unbroken movement, he clutched at a handful of her hair, pushed her face against the wall, and pressed the weight of his body against her. Fingers fumbling at his trousers, he pulled his throbbing cock free of its confinement and, without further ado, pushed the swollen muscle between the woman's buckling legs, burying himself in her wet cunt and thrusting at her for all he was worth.

He continued to ram her even as he endeavoured to unfasten the bonds at her wrists, all the time whispering about how he would fuck her soaking pussy night and day when she was his, and split her wide open with his length of swollen cock.

Once he had untied the redhead, Bertie slid from within her dripping sex and pulled her over to the bed. He sat down on it and wrenched her across his knees, proceeding then to hand-spank her bare bottom with such vigour that globules of perspiration were soon dripping freely from his forehead, kissing the skin of the mistress's back even as his cruel palm stung the flesh of her wobbling buttocks.

He paddled her puffy, swollen bottom-cheeks for what seemed an eternity, even to the silver-haired aristocrat himself. He finally sent her tumbling to the floor only when the desire to once again be inside her had grown too strong to resist. He took her by her hair again then, guiding her onto her back on the creaking bed, and lowered himself on top of her. With a single thrust he was inside her slushy cunt, and pistoned in and out of the squelching pink hole until his shirt was drenched with sweat and every muscle ached from the effort of his endeavour.

Bertie was like an animal, mauling the gasping, groaning redhead as though she were a carcass to be torn apart. He hauled her from the bed when he'd had his fill of fucking her, and dropped her to her knees on the stone floor, holding her in an upright position by her hair. On his instruction, the watching man fetched a thick length of cane from the cupboard. A broad, toothless smile stretched the width of his craggy face as he handed the wicked-looking implement to the aristocrat. Bertie recommenced his vicious flogging of the mistress, clutching her hair ever more tightly within his fist while he lashed her rotund and bulging buttocks, delighting in the way each stroke made the beaten flesh swell, made her whole bottom tremble.

When he'd criss-crossed the length and breadth of the

mistress's magnificent behind with cane marks, he pushed her forward onto her elbows, sank to the floor behind her and pushed his cock back inside her body.

He rode her vigorously, ploughing into her time and again, thrilling to the sight of his cock disappearing inside her oily love-slot...

Eventually, he put her on the bed again, on her back, and made her raise her legs up and over her head, so that her knees were brushing against her temples. Then he used a cat o' nine tails on her bottom-flesh. He cruelly delivered the strokes at an angle which ensured the strips of leather fell across her juicy sex as well as her buttocks, and found himself revelling in the sound of her anguished screams. When he had finally finished, he clambered on top of her where she lay, and for the first time pushed his cock into her anus. He rode her hard, until the tightness of her bum-aperture proved too much for him and he ejaculated into her tripes.

"Let that be a lesson to you," Bertie gasped as he stood up and stuffed his swiftly softening cock back inside his trousers, struggling manfully to gather his composure. "Your days of being favoured are at an end, mistress Kath. When you leave this valley and come with myself and Fran, you will be embarking on a new life of service and suffering, and can expect to be fucked roundly on a daily basis.

"We shall also have to see just how well that pretty mouth of yours can satisfy a man's cock, shan't we?"

The silver-hared aristocrat moved swiftly to the door, gesturing for the watching brute to exit the room with him and to get about his business. "No doubt I shall see you later, mistress, at this evening's circus performance," he added. He turned at the door to look at the redhead. Kath was sprawled across the bed, her raw, swollen buttocks glistening with the gooey white spend that continued to dribble from between them.

"Now, what do you say after you've been taught a lesson,

mistress Kath?" Bertie demanded, enjoying the opportunity to further humiliate his newly acquired slave.

"Thank you, sir," Kathy rasped in response.

"For what, Katharine?"

"For whipping and fucking me, sir..."

Bertie allowed a gentle smile to play across his mouth. He loved it when a woman spoke subserviently to him; it was a real turn-on. Somewhat surprisingly, given the fact that he'd only just ejaculated, he found his sexual appetite suddenly revived by the mistress's words. For a brief moment, he considered the possibility of turning on his heels, re-entering the room, and putting the magnificent redhead back over his knee for another spanking.

Then he thought better of it. The session he'd just had with Katharine Kimble had left Bertie feeling remarkably empowered. For the first time since Fran had spent the night with the Sinfinder, he felt somehow as though he were his old self again...renewed, re-invigorated - and finally ready to deal with the volatile emotions his wife's adultery had stirred within him.

Finally ready, as well, to deal with his wife...

Chapter 15

Morning arrived all too soon for Laura. She and her two fellow prisoners were unshackled, fitted with neck collars and led by three burly overseers from their cell.

Reaching the ground floor, Sally and Lucinda were tugged away in one direction, Laura hauled in another. She was taken to the annexe in which she'd previously received medical attention after the flogging the Sinfinder had given her. There, Bridget and Helen were busying themselves with preparations for the wedding. The mistress, too, was present in the room. Her scowling expression offered conclusive proof that her passion of the previous evening had well and truly subsided.

The overseer gave a particularly savage wrench on Laura's neck collar and sent her spinning across the room towards the flame-haired woman. Kathy Kimble glowered menacingly at her.

"These two bitch-hounds will help you ready yourself for your wedding ceremony," said the mistress. "Your dress awaits you, as, I hear, does your bridegroom, eager for the ceremony to be over so that he can take you to your marital bed."

Laura felt her stomach somersault at the mistress's words. She shuffled across the room towards where Bridget was holding up a long white dress, and Helen a veil.

On the table in front of the two women were white stockings, a suspender belt, and a pair of white silk panties.

"Get dressed," the mistress snapped. "Time is running short. I have been summoned to the Sinfinder, no doubt to discuss final preparations for the ceremony, so I must take my leave of you. You will be sent for when it's time..."

As the mistress left the small annexe, Laura felt tears welling up in her eyes. How she felt as she stood there now, confronted by her wedding gown and the prospect of marriage to a grim-hearted, foul-mouthed dwarf, defied even her own understanding. Prisoner in a terrible society of slaves, her body regularly violated and beaten, her privacy denied her, Laura reflected on the strangeness of her circumstance; a circumstance that would soon see her married into a life of further misery and suffering.

Even as she struggled to come to terms with the dreadful ordeal she was about to undergo, she mechanically went about the task of dressing herself; she knew better than to resist the mistress's will. She slipped on the silk panties, fastened the suspender belt and drew the white stockings up her tanned and shapely legs. Bridget helped her into the dress, and Helen carefully fitted the veil over her head and face. No words were passed between the women, the presence of a pug-faced overseer in the corner of the room ensuring that silence prevailed.

By the time Laura had finished dressing, the door to the annexe had opened and another naked slave had entered. The American recognised her as the broad-bottomed woman who'd played First Lady Harriet Danton in the Oval Office tableau she'd been made to watch a few days earlier. The slave whispered something to the overseer, who nodded his head in understanding and then delivered a stout slap to her bottom as she scurried from the room.

"Time to go," he growled, snapping his fingers and glowering at Laura. Helen handed the American a bouquet of flowers, and the three women followed the overseer out of the annexe.

The small procession made its way along the carpeted corridor and up the huge winding staircase to the second floor of the house.

As they moved along the corridor, the overseer leading the way, the naked Helen and Bridget bringing up the rear, Laura heard the unmistakable notes of the Wedding March being hammered out on an organ.

Reaching the room at the far end of the long hall, their pug-faced custodian ushered them inside.

Laura turned through the door to be met by a sight which both surprised and terrified her.

In the foreground, to either side of a narrow aisle, were row upon row of pews. Filling up the seats on each row were the Sinfinder's slave girls, all naked and standing, facing forward, their bare bottoms presented to the bride's party.

At the far end of the aisle, on a wooden stage raised approximately two feet from the ground, stood the Sinfinder himself, sinisterly cowled in his familiar garb of black, but wearing at his neck a minister's dog collar, and carrying at his hip a wicked-looking birch.

The overseer's grimy fingers wrapped themselves around Laura's arm and with a firm squeeze of encouragement, he moved his reluctant charge along the aisle. Heads turned to view the bride as she edged slowly forward. Bridget and Helen took up positions with the other slave girls on the back pew.

Laura felt unsteady on her feet, as though she were about to swoon; to be enveloped by a comforting unconsciousness. The feeling was momentary. Its passing ripped from her any last vestige of hope that she might in some way manage to avoid the gruesome ordeal to come.

From the front pew to the left of the makeshift church, the small, humped figure of Quinn shuffled into view. The monstrous little man was attired in top hat and tails. The top hat was perched precariously on his stout, oily head; the tails threatened to scuff the dusty floor as he moved into position.

'Please God deliver me from this friggin' nightmare', Laura thought to herself. Her desperation was mounting palpably as every step brought her closer to her terrible fate.

All kinds of images flashed through her mind as she approached her hunched husband-to-be and the bizarrely attired Sinfinder; images of friends and family, of work colleagues, and even of old boyfriends she now wished to Christ she'd married.

For her, life had always been about adventure; about the next great thrill.

Jesus, what an idiot.

The adventure facing her was one she would happily have traded for the mundane lifestyle favoured by so many of her friends. A life strewn with diapers and baby bottles, shopping and cleaning, and straight, conventional, mind-numbingly boring sex with an accountant husband suddenly seemed to her like some unattainable paradise.

As her eyes fixed on the ugly, buck-toothed gremlin waiting to be betrothed to her, a single tear dribbled down her face.

The overseer brought her to a halt next to Quinn, beneath the scowl of the dog-collared Sinfinder. She felt hands behind her, clutching at the material of her dress, and turned briefly to look. From the corner of her eye, she saw the pug-faced guard raising the white gown to her waist. He pinned it there and then clutched hold of her panties, tugging them down to the tops of her tights.

A fairytale wedding this most definitely was not, Laura mused! Not only was she being made to marry a foul-mouthed, hunchbacked dwarf, but the ceremony was also going to be conducted with her bare-bottomed!

Her bridegroom's hand began stroking and squeezing her exposed buttocks, and she felt the bile rising into her throat.

The Sinfinder, glowering at the couple from beneath tightly knitted brows, his eyes still bloodshot, his words still slurred from the effects of the wine, wasted no time in conducting the business of the day:

"Ladies and gentlemen, we are gathered here this morning to see these two young lovers brought together in the holy state of matrimony, beneath the eyes of God." The Sinfinder glanced from Quinn to Laura and back again. "It falls upon me as the Lord's agent in the conducting of this most happy of unions, to ask of ye both that ye pledge thy troth to one another..."

He paused briefly, taking the time to rearrange his flowing black garb before commencing the ceremony proper.

Taking a deep breath, he began: "Do ye, Quinn, take this slave-bitch to be thy lawful, wedded wife?"

Almost before the words had passed the Sinfinder's lips, the dwarf had gabbled his reply, eager to secure the woman standing next to him as his wife. "I do," he panted, his excitement palpably rising. The Sinfinder turned his head and confronted Laura with a demonic stare:

"And do ye, slave-bitch, take this man to be thy lawful wedded husband?"

Faced with the moment of truth, Laura found herself unable to utter even a single comprehensible sound. The question was hardly unexpected, yet for some reason it hadn't once occurred to Laura that she would actually be asked it - and furthermore would be required to furnish an answer!

And what answer could she possibly give? How could she say 'I do' when she knew she'd be condemning herself to a life of purgatory and torment?

Yet what was the purpose in holding back and resisting the inevitable? It would make no difference in the end; the marriage would still continue, with or without her consent.

The time which passed as these thoughts fluttered through her mind proved crucial. A fast, confident response, and the ceremony would have proceeded without incident. Instead, her silence, as her words struggled for supremacy with her conscience, proved absolutely fatal to her. Hands clutching hold of her, she was dragged forward onto the upraised wooden stage and sent tumbling across a table. Cords were fastened to her wrists, her arms pulled up above her head and fastened to the legs on the far side of the table. Her ankles were similarly bound, her legs drawn wide apart and tied to the near-side table legs. Her body was stretched taut and entirely immobilised, her fleshy cunt and puckered bum-crack brazenly exposed to the congregation of sweaty men and bare-assed women.

The next thing she knew, she could hear a terrible whistling sound as the Sinfinder swung his wicked birch rods through the air, and then she felt a lancing, lashing pain across the entire expanse of her exposed bottom.

Laura screamed in agony and banged her head against the table top. "Be ye not tardy in thy response," growled Matthew Hopkirk, "or the rods shall quicken thy tongue!"

Again the savage twigs bit into Laura's trembling bum flesh, cutting a path of savage pain across her nude ass. "If necessary, I shall whip thee until thy arse-flesh bleeds thy answer," Hopkirk spat, once again launching his bundle of rods at the quivering mounds of naked bottom-flesh displayed before him. Laura's eyes poured a waterfall of tears, her face contorting into a terrible, grimacing mask of pain. Time and again, the awful birch lashed her bottom, drawing from her frenzied gasps and soulful howls of anguish.

Twelve vicious strokes burned the flesh of her magnificently presented posterior, each cruel caress causing her fleshy sex to contract instinctively, folding in on itself like a flower hiding from the rain.

The cords were torn from her ankles and wrists then, and her body hauled from its sprawling position. Swiftly, she was returned to her husband-to-be's side, her bare bottom blazing from the cruel touch of the Sinfinder's birch.

As she gasped for a breath that hardly came, Matthew Hopkirk stroked the material of his dog collar and fixed the sobbing bride with an icy stare. "Do ye, slave-bitch," he muttered, repeating his earlier question, "take this man to be thy lawful, wedded husband."

"I do," Laura croaked. The terrible, throbbing soreness in her bottom urged her onward in her effort to utter the dreadful words.

"Who has the ring?" The Sinfinder asked.

Immediately, hands were at Laura again, this time forcing her to bend over until her fingertips rested against the cold stone floor. Fingers plied the flesh of her buttocks apart, cruelly opening her deep and clammy cleft. "She has, Sinfinder!" exclaimed an overseer, with a raucous, guttural laugh, "the ring of her arse!" His cronies, who were dotted around the room keeping a watchful eye on the naked slave girls, joined him in his merriment.

It was only the strange, shrill voice of the Sinfinder General that finally quietened the laughter. Laura winced as the hands on her buttocks clamped her flesh more tightly, the fingers digging into her skin and violently wrenching her buttocks even further apart.

"This... 'ring'," declared the Sinfinder, using his birch rods to indicate towards Laura's exposed ring of anal muscle, "is a symbol of the love that this happy couple share between them. Through this ring, the husband may express his great love and affection for his wife. She, in offering it up to him to do with as he pleases, may reciprocate those glad and joyful feelings." Laura felt the birch rods touch the back of her head. "Say these words after me," the Sinfinder instructed her. "With this ring..."

"With this ring," Laura gurgled in response...

"I thee wed..."

She grimaced, forcing herself to voice the terrible words: "I thee wed." The hands resting on her birched buttocks were intensifying the dreadful pain that continued to course through her.

"And through use of this ring..."

"And through use of this ring,"

"..let me know that thou art my lord and master."

"..let me know that thou art my lord and master."

Her marriage vows at an end, Laura felt the birch rods being removed from their resting place against the back of her head.

"You may kiss the bride," said the Sinfinder to the wildly whooping Quinn.

From her bent-over position, Laura heard the shuffling of feet against the stone floor, and was aware of her hump-backed husband shifting from his position at her side. Almost immediately, she felt hot lips against her bumhole, and the terrible teasing tickle of a tongue dipping into the clammy channel of her rectum.

As her bum-crack was eaten out, she sobbed anew. God, how she hated Quinn! How she hated every oily hair on his misshapen little body, every gruesome morsel of palid, grisly flesh.

"I now pronounce you man and wife!" exclaimed the Sinfinder, a devilish smile that seemed to drip pure acid cracking the craggy contours of his face.

Whoops and shrieks of delight issued forth from the congregation. The sounds of high-pitched squeals informed Laura that even the slave girls gathered in the makeshift church had found something in the ceremony to delight them: the thrill of a morning out, perhaps, away from the smell of dank stonework, the cut of their manacles, the sting of their overseer's spanking implements...

Or maybe it was the sheer elation of knowing that it was Laura, rather than they, who'd been chosen to spend her life with the foul Quinn...

An overseer's hand at her elbow encouraged her to turn from the Sinfinder, presenting the grim-faced overlord with the sight of her red-raw bottom, and to make her way back down the aisle. This time, however, her new husband walked by her side, his jaw soaked with his own saliva, his yellowed, crumbling teeth exposed for all to see as he smiled a proud, self-satisfied smile; the smile of a man with a beautiful new wife to show off.

The 'happy couple' made their way past the rows of bare-breasted, bare-bottomed slave girls and the sweaty, heaving masses of flesh that passed as overseers, and in due course of time exited the room. Their departure was accompanied by the sounds, once again, of the famous Wedding March. Outside the 'church', the mistress met them, clutching hold of Laura's arm and steering her away down the narrow corridor, towards the annexe from where they'd arrived before the ceremony. Quinn was immediately surrounded by overseers. They were all eager to offer their congratulations, and administered a flurry of hearty slaps to the dwarf's misshapen back and shoulders, one or two weighing in with coarse jokes about the wedding night nuptials to come.

Laura was thankful indeed to be away from Quinn; grateful, too, for the chance to have her mind distracted from the terrible thoughts which she herself was having about the night ahead.

Once back in the annexe, she was divested of her gown, veil and undergarments by Bridget and Helen, and once more fitted with the crudely-made leather neck collar and lead.

"Where are we going now?" she asked the big-bottomed mistress as she was led out of the room. They made their way along a corridor down which she'd never before ventured.

"You're on your way to start your new life, bitch," the mistress growled. "I'm taking you to your new husband's home, where no doubt you will be broken-in like the brand new wifey that you are!" The mistress accompanied her cruel words with a haughty laugh and wrenched hard on the lead, causing Laura to stagger. The flame-haired woman led her out through the garden and down to a coppice, at the far side of which was a large wooden gate.

The field beyond was dotted with dilapidated caravans.

Laura felt her stomach churn as she was dragged towards one particularly ramshackle mobile home, situated in the leafy shade of the woodland area that surrounded the pasture.

The mistress flung open the door and urged her captive up the set of steps leading to the entrance. Laura peered inside and felt her heart sink even lower.

Pots and pans littered the floor; plates and dishes - on which the remnants of days' old meals had dried and hardened - were stockpiled on a beer-stained pull-out dining table and on the draining board by the sink. Magazines, newspapers and books lay crumpled and torn in virtually every nook and cranny Laura could see.

To the far side of the caravan - 'far side' was a joke, really; the place wasn't big enough to have a 'far side' - the dreaded 'marital bed' was in a shambolic state; pillows had tumbled to the threadbare rug, yellowing sheets lay twisted and knotted together, and used pairs of pants and socks decorated all four corners.

The mistress shifted closer to Laura and unfastened her neck collar. "I think you'll have your work cut out here, wifey!" she teased. "But then that's what wives are for, isn't it? To keep a nice clean home for their husband and make sure supper's on the table for six. Particularly when your husband's a malignant midget who'll beat the crap out of you if you don't come up to scratch."

Laura felt tears welling in her eyes again and began to sniffle.

"There, there!" the mistress pouted in response to the show of emotion. A sadistic grin crossed the sour landscape of her face as she mockingly made a show of comforting her distraught captive. "You can't expect marriage to be a bed of roses all the time! I'm sure that if you're diligent with your washing, scrubbing, cleaning, ironing and tidying up, hubby won't spank poor wifey's bare botty too hard!"

Laura's body became racked with sobs, her breasts trembling gently as she wept.

Whether through genuine sympathy at the newly-wed's plight, or simply because she'd tired of the game, the mistress stopped teasing her and instead began to snap instructions. "Make the bed," she commanded. "It must always be ready to accept visitors, as indeed must your body. Your husband has been taken into the village by some of the overseers for a celebratory drink. You won't see him again until this evening, but once you do, I'm sure he'll make you wish you hadn't.

"As for now, tidy up as best you can, and ready yourself for the night ahead. Quinn will want his new wife to look beautiful for him on his return, and you'll try hard to make yourself as alluring as possible if you know what's good for you. When your wedding-night ordeal is over, I shall return and take you back to the house for further rehearsals for the tableau.

"You will shortly be visited by the Sinfinder himself. He will take his pleasure of you first, as is his right." The redhead cast a glance around the caravan. "Work hard," she advised. "I think you'll have to here." With that, the mistress clambered out of the caravan into the summer sunshine, closing and locking the door behind her. Laura watched the woman's big broad bottom wobble magnificently as she wandered back towards the garden, and then slumped onto the bed and sobbed.

Remorselessly, the hours advanced. For some time, Laura remained in a slouched position on the edge of the bed, her mind a web of confusion and turmoil, her stomach a churning mass of anxiety. Eventually, tired of waiting in fear and anticipation for the Sinfinder, she decided to tidy her new home, and to scrub clean the food-caked plates and dishes that littered the tiny caravan.

It was as Laura set about her task that the door unexpectedly creaked open.

The dark-cloaked Matthew Hopkirk squeezed his broad frame into the caravan and raised himself impressively to his full height.

"Harlot," he murmured matter-of-factly by way of greeting. The dark pearls of his eyes drank in the sight of

Laura's pert, upturned breasts and her bald pink love-slit. Then his gaze wandered from her, and he inspected the squalor in which his hunch-backed accomplice-in-terror resided. "How many hours have you sat here awaiting my arrival?" he questioned.

"I don't know, master," Laura responded. "It's seemed like a long time."

"And yet your husband's home remains bereft of a woman's touch." There was a dreadful malevolence in his tone of voice; the hint of a rising anger. "You are indeed a most dilatory, slovenly wench."

Laura's stomach became even more storm-tossed as the Sinfinder's words slammed into her with hammer-force. 'Hours spent sitting and waiting instead of scrubbing and cleaning, Laura, you silly bitch,' she chided herself. How foolish could she have been? The mistress had told her that she should busy herself with her newly acquired duties, but Laura had been too dim, too distracted, to comprehend. Instead she'd sat on the bed like a putz, waiting for the Sinfinder, wondering what devilment he would subject her to next.

And now she kind of knew; it would be a devilment that punished her - punished her for her bad housekeeping, for her slovenliness and her laziness; a devilment, no doubt, to be administered to her poor ass!

Matthew Hopkirk stepped forward and reached for her lead with his gloved and sinewy hand. He tugged her firmly - so that she staggered forward - and wrenched hard, forcing her to bend over. Laura dared to look up and behind her and saw him reaching for the birch rods that hung from his belt. Almost before she'd had time to steady herself, the dark-cowled overseer had begun to whip her flesh, and rhythmically flogged her until every morsel of her quivering bottom flamed a lurid crimson and seemed to swell beneath his savage ministrations.

The Sinfinder wrenched the lead again and sent her

spinning across the caravan, tumbling onto the bed. Before she could regain her composure, the dark avenger was upon her, dragging her naked body across his legs until she lay like a little girl waiting to be spanked for childish misbehaviour. She felt his collection of twigs hard against her bottom then, and wriggled and squirmed like a baby girl. The shame, the awful shame of enduring a flogging had become well known to her during her time in the village, yet now...now - as she lay sprawled out across the heavy-set thighs of this strange, malevolent man - Laura's sense of shame was tempered by the feelings of lust that rose within her.

The feelings which always burned within her whenever the Sinfinder General took her in hand...

Several more minutes of birching ensued before she was unceremoniously pushed to the floor. Matthew Hopkirk took firm hold of her then, and tossed her naked sweating body onto the bed.

He threw his cloak to the floor and wrenched at his breeches. Dragging them down to his thighs, he clambered onto the gently groaning mattress beside her.

Gloved hands clutched at Laura's legs, and she felt herself being turned onto her back, her ankles held wide apart. The Sinfinder lowered himself onto her, his thick, throbbing cock hungry for her pleasures, searching for the slimy entrance to her wet and dribbling cunt.

"Your husband wishes a child," he gasped, "and you shall bear him one." Laura's breathing became more rapid, more urgent, as the Sinfinder's twitching shaft teased her soft pink flesh. "Yet the hunchback fears his offspring may suffer the same physical afflictions which he himself endures," Matthew Hopkirk pushed his groin forward, his cock sliding easily inside Laura's hungrily sucking love-hole, "and so it is my child that you shall bear; the product..." he thrust hard, hammering into her until his swollen testicles slapped against her spanked bottom, "...the product of a lusty fuck!"

Laura squealed as the hard shaft began to slam in and out of her. Hopkirk snorted and drooled like a beast, fucking away at her, his hot breath sweet with the heavy scent of alcohol. His gloved hands mauled her soft breasts, traumatising her big pink nipples; his thick growth of pubic hair rubbed against her bald groin, and she wrapped her legs around him, drawing him inside her, and urging him to greater speed, greater savagery.

The Sinfinder gasped and fucked, and hammered her sweating body so hard with his brutally pistoning cock that her skull slammed against the headboard time and again, making her brain ache as her ravaged vagina tingled madly.

The Sinfinder fucked her with short sharp strokes. She felt his testicles slapping against her hot buttocks as he rode her, and found herself wondering how many times he intended to spend within.

She loved the feeling of him deep inside, and found herself revelling in his total, his absolute mastery of her. She was his to command; he could use her as he pleased, and could beat her as cruelly, as mercilessly, as he desired!

Laura knew that she would never again be free. The Farm, the village, the Sinfinder's house of correction; this was her world now - and she must endure it, and accept the inevitability of it.

"Prepare for thy impregnation!" Matthew Hopkirk gasped, and accompanied his announcement with a series of savage thrusts.

Laura groaned at the very sweetness of the thought. She would carry his child, and there would always be a link between them; an unbreakable bond...

...Yet as his cock made her dizzy with its cruel and merciless attacks, she knew as well how foolish she was being; how ridiculous; how deluded by the passions, the terrible, tingling heat, of an unbridled, perverted lust that she simply could not control.

And then he flooded her, pumping his come into the slushy

depths of her hungrily sucking cunt; pumping until his thick length of cock was entirely emptied of its juices.

He was off her then, almost immediately, twisting her away from him, onto her side, and smacking her hot bottom-cheeks with his hand. "Harlot," he gasped, as he struggled to recover from his sexual exertions. The Sinfinder staggered to his feet and retrieved his cowl, once more shrouding his six-foot frame in its enveloping folds. "I will leave you now," he said. "Rest awhile and let the seed inside you do its work. When you have recovered, clean your husband's home. He will return the worse for wear from alcohol, and no doubt will be looking for a reason to whip you. I suggest you do not give him one."

The caravan shook gently as Matthew Hopkirk made his way to the door. Then he was gone, like a dark avenging angel of the night, returning to the hellfires from whence he came.

As she lay on the bed, recovering from the Sinfinder's visit, the horrors of her domestic situation began to crowd in on Laura. The sun was low in the sky, nighttime only a pink horizon away. That was the time when Quinn would return, his short, squat body heavy with liquor, his brutish brain addled and lustful...

...And he would use her then; beat her, perhaps. But certainly take his pleasure of her...

Laura felt a tear trickle from her eye and gave way to her sudden urge to sob.

By the time she pulled herself together, her pillow was soaked through and her misery had given way to fear. She scanned the caravan and realised how much hard work she had to do if she were to ensure a tidy home for her husband's return. She worked quickly, hoping that with every washed plate, every polished surface, she might be saving herself a stroke of the lash.

When the door of the caravan was finally hurled open, the inebriated Quinn remained vertical for just long enough to clamber the steps.

Then he keeled over, and slept face-down in a pool of his own vomit...

CHAPTER 16

By the time Bertie got back to the inn where he and Francesca were staying, his cock was straining at the leash. He carried with him a bag, slung over his shoulder, and had the look of a man spurred on by a barely containable excitement. As he made his way up the stairs to their room, he caught a scent of himself. A heady mix of sweat and sex hung heavily about him, a mix which he felt sure couldn't possibly go unnoticed by Fran.

The diminutive woman was standing by the window when he entered, gazing out towards the dense forest of trees which locals had come to call Witch's Wood. She turned to look at him, revealing a brow furrowed with concern.

"Bertie," she gasped. She decided there and then to take the bull by the horns...

There was no easy way to tell him what she had to tell him. How the hell could she break the news to her husband that she'd fallen in love with somebody else, and with a woman, at that! But she also knew there could be no deceit. She owed him her honesty after all that he'd done for her, and if nothing else, Fran was determined to be honest.

She thought her husband looked curiously dishevelled and somewhat ill-at-ease as he stood there in the doorway, unslinging a bag from his shoulder. Somewhere in the back of her consciousness, Fran found herself wondering what peculiar adventure he'd been enjoying since gliding ghost-like from their room earlier that morning.

She resolved to push her curiosity from her mind, and instead to follow through with her intention.

"Fran, listen to me!..." Bertie urged, unfastening the bag. He was speaking quickly, at the same time gasping for breath as though he'd been running, or exerting himself in some other way. "I've been doing a lot of thinking about everything that's happened to us since we've been here..."

"So have I, Bertie, my love!" Fran gasped, readying

herself for her revelation. Before she could say anything more, Bertie raised a hand to interrupt her, indicating to his wife his need for her to be quiet. "And I know that we've got to resolve this whole business," he continued. He was tripping over his words in his eagerness to vocalise them. "The truth is, Fran, I cannot bear to look at the markings that are on your body, given to you by another man; nor can I bear the thought that you were willing to give yourself to the Sinfinder simply in order to secure the mistress as our property. I thought I could be supportive of you, really I did; I thought I could deal with your...your adultery... because I knew how much you wanted her - how much I wanted her..." He paused briefly, "...but I couldn't. I couldn't, and I cannot, support or forget what you did." He emptied the contents of the bag onto the still-unmade bed. "I was angry this morning, Fran - angry at you, angry at that devil's disciple Hopkirk, angry at the red-haired bitch for what she's caused us to become. And most of all angry at myself, for being too weak to deal with the situation." He paused again, and fixed his wife with a cold, uncompromising stare. "So, I went to the mansion house, Francesca...and I had her. I whipped her and I fucked her, and I made her mine. And I did it to get my own back..."

Francesca's eyes lit up and she exhaled a gasp.

"Oh, Bertie! Bertie, is it true?" she questioned, her heart pounding with a sudden, uncontrollable excitement. "Have you been inside her, my love? Have you had her on the end of that delicious cock of yours?" Fran glided across the room towards her startled husband, falling at his feet. "Oh my darling, I simply cannot help myself," she half-sobbed. "I know now who I truly am, and there really is nothing I can do about it! I had made up my mind to tell you, Bertie, to tell you that things could never be the same between us ever again! I love you, darling, but I cannot love you in the way that I love her! I need her, my sweet, I need her to be mine; I need to be possessed by her!" Her fingers clutched at his trousers, tugging open the buttons in a feverish attempt to clasp hold of his cock. "Let me suck you, Bertie!" she begged. "Let me suck this delicious dick that's ravaged her insides!"

"Good God, Fran!" the aristocrat exclaimed as his wife engulfed his swollen cock. "For Christ's sake, control yourself!"

"I can't!" Fran gurgled between sucks. "Can't you see what she's done to me? She's bewitched me, Bertie, and now I can't get her out of my mind! I must have her! Oh God, Bertie, I can taste her on you, I can actually taste her!"

Bertie staggered momentarily as his wife sucked fervently at his cock. Her response to his confession had dumbfounded him, sending him reeling into a sickening confusion. He swiftly regained his balance, and grabbed her by the hair, pulling her from him and tossing her onto the floor. "Damn you, you little bitch!" he blazed, his addled brain lurching towards the instinctive response of a jealous husband. "If you want her so badly, then you can have her! I had decided anyway that I was going to annul our marriage - that I could never, ever forgive you for giving yourself to Hopkirk. Your days as my wife are over, Francesca! You can go to the very devil, for all I care!"

"Please, Bertie!" she squealed. "Please, my darling, let me become one of your servants! Let me serve beneath the mistress and be hers to command - and you can be my lord and master, and flog me whenever you so desire!"

His face burning red with rage as his wife spoke, Bertie reached for the contents of the bag he'd emptied. "Put this on, you wicked little harlot!" he growled. "I am going to thrash the very life from you - but I shall not make myself suffer the anguish of looking at your exposed flesh, the flesh the Sinfinder's made so merry with! Now get out of my sight and get yourself changed. I'm going to commemorate the annulment of our marriage by giving you the thrashing of your life."

Bertie proved as good as his word. The garment he had thrown at Fran was a tight-fitting all-in-one rubber suit, purloined from the Sinfinder's mansion house on his way out. It covered Fran from her neck to her ankles. Once she had changed into it and re-entered the room, Bertie wasted no time in preparing her for punishment. Fastening her wrists with one end of a long cord, he threw the other end over a cross-beam and secured it to the bed, drawing her arms up high above her head and effectively exposing every inch of her rubber-clad body to his ministrations.

He took hold of his long, swishy cane, then, and began to flog her. He drove the rattan against every quivering morsel of her body, bringing strokes down across first her shoulders and back, then her buttocks and legs, before shifting his position and laying the bamboo across her stomach, the fronts of her thighs, and even her breasts.

He returned his assault to her buttocks, then, thrashing away at the rubber-sheathed cheeks for all he was worth, revelling in the opportunity to exorcise the anger that burned wildly within him; a raging fire that he felt might never be extinguished.

As he whipped her writhing bottom, Fran screamed in a way which Bertie had never heard her scream before.

Soon, he could smell the stench of her hot urine as the flogging made her lose control of herself. She shamelessly filled her rubber suit, with only the occasional trickle of hot, amber piss fashioning an escape route at her ankles.

When Bertie had beaten her for so long and so hard that she'd slipped into unconsciousness, he carefully made a slit in the garment between her thighs. He felt the urine splash his hand on its way to the floor, and wondered at the strange excitement he sensed at being suddenly soaked in Francesca's piss. His erection hardened immediately, swelling until his foreskin seemed ready to split from the strain of it all, and he wasted no time in pushing himself up inside the newly gouged opening, and onwards into her fleshy cunt. Bertie's hands clutched at Fran's breasts for leverage, and he fucked away inside her limp and sagging body with all the energy he could muster, ramming mercilessly at her sodden hole until he could contain the growing pressure no longer, and emptied himself deep within her...

By the time Fran awoke, Bertie had untied her and laid her on the bed. He'd spent the time while she'd been sleeping gazing out of the window, looking into the distance. Through the trees, he was just about able to make out a section of one of the Farm's fallow fields, where the slave girls toiled in the blazing heat, their bottoms aglow from the vicious touch of their overseers' canes.

Bertie had spent his time alone thinking; trying his best to come to terms with his wife's revelation about her love for Katharine Kimble; attempting to work out how he felt about it, and what his next move should be.

He loved Francesca, there could be no doubting that. He had loved her from the moment they'd first met, but he knew as well that he had finally lost her - and lost her forever. The mistress was a wild, beguiling creature - and in his own way, he too had fallen in love with her; certainly it was she who'd pervaded his dreams, who he'd thought about in his quiet moments, those past few days. And it was she who he wished to be inside, and about whose delicious, voluptuous body he desired to uncover every little secret.

When his wife had fully regained her senses, Bertie assisted her out of the tight-fitting rubber garment. He could bear to look upon her body now, covered as it was with fresh marks from the beating he had given her. Francesca's flesh was so comprehensively decorated with his cane strokes that all traces of the Sinfinder's whipping had been concealed.

He bathed her wounds for her, and told her what he'd decided.

"I will not divorce you, Francesca," he said, "nor do I

believe that you would wish me to do so. As you said, you love me still, as I do you.

"But from the time we leave this valley, you shall cease to live as my wife. When we return home, you shall be furnished with a servant's garments and you will live in the downstairs quarters with the other girls - and with the mistress. And yes, in line with your desire, the mistress shall indeed be your superior, and will treat you however she sees fit. Knowing, as I do, how much you crave such an arrangement, I cannot and will not deny it to you. But I cannot pretend your love for that woman has not hurt me, nor can I pretend that there isn't a part of me that truly and madly despises you for what you have done to our marriage. It's for that reason, petty and vengeful though it must seem, that I have decided that all the other girls shall also have superiority over you. They will no doubt take their revenge for the beatings you have given each of them over the years, and I will actively encourage them to treat you cruelly. You will, in short, be the lowest of the low!

"And do not think you have taken my cock inside you for the last time either, Fran. I will have you whenever and wherever I see fit, just as I will any of the other girls. And believe me when I tell you that I shall pay you no favours, nor give you any special treatment, unless it takes the form of beating and fucking you even more soundly than I do the others."

On hearing his decision, Fran embraced her husband as passionately as her burning wounds would allow, and began to sob tears of pure unadulterated joy.

"I would be grateful, Fran," the aristocrat added once his wife had regained her composure, "if, in your remaining time as my wife, you would help me to find a second slave to take home with us - with... me, I mean. Without you there by my side, my life will be greatly changed. A second fresh bottom to chastise should help to keep me busy while I adapt to my new situation."

211

"Of course I shall help you, my darling," Fran chortled. "Oh, Bertie, you've made me so happy, I think I could cry for a week! And yes, yes, my darling, yes - we must select you another slave to take home with us; a gorgeous, beautiful slave that you can whip and fuck whenever you so desire! We will get to the show early tonight, my sweet, and enjoy as many of the tableaux as we can!"

Francesca clapped her hands together in delight and Bertie was momentarily reminded of a performing seal. He pushed his wife down onto her back and climbed on top of her, slotting his once-more-swollen cock into her still-dribbling cunt, and riding her with a vigour which took even Fran unawares.

CHAPTER 17

Laura slept fitfully in her new husband's caravan. Whenever she woke, she peered towards the doorway and was relieved to see that the gruesome figure of Quinn was still slumbering on the caravan floor. As dawn arrived, even the crow of a cockerel failed to stir him, and Laura found herself hoping that he would never awaken again.

She lay there from dawn, unable to sleep, her stomach performing cartwheels as she awaited the inevitable. However inebriated Quinn might have been, he would wake at some point, and then her life wouldn't be worth living.

It was only when the door to the caravan was pushed open, jabbing the prostrate little man's ribcage in the process, that the dwarf finally stirred.

"You filthy little bastard!" spat the mistress as she shoved the ragged, vomit-plastered brute away from the door with a contemptuous push of her high-heeled shoe. "Slumbering like a hog in your own puke while your beautiful new wife lies lusty and frustrated in your bed! I ought to have you horsewhipped for your behaviour."

The dwarf fixed her momentarily with a bloodshot stare, and then sank back into his deep and drunken sleep.

"Well, it seems you got lucky last night," said the redhead, sauntering across the caravan towards Laura, "but he'll make you pay for it tonight, I'm sure. You'll no doubt have his hot come bubbling out of your ears by the time he's finished with you."

The mistress grinned wickedly, her eyes glinting with excitement as she registered the American's reaction to her comment. Laura felt physically sick at the thought of what she'd probably have to suffer that night - not only the savage beatings that would inevitably be administered to her bottom, but also the sensation of the fuck-faced little runt's dick inside of her, using her like a receptacle, filling her up and pumping her full of his filthy come.

"Time to go," said the mistress. "You're taking part in a tableau this morning. You've got a script to learn and a costume to get yourself into, so get that arse of yours moving smartish, you dirty little bitch."

"I need to go to the toilet, mistress," Laura croaked.

"No time for that. I'll try and find you some kind of butt-plug. As for your bladder, you'll just have to hold it."

Laura raised herself from the bed, wincing at the growing pressure in her bladder and bowels, and headed for the door. A sharp slap on the bottom encouraged her on her way, the surprise of it almost making her empty herself there and then.

She moved cautiously past the snoring Quinn, and felt a sudden delight at finding herself out in the fresh air, the hot summer sun kissing her bare back and shoulders.

The mistress escorted her back to the Sinfinder's mansion. Once inside, she directed her to a small closet, wherein Laura found a bundle of clothes and a stapled, typewritten document.

"I'll come for you in a half hour," the flame-haired mistress informed her. "Get into your costume and make sure you know exactly what you're expected to do in the tableau rehearsal. If you make a mistake, causing the tableau to be interrupted while you're punished for your error, the Sinfinder will not be best pleased."

The mistress swung the door to, and sauntered away down the corridor, her high-heeled shoes clicking against the tiled floor as she went.

Laura quickly dressed in the clothes she'd been left - shirt and tie; navy, knee-length blouse; white pants and socks; sensible black shoes; two elasticated bands for arranging her hair, presumably in pig-tails. She was going to play a schoolgirl again, no doubt about it.

After adjusting her clothing, she perused the typed manuscript. It was less a script, more a selection of instructions, giving Laura some notion of the scene in which she'd be participating.

She made herself familiar with the manuscript's contents, and then wondered how best to pass the remainder of time until the mistress came to collect her. The pressure was growing in her bladder and bowels, and Laura found herself praying that she'd be able to hold out until after the tableau.

As she stood in the closet in her navy and white uniform, Laura felt very much the schoolgirl, once more waiting to be taken to the Headmistress's study for a deserved thrashing.

The eventual sound of the Mistress's high-heels clicking against the floor tiles told her that her comeuppance was almost at hand, and she sucked in a deep breath and told herself to remain as calm as she could.

Their journey was a comparatively short one, the Mistress stopping at the end of the corridor and flinging wide a door to reveal a small room furnished with rows of desks. Behind the desks - except for one, presumably Laura's - there sat women in similar navy and white attire.

"A new arrival for you, Mr Belt," said the Mistress, peeping around the door.

"So this is the new girl," said the tall, grey-haired male lounging in the teacher's chair behind a huge oak desk. Laura recognised him to be the man who'd played the American President in the Oval Office scene, and who'd played Mr James in the school-based scene she'd performed in with the Mistress herself.

"And your name, girl?"

Laura found a voice from somewhere and uttered her name. "Laura," she whispered, "Laura Alexis."

"Welcome to your new class, Miss Alexis. My name, as you've heard, is Mr Belt. I hope you'll be very happy and learn many things here." Somehow, Laura doubted it.

"Your desk awaits you." The grey-haired teacher motioned to the empty seat in the second row. "Sit down and we can begin our lessons."

Laura did as she was told, slipping uneasily onto the hard wooden seat. Mr Belt rose to his full six feet height and emerged from behind his huge desk. The Mistress had moved to the far side of the room, and lowered her magnificent bottom onto a plastic chair, ready to observe proceedings.

"Okay, let's begin," said the handsome teacher. "Carol," he looked towards the fortysomething blond who'd played his wife in the Oval Office tableau, "perhaps you'd be so kind as to tell myself and your fellow pupils the answer to the following question: what's thirty-five, plus twenty-three, divided by four and multiplied by three?"

The high-cheekboned blond looked quizzically at her teacher, and then began to count on her fingers, as though she somehow hoped to find the answer to the tricky arithmetical problem simply by counting to ten.

"Come on, please, Carol," urged Mr Belt unreasonably. "We don't have all day. There's a new girl in class; it would be nice if we could show her that we are not a group of complete idiots."

He moved across the room towards the frantically counting blond, and loomed menacingly above her, watching with a certain amusement her futile finger antics. "The answer if you please, Carol - now!"

The blond looked up pleadingly at him, and Laura was certain she heard the slightest tremor in her classmate's whispered reply. "Please, sir," she said, "I...I don't know the answer."

A grim, unforgiving silence followed, during which the teacher fixed his errant pupil with a steely gaze. Carol, for her part, did her best to avoid meeting it.

"To the front of the class," Mr Belt snapped suddenly, "and bend over my desk."

Carol went without a murmur. She sprawled her upper body across the polished oak surface of the desk, reaching out her arms to clasp its far edge. While his pupil was following his instruction, Mr Belt wandered over to a cupboard, and pulled from its cobwebbed darkness a long length of cane. He sauntered across the room and took up a position to Carol's left. "It's shameful that a big girl like you is unable to perform even the most rudimentary of sums," he chided. "As any fool could tell you, Carol, the answer to that simple conundrum is forty-three-and-a-half."

As Laura sat looking at the scene, and in spite of its portents of doom for the welfare of her own bottom, she found herself attempting to work out the sum in her head. Constant failure to do so led her to realise it was anything but 'a simple conundrum'.

"You are a dilatory, backward child when it comes to the finer points of education, girl," Mr Belt continued, swishing his cane through the air, "and I intend to show you that if you will not learn in one way, then you must expect to learn in another."

He paused momentarily before passing sentence: "Your punishment," he announced with great deliberation, "is six strokes of the cane across your bare buttocks."

"Yes sir."

"Then let us bare your errant bottom in preparation for the strokes."

Mr Belt leaned forward and took hold of the hem of Carol's skirt, peeling the garment upward and back and resting it neatly against her lower back. Her broad, white-pantied bottom, splendid in its size and shape, was beautifully exposed to view. The teacher clasped the waistband of her pants and gently edged them down over her buttocks. Carol's alabaster-white bum cheeks trembled like delicious jellies as they were exposed.

"Keep your buttocks nicely relaxed," he told her, shifting his position slightly as he measured up the distance between rattan and bottom cheeks, "and by all means squeal like the shameful girl that you are. It will do you no good; your bottom is going to be soundly thrashed and that's an end to it."

The first terrible stroke landed with a sickening thwack. From the corner of her eye, Laura could see her classmates flinch in response to its sound and power. Each of them knew that it could just as easily be their own bare bottom rippling beneath the cut of the master's rattan.

The rising sense of tension within the classroom was almost palpable.

The second stroke, a lower cut across the broad expanse of bum flesh, caused Carol to gasp out loud. She jiggled her posteriors in a pointless attempt to relieve the pain.

"Keep your cheeks still!" snapped Mr Belt. "If you cause me to miss my aim, you will receive a further two strokes."

He swung again, administering a crueller, more powerful stroke than either of its predecessors had been. The extra savageness was a clear warning to the desperately wriggling Carol - Mr Belt expected his girls to present him with a sitting target. Wiggle your ass and you got more rattan! Laura's heart sank into her stomach; keeping her ass still during a beating was not one of her strengths. She dreaded to think how many extra cuts of the cane she'd end up receiving over the teacher's desk!

Another stroke, and Carol whinnied like a lame horse. Mr Belt paused to feel the stripey buttocks presented so perfectly in front of him. His fingers roamed into the deep groove that clove the woman's bottom, seeking out her wet and clammy secrets. She moaned gently, and Laura could tell that the grey-haired master was tickling her clitoris, working her up into a frenzy before cruelly replacing the sensations of pleasure with the pain-inducing touch of his thrashing bamboo.

When Mr Belt took his hand away, Carol tensed her bottom cheeks momentarily, knowing the fifth stroke was almost upon her. The cane whistled through the air and thwacked against her, causing her buttocks to judder and ripple spectacularly. "Do not tense your cheeks, girl!"

barked the master. "Keep them relaxed and ready for the rod at all times, or it will be the worse for you." The sixth stroke was a mighty shot, catching the sniffling fortysomething 'schoolgirl' across the fleshy peaks of her buttocks and making her squeal like a pig on a spit.

Mr Belt placed his rattan on the desk top and stood back to inspect his handiwork. Carol's ass was a gruesome criss-cross of red-raw weals. The stroke marks showed up all the more vividly in contrast to the whiteness of her legs.

"You may stand up and rub your bottom, girl," said the master.

Carol hauled her body upright, and Laura could see for the first time the tears that coursed down her flushed face. Strands of the woman's blond hair were plastered to her chin, caught up in the rivulets of saliva that had flowed uncontrollably from her mouth. "Return to your seat," said Mr Belt, "and do not give me cause to punish you again this term!"

Carol returned to her seat and sat gingerly behind her desk, grimacing as her beaten buttocks pressed against the hard wooden seat.

The tableau then continued in earnest. Another complex mathematical conundrum left Bridget floundering, and she had soon replaced Carol across the master's desk, her big bum cheeks wobbling in response to the savage cut of the cane.

The dark-haired woman who had played the British Prime Minister's wife in the Oval Office tableau was next to have her bottom bared. She dropped her ruler on the floor - Laura found herself wondering whether it was an accident or if she'd been commanded to do so before the tableau had begun - and was pulled by the ear to the front of the class.

Mr Belt pulled a plastic chair from the far side of the room, settled on it, and dragged the clumsy miscreant across his lap. Her skirt was flipped up and her pants pulled down. He used her own ruler then to spank her big wide bottom, smacking the strip of wood against her bare flesh with a terrible vigour that made the dark-haired woman buck like a wild horse.

When he had coloured the entire surface of her jiggling posteriors, he dropped the ruler to the floor, and set about her smouldering flesh with his hand, spanking her for a full ten minutes.

The teacher moved among the desks then, firing all manner of imponderable questions at the perplexed 'schoolgirls'. A wrong answer, and the bad girl in question was made to bend forward across her own desk. The master would flip up her skirt, wrench down her pants and scold her bottom with a thick leather paddle; a single, powerful stroke, brought smacking down across both cheeks with such resolve that it visibly compacted and flattened the exposed bottom-flesh.

Laura, unable to answer a thorny mathematical problem and a question about Ghengis Kahn, felt the terrible paddle burn her twice. It was as much as she could manage on both occasions to retain her grip on the desk, so profoundly did the pain suffuse her bottom.

Caught then sitting in what Mr Belt regarded as too casual a pose for a well-mannered, conscientious schoolgirl, she was instructed to the front of the class and made to take a trip across the teacher's broad thighs.

She could feel Mr Belt's thick erection nudging at her abdomen as she lay in position, and wondered how much bigger and stiffer it would grow as he beat her.

In truth, she was hardly able to tell, so much did she wriggle throughout the ordeal. The teacher had a huge hand, and splatted it against her bottom with so much power that she was unable to concentrate on anything but the awful pain in her ass.

The big palm had covered the entire area of her cheeks with burning spanks in no time at all, and continued to slap down against the tenderised flesh with an unremitting gusto.

As the giant hand spanked away at her buttocks, she stoically gritted her teeth against the still-growing pressure in her bladder and bowels. Tensing her body as much as she possibly could, Laura found herself hoping to God she could avoid the awful shame of pissing and crapping herself. It had been more miserable hours than she could remember since she'd last been allowed to urinate. And her stomach had churned so often in the previous twenty-four hours - as she'd faced up to the terrible ordeal of her marriage to Quinn and the awful thoughts of the wedding night - that she was surprised the contents of her bowels hadn't turned to pure liquid long before.

Mr Belt's spanking hand was now pushing her to the limit of her endurance.

The hand drove against her mercilessly, spanking her buttocks until they seemed to Laura to be the size of huge beachballs. She gritted her teeth, tried hard to distract her hoping against hope that the vigorous beating would be brought to an end swiftly. Not that she knew what she'd do then, of course. Ask to be excused? That, surely, would prove to be a punishable offence, she thought to herself. And knowing what a sick bunch of fuckers her masters were, it wouldn't have surprised her one bit if the punishment for asking to be excused was to have to empty herself in front of her classmates!

All of a sudden, the whole issue became academic...

As the master's palm continued to slap her ass about, Laura groaned and felt her bladder give way...

Her bare legs were suddenly sheathed in a cascade of hot urine. And as her floodgates opened, she could hear her classmates gasping with astonishment.

"You filthy girl!" snapped Mr Belt, as he lifted his suddenly soiled hand from her trembling buttocks. "You dirty little bitch!"

Laura was hardly aware of the tears of shame that poured from her eyes - her concentration was focused almost entirely on what was happening in her lower regions, as her bladder and continued to empty itself.

When her mind finally ceased leaping somersaults, and she felt the true shame of her situation crowd in upon her, she could hear the delighted sniggers of her 'classmates', and the raucous laughter of the watching Mistress. "Open all the windows, girls," the redhead commanded. "The stench is quite foul! What a disgusting, wicked madam!"

And in her humiliation, the very worst part of it all for Laura was that 'Mr Belt' had held her in place over his knee throughout, as her urine had squirted from her. She had emptied her bladder while lying across a man's knees, and had no doubt pissed all down his legs as well as her own!

"This terrible crime will not go unpunished," snapped the mistress, holding her laughter in abeyance while she scolded the miscreant Laura. "The Sinfinder views most seriously the crime of slave wenches emptying themselves without first gaining permission. You will be fortunate indeed, you wicked girl, if he does not flay the very hide from your wilful bottom! Now get up!"

Laura hauled herself from across Mr Belt's legs, slipping and sliding in the puddle.

Laura was too ashamed to look up, to meet the laughing faces of her classmates. Nor could she bring herself to look into the lustful eyes of her grey-haired spanker.

"Let's get you cleaned up," said the mistress, striking a surprisingly sympathetic tone. "You are sure to be beaten soundly for this, perhaps even publicly flogged. The Sinfinder will want a clean bottom upon which to have the cuts of the whip laid ..."

The only positive aspect for Laura of the ordeal which followed was that, in the light of her 'wanton' public urination, the Sinfinder decreed that she would not live as the malevolent Quinn's wife, as originally intended. The gruesome little dwarf begged and pleaded with the grim-faced Sinfinder, imploring him to reconsider. When it became apparent that his pleas were falling on deaf ears, he begged at least for one night with his wife, so that she might give him the pleasure that was rightfully his to demand. Matthew Hopkirk remained impassive and unmoved. Her crime, he said, was of such magnitude, that she was to be condemned to a state of constant punishment. She would have neither time nor opportunity to gratify the brutish Quinn's terrible lustings.

"Let ye know this," the Sinfinder General decreed, his eyes burrowing into Laura's very soul as he spoke, "for your most heinous crime, the punishment is severe indeed. Ye are to be taken from this place, and publicly and most profoundly whipped. When the full measure of strokes hast fallen upon thy flesh, ye are to be made much use of within thy woman's hole, until thy orifice can hold not one drop more seed. Thereafter, ye shall be placed within a grim and terrible prison for the period of five summers - and thy offending back-hole shall be displayed and most scurrilously used by all who shall desire it."

Laura's heart thumped like a hammer, threatening to pound its way from within her chest. For all that the Sinfinder had decreed, it was his pronouncement that she were to be whipped which had struck the most profound chord with her.

There was just something about the formality of her sentencing that made her feel sick, made her feel that she had just been condemned by the hangman himself. Muscular overseers frogmarched her from the Sinfinder General's lair, returning her to the dank little cell she'd shared with Lucinda and Sally. She was pushed to the wall and fastened in the traditional manner, cruel clamps biting into her nipples and clitoris. The rough and ready overseers flipped a coin to see which should enjoy her delights first, and then each took a turn fucking her, until her cunt burned and throbbed

223

and her eyes watered.

Laura was then left alone in the cell for several hours, with only the occasional noise from beyond her prison door, and the accompanying pang of fear deep in her gut, to relieve her boredom.

She was visited in the evening by a guardsman who brought her a dish of watery soup and some crusty bread. He spooned the warm slush into her mouth, then held bread beneath her nose for her to bite and chew upon. While she did so, he felt her bottom with his rough-skinned hand and fondled her cunt-flesh with his stumpy fingers.

"These arse cheeks o' yourn'll be feelin' it soon," he mocked, in a strong Cornish accent, "and this dirty crack, I shouldn't wonder. You're goin' t' get a right proper whippin' and no mistake!"

The brute's own words seemed suddenly to work him into a frenzy. Throwing the remains of the bread to the stone floor, he pushed his hefty body against Laura's, mashing her clamped nipples to the brickwork, and began to rudely distend her vagina with his thick fingers.

"Let's have you, shall we," he gurgled from between gritted teeth, "let's have you in this cunt o' yourn so's you get used t' the feel of a man's prick in there!" As she gasped and squealed in response to the rough intrusion, the thought flashed across Laura's addled mind that there was hardly a need to 'get used to' the feeling of a prick inside her. After all, since her arrival in the valley, there had seemed very little time when her body hadn't been stuffed with one length of cock or another!

It was just as the grizzly brute prepared to push his erect muscle into her that the cell door swung open.

"What were you told, you big brute!?" snapped the Mistress. "Did you not hear the Sinfinder decree that this bitch was not to be used, that her hole was to be left empty in preparation for her punishment? Get out of here. Use another of the bitches in her filthy hole if you wish to be rid of that ugly stiffness. Do not let me see you sniffing around this piece of ass again tonight, do you hear!"

As the cell door slammed shut and the overseer bade a hasty retreat along the corridor, the Mistress moved in close behind Laura.

"Thank your mistress for saving your miserable arse," she whispered in the American's ear.

"Th-thanks," murmured Laura tentatively, "thanks for saving my miserable ass." She felt the woman's gloved hand slip between her thighs, and gently groaned as fingers began to explore her fleshy sex.

"I've got something for you," said Kath. "A little pleasure before the pain. Open your legs wide."

Laura edged her legs apart cautiously, acutely aware of the wall-clamp that cruelly nipped her clitoris. Almost before she'd properly adjusted her balance, one gloved hand had cupped her left breast, and a hard object had been pressed against her sex.

She was wet - she was always wet, in spite of the terrible things that were continually done to her - and the object slipped inside her body with considerable ease. Laura exhaled a languorous groan, and revelled in the delicious feeling of having her sopping cunt stretched and probed by her mistress's bulging invader.

The redhead gently moved the object in and out of her sodden sex, every minute movement drawing an ecstatic purr from Laura's parched throat.

She unclipped the American's breasts and began to caress them tenderly; stroking the sore nipples, gently massaging the flesh until Laura thrust her bosom forward, urgent for the touch of her lover's lips.

Her body began to undulate, then, and she wished the mistress would remove her clitoris clip; she wanted to thrust down onto the gently fucking dildo, wanted to bring herself to a shattering, breathtaking orgasm; but the clip meant that she could only respond with the slightest of movements, making her yearn all the more for a gratification she could never achieve.

Hot kisses peppered her neck and shoulders, warm breath caressed her skin. "Please, mistress," she found herself moaning, "please let me come!"

"It is enough that you should be allowed this pleasure," the flame-haired woman gasped. "You are to be punished tomorrow and then incarcerated," she twisted the dildo inside Laura, expertly working the American into a frenzy, "your days of enjoying orgasms, my sweet, are well and truly over!"

The Mistress gave Laura's left nipple a sudden, savage twist and pulled the dildo from within her dripping cunt. Laura exhaled a sigh, and realised any hope of satisfaction had evaporated.

"Get whatever sleep you can, bitch," the woman said. "You'll need to be fresh tomorrow."

The cell door slammed shut.

Laura listened to the Mistress's stiletto heels clicking against the tiled floor as she made her way back up the stairs into the house.

And then, eventually, the only thing the American could hear at all was the terrible sound of her own miserable sobs...

Sleep, not surprisingly, came fitfully to her. She was managing a rare doze, in spite of her manacles and her standing position, when the cell door was next flung open. Two burly overseers, both carrying objects, entered with great purpose, followed by Kathy Kimble. The men unfastened Laura and swung her around to face the red-haired mistress.

"It's time," said Kathy, a gentle smile etched across the hard contours of her face. She nodded towards her henchmen, and they set about their work. Each grasping one of Laura's arms and clasping the back of her neck, they forced her down onto her haunches. Her hands were then fitted into a lightweight set of stocks, which one of the men had swiftly positioned behind her head and across her shoulders. A collar, with two short cords, was then fitted around her neck; the cords were pulled tight, the free end of one being attached to the big toe of her left foot, the other to the corresponding toe of her right foot. In this way, she had been successfully secured in a squatting posture.

A hand reached under her from behind. In her uncomfortable position, her buttocks were wide apart, her anus distended. She felt a finger dab her bumhole with something cold, and then felt an object being pushed up inside her bottom. As it was being carefully inserted, Laura heard the gentle tinkling of bells, and registered a quiet chuckle of delight from the flame-headed mistress.

"Wonderful," Kathy Kimble muttered. "With rings on her fingers and bells hanging from her arse, she shall have music wherever she goes!" The mistress clapped her gloved hands together as if to imply she meant business. "Right," she said. "Your punishment awaits. A crowd is gathered in the Sinfinder's lair, waiting for the entertainment to begin, so we shouldn't keep them waiting. Chop chop!"

Laura was well aware of the two overseers sniggering behind her, their jocular mood being perfectly reflected by the mistress's thoroughly amused grin. Laura could hardly move. Her hands were in the stocks and if she over-extended herself in attempting to move, she would undoubtedly lose her balance and topple over. The only way she could hope to make progress in her ridiculous squatting position was to edge herself forward inch by inch, carefully shifting her body weight from her left side to her right side and then back again.

At her first movement, the bells dangling from her bottom-hole tinkled merrily, as though ringing out their delight at her terrible discomfiture. "Listen to those lovely bum bells!" laughed the mistress. "My, what a musical arse you have!

Let's hear that lovely bell of yours tinkle again, shall we!"

Laura edged herself forward, the little bells jingling as she struggled to retain her balance. Slowly, excruciatingly, she shuffled her way through the cell door and out into the corridor, her face a mask of grim concentration.

Faced with the challenge of mounting the staircase from the cellar, the American bravely attempted to lift her left leg onto the first step. Her three captors watched her efforts from behind, and laughed out loud when she overbalanced and toppled onto her side.

The burly overseers lifted her up between them and carried her to the top of the stairs, depositing her on her feet in the compulsory squatting position once again. With the mistress leading on ahead, and the laughing henchmen bringing up the rear - and no doubt delighting in watching her ass-bells jingle! - Laura edged along the corridor like some sort of pathetic, injured animal, a whimpering beast being degraded and humiliated for the enjoyment of her mocking captors.

Every now and then, one of the overseers would stoop down and jingle the bells that hung from her bottom, asking the gasping, straining woman to jiggle her ass and play them a tune. The mistress, meanwhile, took great delight in leaning over and fondling Laura's breasts, teasing and twisting the nipples so that the captive American required all her powers of concentration to focus on the matter in hand; keeping her balance and reaching her destination.

Eventually, after an interminable age, she wobbled into the open doorway of the Sinfinder's lair, her grim-faced look of determination being met by dozens of staring eyes and highly amused visages.

At the far end of the room, seated in his huge chair, lounged Matthew Hopkirk, the sight of his sombre countenance striking a terrible fear into Laura's heart. In front of him, taking centre-stage, was a wooden contraption, a horizontal bar affixed to two vertical posts at crotch height.

Laura instinctively knew its purpose. Before long, her

body would be positioned across it, presented for punishment!

The burly overseers scooped her squatting frame up into the air and carried her into the room, past the groups of guardsmen and naked slavegirls who had gathered to watch events unfold. Laura was lowered to the floor in front of the wooden construction. From her squatting position, just able to see over the top of the horizontal beam, she looked into the dark eyes of the Sinfinder General, and saw reflected there a vision of her own miserable future.

"Ye who have sinned," he murmured, "will here, today, have that sin purged from thy body." As he spoke, a naked girl appeared from a group of slave women to Laura's right and settled down on her haunches next to the wooden contraption, resting a bowl of water on the stone floor. Risking a furtive glance, Laura recognised the new arrival to be Bridget, and felt strangely calmed by the gentle, friendly smile she saw playing around the brunette's lips.

"Unfasten her," instructed the Sinfinder. The two brutes who had fetched Laura to the terrible torture chamber set about removing the collar from her neck and the stocks from her shoulders. She gasped with relief as the collection of bells was plucked from her anus.

Their hands under Laura's arms, the henchmen pulled her up to her full height, the sudden movements of her stiffened limbs causing her to grimace in discomfort.

The Sinfinder leaned forward in his chair and fixed Laura with an icy gaze. "It is the judgement of this court," he growled, "that ye shall have administered unto ye twenty strokes of the rattan, and that ye shall thereafter be plundered in thy shameful hole, and therein defiled until ye are plugged full with seed."

The sentence decreed, Matthew Hopkirk reclined in his chair once more, a gentle nod to one of the overseers standing behind Laura conveying his desire for proceedings to commence.

"Bend your body over the bar," barked the brute standing at Laura's left shoulder.

The moment had arrived.

Laura felt a terrible knot tighten in her stomach. She gritted her teeth, moved towards the wooden contraption, and leaned right over the horizontal beam, until her palms were resting against the floor to its far side. Manacles were fitted around her wrists and fastened to metal rings set in the floor. Behind her, her legs were pulled wide, her ankles fastened to the vertical posts at either end of the horizontal beam.

How perfectly she was presented for punishment! Her buttocks were taut and angled beautifully for the cut of the cane, while the wide-apart positioning of her legs ensured her fleshy pink cunt and wrinkled brown bumhole were lewdly exposed for all to see.

"Be brave," whispered Bridget. "I have been told to dab you with cold water from time to time, and to talk to you, to ensure that you don't faint during your beating. Would you like me to dab you now?"

Laura shook her head slowly. "No, honey," she said. "Don't dab, just help! Please - help me!"

"Let the punishment commence," declared Matthew Hopkirk.

"Be brave," Bridget repeated. "The overseer who has been chosen to cane you is a big man. He'll lay the rod on hard. You must be resolved to take it."

Laura could hear the movement of feet behind her, and felt her heart skip a beat when she heard the sound of a rattan slicing the air. A practice stroke, but what a savage one! Her bottom would never be able to take such punishment!

She bit her lip and sucked in a mouthful of air. Of course she could take it, she told herself. She had been beaten more times than she cared to remember, with all manner of cruel implements, by all manner of cruel people; why should this be any different?

It was the terrible ceremony of it all, that was what made the difference. All those people, she thought to herself, gathered there for the express purpose of watching her punished! And her punisher - whoever he was - had no doubt been hand-picked by the Sinfinder to make her suffer. The brute would be determined to vindicate his master's faith in him - a vindication, she knew, which would be arrived at through the thorough caning of her poor bottom!

Her wandering thoughts were interrupted by the sudden feeling of the cane being pressed against her buttocks...

...This was it - this really was it, Laura thought to herself. She felt the cane being lifted from her flesh, and held her breath for what seemed to be an eternity.

Swish, crack!

The wicked implement sliced into her bottom. In the instant before she was consumed by sharp, searing pain, Laura's bemused mind struggled to reconcile the savage swishing sound with the heart-stopping sensation of the rattan impacting on her flesh. The pain of the stroke stabbed its way through her, burning deep into the flesh of her bare buttocks.

She gritted her teeth, clenched her fists and grimly resolved to hold the posture demanded of her.

Again the terrifying whistle as the overseer launched his cane at her bottom-cheeks.

Swish, crack!

The cut struck higher than the first, biting savagely at the less fleshy portion of her bottom. She wheezed as an incomparable pain danced across her perfectly presented moons.

"Fuck!" Laura expelled the expletive quietly, within a huge exhalation of breath. Fresh tears welled up in her eyes. She could hardly believe the pain she was suffering and felt certain she would once again wet herself if the flogging continued.

She bit hard at her lip, and concentrated her efforts on controlling her bladder and her tear ducts.

The overwhelming stillness of the chamber - full though it was with people - was shattered for a third time by another powerful slicing sound. The monstrous implement was once more propelled at her soft buttock-flesh.

Swish, crack!

Lower that time, on the fulsome crown of her bum. Laura sucked in a huge mouthful of air as the whole of her ass begin to smoulder.

Swish, crack!

Again she sucked in air. Another line of fiery pain burned the width of her naked hemispheres.

Swish, crack! The fearful swishing sound again; then, the awful, gut-churning noise as the vicious cane impacted on already-scorched flesh; then a dreadful pain, lacerating her nerve endings - and from her own mouth, forcing its way up through her parched throat, a fearful, gurgling whine, merged with a stammered plea for leniency.

Swish, crack!

There was no leniency to be had. No quarter given. Instead, more savage, searing pain consumed her. Her flesh seemed almost to sizzle as the barbaric implement of torture was brought down time after time across her swollen, throbbing hillocks.

Even as tears tumbled from her cheeks onto the stone floor, and her knuckles turned white - so tightly was she clenching her hands into fists - Laura couldn't help but imagine the sight she was presenting; bent double over the bar, her legs stretched wide apart, her bottom thrust out and up, cunt twitching, anus throbbing - and all the while, a brutish overseer lacerating her miserable ass cheeks with stroke after grotesque stroke of his evil cane.

Her bottom suddenly felt so big! Her bum cheeks so swollen and puffy! Laura was no longer aware of anything physically except her poor throbbing bottom, and felt certain she could be no more than a couple of strokes away from passing out.

The caning was proving every bit as terrible as she'd imagined it was going to be!

The rattan cracked against her swollen nates once more, cutting into the tender crease where her buttocks sloped into her thighs.

"You're doing so well," Bridget encouraged, using a sponge to dab cooling water onto Laura's forehead. "He's beating you with everything he can muster! Your poor bottom must be hurting so much!"

"Make him stop!" Laura gasped, as tears poured down her face. "Oh Christ, please make him stop! My - my bum can't take much more!"

"It's got to, Laura," urged Bridget. "You have to be strong. You're going to have to take the full twenty on your bottom, you know that. Just try and blank your mind..."

The terrible onslaught continued. A deathly silence embraced the chamber between each stroke, as overseers and slavegirls alike stood watching the ferocious caning proceed - their breath baited, their hearts pounding fiercely with a sickening mix of excitement and repulsion.

"Please..." she murmured. "Please, no more. My - my bottom...please..."

The brutish overseer paid her no heed, instead mercilessly swinging the swishing rattan through a huge arc and lashing her buttocks over and over again. For the final three strokes, the shaggy beast took a run-up. His heavy boots clumped against the stone floor as he charged towards his victim, his powerful arm unleashing the wicked bamboo with a sickening ferocity that made the onlookers gasp. Laura bucked against the beam, thrust her face towards the ceiling and screamed from the very depths of her soul for mercy. All the while, her tortured, swollen bottom burned with a fire she had never imagined possible.

And then she slumped, to as great an extent as her pain-racked body could do so while stretched across the wooden contraption.

Bridget bathed the back of her head and the nape of her neck with water, and soothed her with comforting words. "The pain is over now," she whispered, "the overseer's put down his cane. Be strong, Laura; what's to come next is bearable, you know that. You can endure the shame of it, I'm sure you can."

As she lay there panting, Laura felt heavy hands against her caned buttocks, and knew that the second part of her ordeal was about to commence.

The Sinfinder had made it quite clear; she was to be fucked until her vagina could hold no more sperm - and doubtless there'd prove to be no shortage of willing overseers ready to make a deposit inside her traumatised love-slot!

She felt the overseer's cock against her cunt-opening, winced as he squeezed the flesh of her buttocks to gain more leverage, and groaned in pain as he pushed his thick muscle up inside her. He thrust at her crudely until the full length of his penis had been accommodated by her yielding cunt.

She was roundly fucked then; savagely, in front of a roomful of people. The wooden beam creaked rhythmically as the overseer's cock plunged time and again between her thighs.

"Good girl," encouraged Bridget, caressing Laura's bobbing head. "Keep your hole relaxed, and push back against him if you can. Milk him as quickly as possible. The sooner you're full up, the sooner the whole thing is over."

Laura did her best to thrust her ass back into the overseer's groin. She was desperate to feel his hot jet of come splash the walls of her vagina; desperate to feel his cock slip out of her hole. She found herself hoping his balls were fit to burst; the more spend he pumped into her, the nearer she'd be to having her pussy filled up, the fewer cocks she'd need to take.

The grizzly brute fucked away at her for what seemed an eternity, so much so that even Bridget was quietly urging him on, exasperated by his inability to reach a climax. Laura tried everything to draw his seed: tightening her vaginal muscles around the thrusting cock; wriggling her ass from side to side - as much as her spreadeagled position would allow - and even spurring him on verbally. "Come on, honey," she enthused, "spunk inside of my cunthole! Come on, fuck my pussy with your great big cock - teach me a real good lesson! Punish me, honey - punish me by fucking my naughty cunt with that big ol' dick of yours!"

After fifteen minutes of violent, savage thrusting, the sweat-drenched brute finally unloaded himself into Laura's vagina, his huge cock pumping thick globules of spend deep inside her.

Almost as soon as he'd slipped from her, other hands were mauling her buttocks. Another cock slipped inside, and before she could even gather her strength, she was once again being vigorously taken. Her head recommenced its bobbing movement as the new assailant slammed into her, pushing her forward over the groaning wooden beam.

"Come on," she gasped, "fuck me, honey! Make me take your come inside of my naughty little cunthole! Fuck my pussy 'til I scream, you big horny brute!"

"Silence her!" growled the Sinfinder, evidently tiring of her attempts to influence proceedings. Even as the brute behind her continued to thrust, another overseer snatched at her hair and pulled her head up. He wrapped a thick cloth around her mouth, tugging it tight and fastening it at the back of her neck, effectively gagging her.

The terrible ordeal proceeded without respite. One after another, thick, erect cocks were slipped into Laura's vagina, and each remained there, thrusting backwards and forwards, until it had finally emptied itself.

Had Laura possessed knowledge of the time, she would

have realised that her ordeal lasted for well beyond two hours in total, during which period many of the watching slavegirls began to weep openly, in sympathy with the American for the cruel torture she was being made to endure.

Finally, after what seemed to Laura to be an eternity, the session was brought to a conclusion. Her head filled with blood, her cunt heavy with sperm, she felt herself being swiftly and efficiently unfastened and suddenly hauled upright.

On the Sinfinder's instruction, she was carried from the chamber, and taken immediately to the small annexe, where the wounds to her buttocks were carefully tended and dressed by the gently smiling Bridget.

The days immediately after her ordeal seemed sweet indeed to Laura. She was neither beaten nor used sexually, but instead confined to the house's annexe while she recovered from the caning.

After a week or so, brutish men barged into the room, manacling her wrists and fitting a neck collar, and Laura knew that her period of recuperation had come to an abrupt end. She was taken to a part of the house she had never been to before, and tugged into a small, dusty room.

Positioned centrally was a large wooden box - a cage, almost - two opposite sides of which were slatted from top to bottom. The third side had a porthole-shaped opening at crotch level, and Laura was reminded of the restraining box in which the female villager had been imprisoned on Devil's Hill. The fourth side was open, though a panel rested against the far wall, ready to be fitted into position. A heavy roof was balanced atop the three panelled construction.

"Inside," ordered one of the men, wrenching on Laura's neck collar to encourage her to follow his command. She staggered across the room, and cautiously entered the box. Two of the men accompanied her, swinging her around and pushing her against the panel with the porthole-shaped opening. Hands pressed against her abdomen and forced her backwards, until her bottom was poking through the hole. The man still standing outside the wooden 'cage' gripped her buttocks firmly and pulled, ensuring her bottom was thrust out from the opening as far as possible.

Inside the box, the two men fastened a thick leather strap across Laura's groin, locking both ends into metal rings fitted to the panel to either side of the American.

In this way, Laura was trapped, unable to move her bottom from its position wedged through the porthole, exposed in the outside world. The two men left her then, fitting the fourth panel into place and casting Laura into semi-darkness, with only the light that slanted in through the narrow slats serving to illuminate her murky prison.

When first sentenced, Laura had been condemned by the Sinfinder not only to the dreadful whipping that she'd had to endure, but also to a period of incarceration. Five summers, he had said. Five summers!

For the first time, the awful reality of Matthew Hopkirk's words struck at Laura's very soul. She was to be incarcerated for five years - and this dreadful box was to be her prison!

As the terrible truth dawned upon her, she held her head in her manacled hands and began to sob... like she had never sobbed before.

"Roll up, roll up!" wailed the malevolent Quinn, wildly waving his top hat in the air. He was standing in the crowded big-top, doing his very best to attract the attention of the many men and handful of women who were wandering around inside the enormous tent.

The Sinfinder General's circus of sex continued to perform, playing to its private and extremely select audience at a secret destination in the English countryside. Various tableaux had already been performed. As a number of top-hat-and-tailed overseers rearranged the main stage for another 'show', the audience were meandering at their leisure, enjoying watching the various beatings and whippings to which many of the naked slavegirls were being subjected in the specially constructed booths.

"Ladies and gentlemen," Quinn shouted from his position to the far side of the tent, standing next to a curtained booth of his own, "for your delight and delectation, we present an entirely new addition to the Sinfinder's Circus of Sex Slaves. Captured in the wilds and caged for your enjoyment, the Sinfinder General takes great pleasure in presenting..." Quinn clasped hold of a long cord that dangled from the top of the curtained booth, "...The Ass!"

With a gentle tug on the cord, the malevolent dwarf drew back the curtain, revealing the large wooden box from which Laura's bare bottom was blooming magnificently. "This phenomenon, ladies and gentleman," Quinn continued at length, "is not a woman, nor is it a man...it is, quite simply, an ass. A bottom, ladies and gentlemen, to be used as you desire.

"Here, hanging on these hooks, are a variety of implements - a whip; a cane; here, a paddle; a birch; a slipper, and a hairbrush. Use them as you please, to make The Ass dance in wild abandon.

"And here, to this side of the bare and beautiful bottom-cheeks, a pair of rubber gloves - perhaps some amongst you gentlemen would like to fist the bumhole. Sachets of lubricant, for those who wish to take their pleasure of the bottom's tight opening, are available, as is this hose and a bucket. Ladies, why not give that bottom a thorough cleaning out! Apply a cleansing enema to the rectum and watch the bottom empty itself into this handy receptacle!"

From inside her grim little prison, Laura listened to the speech she had heard her estranged husband give so many times before. What would she have to endure on this occasion, she wondered. The show had been running for many weeks, and she - or rather, her bottom - had become an enormously popular addition to the Sinfinder's range of bizarre circus acts.

Her life since her imprisonment had been a lonely, miserable, soul-shattering experience. Kept always inside her box, she was fed through an opening in the slats, and allowed an hour's-worth of verbal communication per day. Her bottom, fitted through the porthole and always accessible to the outside world, was used regularly throughout each day, being flogged, fucked, licked and fisted. A tube was fitted inside her every morning and her bowels emptied. As for peeing, she did that on the floor between her feet, an overseer hosing down both her and her prison twice daily.

She was, she knew, no longer a woman. She was, as she had been introduced, an ass - The Ass! A bare bottom, to be used as was seen fit. In her hand she held a small block of wood, which she had been instructed to clench between her teeth whenever her backside was beaten; being only a bottom, she could hardly be allowed to howl and scream and beg for mercy. Biting down on the wood kept her quiet, ensuring the only sound within her wooden prison was the gentle splash of her tears as they struck the floor.

"You sir," Laura heard her husband begin, "can I perhaps interest you in enjoying the pleasures of The Ass - always assuming your good lady wife is in agreement, of course?!"

"Well, I must confess..." the customer began, "I must confess I do have rather a fancy for giving that arse a damn good fucking!"

"Bertie!" exclaimed a woman's voice - presumably that of the man's wife, Laura thought to herself. "I am surprised at you! Still, if you really fancy having a dabble..." she paused momentarily, before adding, "but I must insist that the hole is properly clean before I allow you to put your precious percy in there, my sweet! So I think we'll get the hose and some soap into that arse before we do anything else!"

"How about giving it a few swipes with a length of rattan

first, eh Fran?" Bertie suggested to his wife. "Just to get it wriggling around a bit!"

"An excellent idea if I may say so, sir," Quinn interrupted. "I often take the cane to The Ass myself, and can assure you it dances most splendidly. Here's the very implement, sir. Now be sure and thrash these splendid buttocks just as hard as you can!"

Inside her prison, Laura exhaled a languid breath and scraped her fingers through her hair. "Let's have the target area thrust right out, please!" Quinn demanded of her.

She pushed her bottom as far through the porthole as it would fit, her buttocks peeling apart sufficiently to allow fresh air to caress her sore and battered anus.

"Oh, Bertie!" she heard Lady Francesca Cartwright cry with delight, "this is it, my darling, this is what we've been looking for! The perfect new toy to keep you amused! We must buy it, Bertie, we must buy it and take it home with us!"

Then Laura raised the small block of wood to her mouth, and purposefully sank her teeth into it...just in time to hear the familiar swish of a bamboo rod descending through the clammy summertime air.